THE HALLWAY WAS PRE͟... ͟...͟... ARE NOT TALKING about a high-rent establishment, and I had to squint to see a rest room sign. What I saw was movement from the stairs, somebody coming out of the shadows.

I don't think it would have made me stop in my tracks if the person hadn't moved as if he didn't want to be seen. I knew it was a he. He wasn't too tall, but he had broad shoulders and a head too sharp around the edges to belong to a woman. Yeah, it was a man. And when he stepped into the faded light, I saw what man. Coach Mayno.

The second it registered I started to back up.

"No, L'Orange, don't go." he said. "You have to listen to me—you owe me that."

I kept backing—until I bumped the wall.

"Relax, L'Orange," he said. "I'm not going to hurt you. What do you think I am?"

The voice went right up my backbone. I'd heard those words before from him, said to somebody else: *I'm not going to hurt you—you know that.*

Dear Parent,

Thank you for considering Nancy Rue's book for your teen. We are pleased to publish her *Raise the Flag* series and believe these books are different than most you will find for teens.

Tragically, some of the things our teens face today are not easy to discuss. Nancy has created stories and characters that depict real kids, facing real-life issues with real faith. Our desire is to help you equip your children to act in a God-pleasing way no matter what they face.

Nancy has beautifully woven scriptural truth and direction into the choices and actions of her characters. She has worked hard to depict the issues in a sensitive way. However, I would recommend that you scan the book to determine if the subject matter is appropriate for your teen.

Sincerely,

Dan Rich
Publisher

Raise the Flag Series BOOK 1

DON'T COUNT
ON HOMECOMING
QUEEN

Nancy Rue

WATERBROOK
PRESS
COLORADO SPRINGS

DON'T COUNT ON HOMECOMING QUEEN
PUBLISHED BY WATERBROOK PRESS
5446 North Academy Boulevard, Suite 200
Colorado Springs, Colorado 80918

A division of Bantam Doubleday Dell Publishing Group, Inc.

The characters and events in this book are fictional,
and any resemblance to actual persons or events is coincidental.

Scriptures are taken from
The Holy Bible, New International Version (NIV)
© 1973, 1978, 1984 by International Bible Society,
used by permission of Zondervan Publishing House,
and *The Message,* © 1993 by Eugene H. Peterson

ISBN 1-57856-032-2

Printed in the United States of America

1998—First Edition

1   3   5   7   9   10   8   6   4   2

For my inspiration, the Footnotes Girls—
Mairin, Chamaea, Ana, Vanessa, Michelle, and Marijean

PROLOGUE

September 22

I WANT TO SAY SOMETHING RIGHT OFF SO NOBODY thinks I'm a hypocrite: I really did go to the flagpole that morning because I believe prayer changes things—maybe everything.

But I also went for a couple of other reasons.

Like one—My dad's a pastor. He'd dropped enough hints about See You at the Pole to sink the *Titanic*—stuff like, "I'd sure like to see something like that take hold here in Reno. We definitely need it." He didn't exactly say, "Tobey, girl, now you go." But it's the kind of thing the preacher's kid just does, you know?

Besides that, I was kind of a show-off.

Not like stand up on the table in the cafeteria and do the Macarena. More like prove that I'll do what I want no matter what other people think. That's why I ran cross-country track, which not that many other girls did, and why I competed in speech contests, which unlike a lot of people I could pull off without looking like a geek, and why I sometimes wore army surplus combat boots with a dress.

And besides all that—I went to the flagpole thing because I thought Damon Douglas would be there.

He wasn't. I checked that out the minute I arrived.

There was no buff, blue-eyed Damon. Just five other girls, all of them blinking out at the fading lights of the casinos in the Reno smog and looking like they couldn't remember any of the reasons why they'd shown up.

I tossed my backpack on the grass on the King High School front lawn next to theirs. It looked like a pile of luggage waiting to be loaded onto the next 747. It always looks like that when there's a bunch of high school students assembled. We all haul around half of what we own like we're expecting a natural disaster.

But there, the similarity among us ended. I didn't even know any of these girls, except one—and, frankly, I'd never really wanted to know her. I was reminded why as soon as she opened her mouth.

"L'Orange," Norie Vandenberger said to me, "thank God you're here. You probably have the rules for this thing."

She looked at the rest of the group with her piercing brown eyes. "Chill," she said, although none of them had so much as twitched an eyebrow. "I wasn't swearing. I really do thank God she's here. I sure don't know what we're supposed to be doing."

Norie tossed back her short crop of hair the color of espresso, folded her arms over the olive green T-shirt that said "God loves you—why don't you return the favor?" and looked at the rest of us as if she had given somebody her cue to say her line.

But none of the other four seemed to know what to say.

I shrugged. "I don't know the 'rules,'" I said. "I think we're supposed to, you know, pray."

"Have you ever done this before?"

That came from an African-American girl—gorgeous girl. Hair cut really close to her head, the way only incredibly beautiful women can wear it. About three pierced earrings in each ear, only she made it look classy. Big ol' round black eyes that said, "Don't mess with me, girl. I don't have time for it."

"No," I said. "Well I take that back. Yeah. They announce See You at the Pole every year, but the last two years I came and nobody else was here."

"So what did you do—stand out here and pray by yourself?" Norie said.

I wish I could have said yes, just because this girl always got on my nerves so bad. It was the sarcasm thing—she did it in English all the time. Everything Mr. Lowe said, she was all over it with all this cynical—

"So what do we do?"

We all looked at the Hispanic girl, the one with the shy eyes and the flawless skin and the chopped-off-at-the-chin hairstyle that was totally cute on her but would have made me look like a refugee.

"I think we can do anything we want," I said to her. "I mean, that's why there aren't any adults allowed—it's supposed to be student-led."

"So you're the leader type," Norie said, smiling squarely. "Lead."

That seemed to be okay with everybody, including the short little thing with the lips people have plastic surgery to get, and the thin, willowy blonde in the ironed jeans. She looked familiar to me.

I must have rung a bell with her, too, because she smiled at me and said, "You are really good at this. I saw you lead that workshop at the youth conference—you know, up at Tahoe."

"That's where I've seen you before," I said.

"Fabulous—you two have bonded," Norie said. "So lead us in prayer."

I was starting to bristle, you know, the way you get when you've been wearing your bra for too long or something. But I didn't show it, I know. That's not my style. Why let people know they're getting to you, when you can usually get a grip on the situation and turn it around?

I flashed them all a smile. "Okay," I said. "I guess we ought to decide what we want to pray for."

"Aren't we supposed to—" Willow Girl started to say.

But I held up my hand. "I think we ought to take the 'supposed to' out of it and just go with the way the Spirit leads us."

"You're talking about the 'Holy' Spirit, right?" Norie said.

I nodded.

"Good," she said. "I just wanted to make sure you weren't referring to the 'Great' Spirit. I have no Native American blood."

"I do," said Lips.

We all kind of gaped at her for a second. It reminded me of kindergarten when the teacher would say, "Today we're going to talk about rabbits," and somebody would yell out, "I have a cat at home!"

"So—" I said. "Do you want to just say what you want prayers for and then we can just—start?"

"I can get to that," said the African-American girl. "Could we pray for—"

"Name," Norie said.

The girl looked at her blankly. "What?" she said.

"Your name—what is it?"

Gee, Norie. I thought, *if we paid you more, could you be a little ruder?*

"I'm Brianna. Brianna Estes."

"Thanks. Go on."

Brianna swept Norie once more with her enormous black eyes before she said, "I'd like to pray about all the racial stuff that's starting to stir up at this school."

I saw the Hispanic girl nod. The Native-American-with-the-Cute-Lips nodded, too, but I decided she probably nodded at everything. Had to be a freshman.

Norie jerked her chin at the Hispanic girl. "You want racial peace, too, uh—"

"Marissa," the girl said quickly. "Marissa Martinez. And yes—please. Not like, about fights and all, but just, being treated better. Not being judged because I'm Mexican."

"Gotcha," Norie said. "Next."

Willow Girl crossed and uncrossed her arms and rolled her translucent blue eyes up at the sky.

"Did you want to say something?" I said to her. I smiled at her and gave Norie a warning look. This girl looked so fragile, one politically correct little jab from Norie and she'd probably crack like an eggshell.

"Just—I want to pray for, you know, like, kids on drugs and stuff," she said.

Norie snorted. "Do you even know any kids on drugs?"

I opened my mouth to protest, but Norie held up both palms. "I was just asking," she said.

"We'll pray for kids on drugs," I said. "Anybody else?"

"Wait—what's your name?" Norie said to our blonde.

"Shannon D'Angelo."

"You don't look Italian," Norie said.

Not that it's any of your business, I wanted to say to her.

"So what do you want prayers for?" I said instead.

To my utter amazement, Norie suddenly looked at the toes of her Doc Martens. If I hadn't known better, I'd have said she was embarrassed. If I'd been a better person, I would have felt bad. I didn't.

"You don't have to tell out loud if you don't want to," Shannon said.

"Yeah, I do," Norie said. "That's why I'm doing this, you know, so I'll have to say to somebody, 'I'm a Christian.'" She looked up at us from under her bangs. "I haven't been one that long."

That would fall somewhere in the No Kidding category, I thought. And then I did feel bad.

"Take your time," I said. "It can be weird at first."

"And I can be weird at first. Guess it figures."

Lips giggled and then covered her terrific mouth with both hands.

"Okay—" Norie said. "I want prayer for the pressure." She critically surveyed the group. "I don't know—some of you might have felt it around here—the way they push you to be excellent at everything. I'm surprised they don't grade you on how you go to the bathroom."

"They do," Brianna said. "In my math class, every time you ask for a pass, he takes off two points."

"Okay, we'll pray about the pressure," I said. I looked at little Lips, who was fiddling with the clasp on her overalls shorts.

"Do you want prayers?" I said. "You don't have to—"

Evidently she did have to, because she blurted it out like she'd been holding it in for days. "I'm new," she said. "I mean, not just because I'm a freshman but—I just moved here."

"From where?" Marissa said. She cocked her head—kindly— and I decided I liked her. It was nice of her to try to make the kid feel comfortable.

"A lot of places," Lips said. "I was in Lovelock right before here."

"I'm sorry," Norie said dryly. "So—what's your name?"

"Cheyenne," she said.

"Of course—the whole Native American thing," Brianna said. "That's cool."

"I'm not all that Native American," Cheyenne said. "Maybe an eighth or something. My mother just named me that because she was in her 'Save the Indians' phase when I was born."

"What phase is she in now?" Norie said. For a second I thought she was going to whip out a pad and pencil and do an interview. Being editor of the school paper was her big thing.

"Guys, it's getting late," I wedged in. "We probably ought to get started."

"What about you?" Norie said.

I blinked at her. "I'm Tobey L'Orange."

"I think most of us know that."

They all nodded in agreement, except Cheyenne who nodded because everybody else did.

"I meant, what do you want prayer for?" Norie said.

I stared at her for a second. Absolutely nothing came to mind—not for myself anyway. I had such a perfect life, it almost made me feel guilty. I had really decent parents and a fourteen-year-old brother who didn't drive me too nuts. I made A's in school and had great relationships with all my teachers. My Christian friends all went to Foothills Christian Academy or were home-schooled, but that didn't keep me from being, well, pretty popular at King. Enough to be elected Junior Class President and to the Judicial Board which ran all the elections. I didn't hang with kids who did drugs; I didn't even know we had racial tensions; and I did what I did because I wanted to, not because anybody was pushing me.

I didn't want to appear smug, but—I didn't have anything to pray for.

They were all looking at me expectantly, like if I didn't put in a request the whole See-You-at-the-Pole thing would go bust.

"I want to pray for the school, you know, just in general," I said finally. "That it'll give every kid what they need."

Norie grunted. "Who decides what they 'need'?"

I said the first thing that came into my head. "God."

She looked at me hard, out of those penetrating eyes, and then she said, "Okay—I can dig that."

Shannon glanced over her shoulder at the still-mostly-empty student parking lot. "Shouldn't we get started?" she said.

"Yeah," I said.

And then we all looked at each other. Cheyenne edged closer to Marissa, which seemed to be the cue for everybody to scoot in together, even Norie. We got shoulder-to-shoulder so that the flagpole was right in our faces, and Cheyenne giggled.

"Do we, like, bow our heads?" Norie said.

"That would be good," I said.

Heads ducked, and then we stood there in silence. It was windy, as usual up there on the hill above Reno, and the flag flapped overhead and the rope clanged against the pole like some kind of urgent death alarm.

At five-feet-ten I was taller than all of them standing there, and it made me feel even more like I was supposed to be in charge. I scrambled around for the first words, but before I could get my mouth open, Norie started to talk. It took me a good thirty seconds to realize she was praying.

"So—here we all are—all six of us. I'm sorry more people didn't show up, but I guess You know how hard it is for people to own up. You aren't exactly the trend right now."

Cheyenne giggled. I heard Marissa laugh, too, and Brianna gave a sophisticated grunt.

"So I guess we'll get started, God," Norie went on. "We really hope You'll take a look at this whole prejudice thing."

"Turn the hearts of the racists, Lord," Brianna said. "Take all the hate and the fear and the narrow-mindedness out of them, before somebody gets hurt."

I was surprised at the fervor in her voice, and I sneaked a glance at her. She had her eyes closed, but her face was lifted right up to the sky, like she wanted God to see how intense she was. It made me want to keep praying.

"And Lord," I said, "would You be in the presence of every kid that's even thinking about taking drugs right now—"

"Oh, Lordy, Lordy, YES!"

My lips froze, and I could feel Norie stiffening on one side of me and Shannon going rigid on the other. The voice hadn't come from inside our circle. It was somebody on the walkway, cackling like a hyena.

"What are ya doin', Jesus Freaks?" somebody else said. Obviously a kindred spirit to the first kid.

I looked up at our group. Only Cheyenne was looking furtively at them over her shoulder. Everybody else was pretending they hadn't heard, except Marissa who had her eyes scrunched closed like she was expecting to be shot.

"Go on, L'Orange," Norie said. "Ignore them."

"Pray for 'em," Brianna whispered. "They need it more than we do."

So I did. And Norie piped up and put in a good word for Cheyenne and all other new kids. Brianna lifted up the pressure issue, and Marissa offered a barely audible prayer for all the kids at King getting what they needed.

The whole thing was punctuated with jeers from arriving students who passed us on the walkway. Any other time, I thought, most of those kids would barely speak until noon.

"And so, God," Norie said about then, "we just offer all these prayers, hoping you'll hear them—"

"Wait," Cheyenne whispered hoarsely. "I have one more."

"Hey, what's this, a Sunday school class?" some kid called out.

"Go have your tongue pierced," Norie muttered. "Go ahead, Cheyenne."

But Cheyenne shook her head, sending strips of black hair swaying across her shoulders. "Never mind," she said. "That's okay."

"Don't let them get to you," I said. "We're out here doing a good thing. It's nothing to be embarrassed about."

Cheyenne gnawed on her full lower lip.

Marissa reached over and grabbed her hand.

Cheyenne stared at it for a minute, and then like a little kid about to cross Interstate 80 she groped for Brianna's hand. Norie shrugged and took Marissa's other one.

Before any of us really realized what we were doing, we were all holding hands.

"Isn't that sweet?" somebody said from the walkway.

I really wanted to look up and smile at him, just to let him know he wasn't bothering me a bit. But it would've been like breaking the circle, and I have to admit for those couple of minutes it felt good to be in it.

Maybe it was the public witness. My dad would've been proud.

Maybe it was the spotlight we'd created for ourselves, and that I liked being in.

Or maybe it was the energy a bunch of females can create when they're all feeling the same thing at the same time.

Frankly, right now I don't think it was any of those things. If I'd been able to foresee then what was going to happen in the next month of my life, I'd have known it was something different.

Something totally different.

"I just wanted to say," Cheyenne whispered, "thank you for this group. It's nice to know I have Christian friends."

"Amen," Brianna said.

And then the bell rang, and we went our separate ways.

CHAPTER ONE

I WAS AN AIDE IN PE FIRST PERIOD. COACH GATNEY TOLD me it was a waste for me to be in study hall when she could use somebody like me to keep "those little chickies" in line.

More like "those little vultures." They were already going after some poor little Hispanic freshman in the locker room when I walked in.

"I don't mean to be rude," Emily Yates was saying to her, "but why do you all wear your hair like that?"

Emily shot her hand straight up from her own forehead to imitate the sort of stiff wall Angelica Benitez had made with her bangs and a can of hair spray.

Okay, so it wasn't a good look for her, maybe for anybody. But it wasn't worth crushing the poor kid's feelings over it. I glared at Emily around my locker door. She ignored me. I went on to Step Two. "By 'you all,' you mean Angelica's whole culture?" I said.

Behind us, I heard Hayley Hatcher whisper, "Yeah, all the Beaners."

Emily caught it, too, and grinned. I didn't point out to her that she should talk about 'dos, what with hers reacting to a recent perm by going out of control. I just smiled at Angelica and pulled my King High T-shirt over my head.

"Hey, Tobey," Emily said. "What were you guys doing out there at the flagpole this morning, having a séance?"

"They were trying to reach Elvis," Hayley said. She snickered through freckle-covered lips at Jennifer Oakman. Jennifer rolled her eyes. That was the only expression I'd ever seen on Jennifer's face besides the mouth lolling open as if she were either bored or catatonic.

"No," I said with total calm, "we were praying."

Every door in the locker room stopped clanging—a feat in itself—and everybody stared at me. I pulled on my shorts and reached for my tennies.

"Is that a problem for anybody?" I said, still smiling.

Jennifer rolled her eyes, and Hayley said, "Whatever."

"So, like, why were you praying?" Emily said.

"Because there are people who need it," I said. "We were praying for the school—"

"Did you pray for me?" she said. "I need a guy."

"You should have prayed for Angelica's hair!" Hayley whispered loudly.

I glanced at Angelica. She was so intent on tying her shoes, I knew she had heard.

"Well, I don't mean to be rude," Emily said, "but I thought it was kind of weird."

"Isn't it against the law to pray in school?" somebody else said.

I picked up my clipboard. "Nope. I do it all the time. Nobody can control what goes on in your head, right?"

"Yeah, well, they try," Emily said.

"I know," I said. "That's why we were praying."

It was such a good line to exit on, I couldn't resist leaving the locker room with a hint of a swagger. Ten to one they started to snicker about me the minute the door shut, but that was okay. I was feeling pretty proud of my sweet self.

"Got those little chickies in line, L'Orange?" Coach Gatney called to me down the hall.

"Yes ma'am," I said.

"I love those manners," she said.

She gave me the Gatney Grin, really wide with a big ol' space between her two front teeth and her nose crinkling up. She was fortyish and so tanned she was starting to look like luggage, but she had this bounce I really liked. We were more like buds than teacher-student. Right then, she slung an arm around my neck.

"Sometime I want you to tell me how you get your hair that color," she said. She rolled her eyes up at her own frizz of burger brown.

"I was born with it," I said. "I don't even know what color to call it."

"Strawberry blonde," Coach Gatney said. "If I didn't like you so much, I'd hate you for it. That and those eyes. Nobody should have eyes that brown."

She did the gap-toothed grin and let go of me. "Let's get those little chickies out here. We have a class to do."

I corralled the little vultures, took roll, and sent them off to the equipment room for volleyballs. As I was compiling the absence slips for Coach Gatney, I felt a tap on my shoulder. When I turned around, it was Angelica, trying to figure out a place to hang her arms. She finally crossed them over her chest.

"Hi," I said. "What's up?"

Her face immediately softened into this sweet smile. She looked almost like a baby, like all I'd had to do to get that grin was acknowledge her existence. In spite of the bad hairdo, she was pretty.

"I just wanted to tell you, I thought you were really cool in there," she said.

"In where?" I said.

"In the locker room."

"Oh." I shrugged. "I didn't say that much. If they had gotten on your case any more I would have—"

Angelica put her hand on my arm. "I don't mean that. I mean, when they were giving you grief about being at the flagpole praying. I thought you were so brave."

I smiled. "It's not really that hard," I said. "If you know what you believe in is right, you just go for it."

She looked as if she wanted to say something. She probably would have if Coach Gatney hadn't started to yell. "L'Orange!" she screeched at me. "Go in my office and get my whistle, wouldya?"

"Yes ma'am," I said.

"Yes ma'am," Emily said behind me, in a very bad southern accent.

I rolled my eyes at Angelica. She gave another one of those sweet smiles.

I guess you could say I was pretty much feeling my Cheerios about this bravery thing. I was wishing, as I opened the door to the coaches' office, I'd taken even a little more leadership at the flagpole. Coach Mayno, our cross-country coach, was in there.

"Hey, Tobe!" he said.

"Hi, coach," I said. "I'm looking for Coach Gatney's whistle."

"You have to run off with it this minute?" he said. "You can't talk a second?"

He smiled at me, and I put off the whistle errand. When Coach Mayno smiled, it was hard to resist. A lot of the girls on the team referred to him as a "babe." I just thought he was pretty good looking, you know, for a thirty-something guy. He had been working out since birth so he was totally in shape, and he was blond and blue-eyed, with this "talk-to-me" smile. He also had an ego about the size of Montana, but then, who cared? He was a fun coach to work with.

"You'll be at practice today," he said.

"No sir," I said. "Remember, I told you, I have to go to that speech contest fifth period, and I won't be back until after practice."

"Speech contest?" he said, eyes twinkling. "That's no contest—you can talk the arm off anybody I know."

"But it's what I say that counts."

"I don't care what you say. All I care about is whether you can run."

He was still grinning, but I knew he wasn't totally teasing. I'd seen him get kids out of major tests so they could go to a race. He could be very persuasive.

"Let me talk to Lowe," he said.

"It won't make any difference," I said. "Mr. Lowe didn't set up the contest. The Lions Club did."

"Lions Club! What the heck are you doing going to the Lions Club?"

I grinned back at him and reached for the whistle on the desk. He grabbed the back of my neck like a big ol' playful bear and held my head down.

"You turnin' into a women's libber on me?" he said.

"No!"

"You better not," he said. "You're way too cute to be walkin' around with hairy legs and an attitude."

I wriggled away and left him laughing behind me. I was still grinning when I got back to the gym. It did feel really good to be, well, "in" with cool people. Even teachers.

The speech contest was like most of the ones Mr. Lowe took us to. The Lions fed us the same greasy chicken, unsalted rice, and big honkin' pieces of chocolate cake the Kiwanians and Rotarians did and then sat back and smiled like a bunch of proud fathers while we gave our speeches on "The American Dream." When I was done with mine and was going back to my seat, I heard one guy say, "Isn't she about precious?"

"That one old dude said you were 'adorable,'" Gabe McClelland said in the car on the way home.

"'Precious,'" I corrected him. I jabbed him with my elbow. "And don't start with me."

"Why not?" he said. "You always take at least third place just because you're . . . 'adorable.'"

Mr. Lowe grinned at him in the rearview mirror. "'Precious,'" he said.

"Whatever," Gabe said. He flipped his ponytail. "I could probably take third place, too, if I got all gussied up."

"Got a haircut," Mr. Lowe said.

Gabe didn't rub Mr. Lowe's bald head and say, "At least I have hair." Now if it had been Coach Mayno, we could have gotten away with something like that. Mr. Lowe was more . . . dignified.

"Yeah," Gabe said instead. "Like if I got a haircut."

In the front seat, Roxy Wainwright sniggered. "Like if you gave a decent speech."

"Hey!" Gabe said. "Didn't I give a decent speech, Mr. Lowe?"

Mr. Lowe nodded solemnly.

"Do you think I'll win anything?"

Roxy gave this huge guffaw. Mr. Lowe just said, "I don't know, Gabe. We'll have to wait until the results come in a couple of weeks. Some of the other schools haven't done theirs yet."

"Like they should even bother entering," Gabe said. "King takes everything in this town."

That was pretty true. Martin Luther King High School was nicknamed "The Academy on the Hill" because Mr. Holden, the principal, ran it as if it were a prep school. For some reason, I thought about Angelica. No wonder she was having a hard time with all those yuppies' kids. And that little girl with the pretty lips at the flagpole—what was her name—Shawnee or something? She was fair game for all the preppies. Not to mention the Hispanic girl . . . Marissa, yeah, that was it. And Brianna. She was one of about, what, forty black kids in a school of fourteen hundred students? Funny how I'd never thought about any of that stuff before.

"I will say this," Mr. Lowe was saying, "I'm always proud to take you three to these contests. You really represent King well."

"Because we look like we just got out of Sunday school?" Gabe said.

I groaned. I know Doberman pinschers who are more spiritual than Gabe McClelland.

"No," Roxy said, "because Tobey makes us all look good. One glance at her, and they know where she's coming from." She whipped around and suddenly looked embarrassed. "Not that that's a bad thing," she said. "You're totally cool about it. I mean, you're not churchy or anything. I don't ever feel like, 'Oh, man, here she comes—hide before she starts preaching and trying to save us.'"

"Roxy," Gabe said, "shut up before you hurt yourself."

That went right over Roxy's red head. She leaned over the

backseat and said, "So, what's happening with Damon? Did he ask you out yet?"

"Damon who?" Gabe said.

At that point, everything that was "totally cool" about me went straight down the tubes. I started stammering and blushing, and my hands turned into a pair of sweaty dishrags. None of it escaped Gabe.

"Ooooh," he said, green eyes leering. "Are we talking true love here? A little hanky-panky among the saints?"

"Knock it off," Roxy said. "Here, trade places with me. Tobey and I have to talk."

Without waiting for an answer, she hurled herself over the front seat into my lap and gave Gabe a shove.

"It wasn't my idea, Mr. Lowe," Gabe said as he crawled up front. "Honest, it was all Roxy."

Roxy waved them both off and brought her little turned-up nose close to mine. "Well?" she said. "Has he called?"

"No," I said.

"What a loser. Why don't you call him?"

"I hate calling boys."

"You call me," Gabe said.

"You don't count," Roxy said. "Now mind your own business."

Gabe scowled and turned to Mr. Lowe. "So, how 'bout those Mets, eh, Mr. Lowe?"

"Just call Damon," Roxy whispered to me. "You know he likes you. He's been asking all these people about you."

"Why doesn't he ask me about me?" I said.

"Because he's new. He doesn't want to make a total fool out of himself. What if you were a real witch or something?"

I went after my fingernails with my front teeth. "Yeah, I guess you're right."

"But he's a total hunk," she said. "You had better make a move before somebody else does."

I could feel my eyes widening. "Like who?"

"I don't know, like anybody. I mean, he's got shoulders for days. A lot of girls are into shoulders. And the eyes, the eyes, they have like blue and gray and gold all in them, with those eyelashes—have you noticed? Why do the guys get the great eyelashes?"

"Yes, I've noticed," I said pointedly. "You obviously have, too."

Roxy raked her hand through her mop of red curls. She has a habit of doing that every five seconds. "Don't worry about me. I like them a little crazy, which Damon is not. No, who you have to worry about are girls like Emily Yates."

"Emily Yates!"

"Oh yeah. As soon as she gets an eyeful of him, she'll be all over him. I mean, she chases anything with testosterone, but she'll go into hyperdrive for somebody like him. Especially fresh meat like that."

"Roxy!" I said. "Could you be any more crude?"

"Sorry." She raked her hair again. "Look, all I'm saying is, you had better get on it, or you're going to lose out, and I'd hate to see that."

"Why?" I tried to pull myself together. "I'm not going to freak or anything, if this doesn't work out."

"You won't freak. You never freak. But you deserve to have, like, a real boyfriend. You always run around with a bunch of people, which is fine, but you need a guy in your life." Her eyes, hazel and round, glistened at me, and she gave me a poke. "Is that what you were praying for at the flagpole this morning?"

"No!" I said.

"Sorry," she said. "I didn't know that was one of your taboos or something."

"It isn't," I said. She was getting a little too close to the truth. One of my main reasons for hauling myself out of bed at 5:30 A.M. was because my subtle inquiries had uncovered that Damon Douglas went to church, so I thought maybe . . .

Then I pulled my nails out of my mouth and got a handle on the blushing thing. This was stupid. If he wasn't a Christian and didn't share my morals, I wasn't interested in dating him. And with the Christian population at King being practically nil, what were the chances of that?

"I'm such a dork," I whispered to Roxy, as Mr. Lowe pulled the car into the school parking lot. "I'm all flipping out over some guy!"

"You are not flipping out," Roxy said. "What you're doing is finally being a normal, red-blooded American girl. If you were flipping out, well . . ." She gave the mop a final rake. "It just wouldn't happen. Tobey L'Orange does not flip out."

I grinned at her and thought she was probably right. Yeah, I was feeling braver by the minute.

CHAPTER
TWO

MY BROTHER, FLETCHER, KIND OF SLUNK TO THE DINNER
table that night and took a sudden fascination with the broccoli
casserole. I cut him no slack.

"Thanks for ditching me this morning," I said.

"It was too early," he said.

My father frowned at him over the basket of French bread.
Dad's getting-higher-every-day forehead wrinkled all the way up
to the graying, used-to-be-the-color-of-mine hair.

"Dad, it was!"

Now, you talk about freak, Fletcher could do it at the drop of
a ball cap. We're talking, you asked him if he had seen your CD
or your hair scrunchie, and he turned beet red and yelled, "I
didn't take it!" At this point, he was white-knuckling his fork.

"Relax, Fletch," Mom said in her usual, deep, everything's-
going-to-be-all-right voice. "Nobody's going to drag you before
the firing squad."

"I might," Dad said. "Pass the butter, please."

"Man, come on. I was up late doing homework! Hopkins
loads on the math like we don't got any other classes!"

"Mr. Hopkins," Dad said.

" 'Don't *have* any other classes,' " Mom said.

I grinned. I was loving it.

Fletcher narrowed his eyes at me—big, pale blue ones like

Mom's—and kind of jerked his head back like he had started to do since he got the new haircut. I guess he liked the way it felt when all that corn-silk hair (also like Mom's) slid back over the part that was shaved. I frankly thought it made him look like something out of *Oliver,* but I'd heard freshman girls actually say he was "so-o-o cute." Huh. Only because he looked like Mom. I, on the other hand, was the spitting image of Dad.

"So how did it go at the flagpole?" my dad, the Rev. Grant L'Orange, said. "Did anyone else come?"

"Yes," Fletcher said. "So don't let her try to tell you she stood there all by herself."

"How do you know?" I said. "Were you one of those people shouting stuff at us?"

Fletcher stopped in midbite of his chicken breast. "No! I heard it from a girl in my math class."

"Really?" Mom said. "Someone else in your math class was talking besides you?"

"What is this, Cap on Fletcher Night?"

"What girl?" I said.

"I don't know—some freshman. She has a weird name. Shawn or Shane."

"Shawnee," I said.

Fletcher shook his head. "No, that isn't it. It's—"

"So what did she say?" Dad said. He had more patience as a pastor than he did as a father, although who could blame him with Fletcher driving us all practically to addiction sometimes?

"She just started talking about how she met all these really cool girls at the flagpole." He glinted his eyes at me. "When she said that, I figured you didn't go either. Anyway, she was saying how cool it was praying for everybody on the planet."

"How did the other kids react when she said that?" Mom said.

"They just totally dissed the whole thing."

My parents gave each other bewildered looks across the table, Dad bulging out his brown eyes, Mom crossing her blue ones.

"That means they gave her a hard time about it," I said.

"Oh," Dad said, "that's too bad. I hate to see somebody stick out her neck and get it chopped off."

"Attractive image," I said.

"Yeah, well, maybe she shouldn't stick out her neck then," Fletcher said. "Y'know, if she can't handle it."

"You sure didn't stick yours out," I said.

"I know—'cause I hate it when people start cappin' on me."

"Are we going to be tested on all this new vocabulary?" Mom said.

"Don't bother," I said. "It's his own language."

Fletcher grunted. "At least I don't go around saying, 'he's all' and 'she's all.'"

"Are we all going to be able to leave you all alone for three days next week?" Dad said. "You're not going to kill each other, are you?"

Poor baby. He totally tried to keep up with us, and about half the time he got it all messed up. I had to love him for trying. Fletcher, on the other hand, gave him no space.

"Whatever, Dad," he said.

"Are you really leaving me alone with him for three days?" I said.

"That was the plan," Mom said. "Somebody finish up this broccoli."

"I hate broccoli," Fletcher said. "Where are you going?"

"Where do you disappear to during family conversations?" Dad said. "Does your spirit leave your body and fly off somewhere while I'm giving out information? We talked about this yesterday, right at this table."

Fletcher grunted at his plate.

"I have a show in San Jose," Mom said. "Dad's going to do a seminar at a church right down the street from the convention center; so we're going together."

"You're gonna sell teddy bears for three days?" Fletcher said.

I could see the wheels turning in his head, wondering who was going to feed him for three days.

"We're taking one day in San Francisco to get back our sanity," Dad said.

"Forget it, Daddy," I said, waving my fork at Fletcher. "You'll lose it again the minute you walk back in here."

"Hey!" Fletcher said, blood pressure visibly rising.

"Bless his heart," Mom said. She patted Fletcher's arm for about five seconds and then looked brightly around the table. "All right, who has dishes tonight?"

Fletcher and I pointed at each other. "No," I said. "I have garbage duty."

My parents tried to be gender-blind when it came to our chores. I took my turn mowing the lawn and taking out the trash, and Fletcher did his share of washing the dishes and folding the laundry. And his share of griping and moaning.

I wasn't wild about taking out the trash myself. There we were, in this almost-upper-middle-class neighborhood in which all the men competed to see who could get their lawns the most manicured and who could line up their Reno Disposal garbage cans the neatest on the sidewalk. I was the only teenage girl on the block doing it, and I was lucky to drag the cans to the street without dumping the L'Orange family waste. I usually jammed the containers out there and ran.

But I changed my attitude right at the curb that night. Because a steely blue Chevy S-10 pickup truck was coming down our street.

There were probably at least a thousand steely blue Chevy S-10 pickups in Reno, but most likely only one that still had New Mexico license plates. I let go of the garbage can and, quick, shook my hair out from behind my ears. As my hands broke out in a sweat, I simultaneously hoped I didn't have any broccoli between my teeth and prayed the truck would stop.

It did, right at our curb. A dark, wavy head poked out the window, and these eyes—these eyes—all gray and blue and gold and surrounded by curly eyelashes—shone at me.

"Hey!" Damon Douglas said. "Do you live here?"

"No," I said. "They just hire me to take out their garbage."

He grinned. Yikes, it was one of those one-corner-of-his-mouth-at-a-time smiles. I smiled back and dusted off my hands on the back of my shorts as I strolled casually closer to the truck.

Don't be fooled. I was a Jell-O salad inside and melting down fast. I'd only been daydreaming about this guy ever since he had showed up at cross-country track practice the first week of school. And now he was sitting in his truck a foot from me. So much for totally cool. So much for brave.

"No, seriously," I said. "This is my house. I didn't know you lived around here though."

That was actually a lie. I knew he lived at 1420 Valley Wood Drive. I also knew he was an only child, had geometry second period with Mr. Hopkins, and had locker number 505. That was all compliments of Roxy.

"I think I live here," he said. "Sometimes I wake up and think I'm still in Santa Fe, but it's getting better."

I nodded stupidly and fumbled for something to say. That's rare for me, but then, it was rare for me to have a total crush on somebody, too.

"So how come you weren't at practice today?" he said.

"Oh, I had to go to a speech contest," I said.

"You're into all kinds of stuff, aren't you?"

Is that a bad thing? I wanted to say. But I stopped myself from asking if he would like for me to give up every club I belonged to and tried to look nonchalant.

"How was practice?" I said.

"Good. I like Coach Mayno. He's so into it."

"Yeah, he's pretty cool."

"How do you get him to do the private lessons thing?"

I shook my attention away from his wonderful eyes. "What private lessons thing?" I said.

"After practice was over, he told that little freshman girl, what's her name? Angela?"

"Angelica?"

"Yeah, he told her to stay so he could work with her some more. I could use some of that. I'm an okay runner, but I think I need some help. I was a sprinter in New Mexico." He bobbed his head. "Okay, so Damon, get back to the point. The point is, do you know where to sign up for that?"

"I didn't even know he gave private coaching," I said. "I have a hard enough time just doing the regular practice. I thought I was going to die the first week."

"Get out," Damon said, eyes shimmering—I mean it, they were totally shimmering. "I've watched you run. You're about the best of the girls."

I tried not to fall face first into the image of Damon Douglas watching me run. "That's nice of you," I said. "But I'm not into it like Angelica obviously is."

"You would probably handle it better than she does," he said.

"I don't get it," I said.

"Well, she's going off to the track with him, and all these girls are talking behind her back about how she's kissing up to the coach, only she can totally hear them, you can tell that."

"How?" I said.

"She looked as if she was about to cry. People can be so mean, you know?"

"Yeah," I said eloquently.

"I know you were probably raised this way, too," Damon went on. "My parents brought me up Christian. I was taught not to put people down twenty-four-seven."

It was hard for me not to do an end-zone dance and yell "Yes!" I controlled myself and nodded adamantly. "I was, too," I said. "I got in some girls' faces this morning for capping on Angelica about her hair."

Damon smiled, slowly, one corner of his mouth at a time. I, meanwhile, was having a wigged-out discussion with myself. *Do I sound like the Politeness Police? Am I coming on too strong? No, don't be a geek. Be yourself. If he doesn't like you for who you are, then . . . change!*

But I got a grip on my pumping hormones and smiled at him. *Just be cool, Tobey. You can do this.*

"So," he said, "are there any other kids from your church at King?"

"No," I said.

"Mine either. I thought I was the only Christian on campus until I heard your dad was a pastor."

"I know of five," I said, "Well, six now including you. They showed up at the flagpole this morning."

He mouthed the word "flagpole."

"See You at the Pole," I said. "Have you heard of it?"

"Oh yeah," Damon said. "Was that this morning?"

I nodded.

"I'd have shown up if I'd known about it," he said.

I found myself thinking I was glad he hadn't. All he would have had to do was get one look at gorgeous Brianna, or sweet Shannon, or model-material Marissa, and I'd be history.

You're an idiot! I told myself. *Just—chill!*

"I better go," Damon said. "I have my mother's ice cream from Safeway. It's probably melted by now."

"Nothing like chocolate chip mint all over your front seat," I said.

He wiped me out with his gray-blue-gold eyes. "How'd you know it was chocolate chip mint?" he said.

I just grinned and waved as he drove off. It didn't occur to me until later that he had been driving in the wrong direction to have come from Safeway.

Roxy assured me on the phone that he had probably been out cruising, looking for my house. "I'm telling you, he's got it so bad for you," she said.

I prayed that night, for the school, like I promised I would, and for Mom and Dad not to be sent over the edge by Fletcher. And for Roxy to be right.

I had to get to school early again the next day to pick up my absence slip for being out of fifth and sixth periods. I was standing in line at the front counter when somebody behind me said, "You practically need an accountant to keep your attendance straight at this school."

It was Norie. I stifled a groan.

"Hey," she said, "did you catch any static for being out at the pole yesterday?"

"A little," I said. "It was no big deal."

"That's cool," she said. "I got some in American history, but then, those AP types are always ready to hassle you about something. We got into this big discussion about the separation of church and state. I set them straight."

"I'm sure you did," I said.

We inched closer to the counter where a dark-haired girl with her head bent down was checking people off.

"I wonder if anybody else got ragged on," Norie said.

"My brother told me Shawnee did."

"Who's Shawnee?" Norie said.

"The little Native American girl."

"Cheyenne," Norie said. She looked amused. "You were really paying attention. Anyway, what happened?"

"My brother didn't, like, go into detail."

"They never do. It's a male thing."

"He just said they 'dissed the whole thing,' and she totally got her feelings hurt."

"Jackals!" she said. "I can't believe they did that to that sweet little kid. She's just a baby!"

I had to tell myself to shut my mouth. It was hanging open about down to my chest. Norie's eyes were blazing. She was genuinely ticked off. I pulled her toward the counter so she wouldn't hold up the line.

"Hi," said the dark-haired check-off girl.

"Marissa!" Norie said. "What are you doing here?"

"I'm an office aide fifth period," she said. She cocked her silky bobbed head. "Sometimes I come in and help out before school if they're really swamped."

"Which we are today, ladies, so if you'll save your conversation for just a little later?" That came from a woman next to Marissa I'd never seen before. She obviously worked in the office. That place was Fort Knox. You didn't get behind the counter unless they buzzed you in. She was about, well, less than thirty, and she was wearing the neatest dress—all different South American looking colors, kind of flowy. I was thinking it would look great with a pair of Birkenstocks. Norie looked like she was thinking the chick ought to move on and mind her own business.

The woman smiled a crinkle-up-your-blue-eyes smile and put her hand on Marissa's shoulder. She didn't have her nails professionally done like most of the other women who worked in the office. I glanced at her nametag. All it said was "Ms. Race."

"All right, Tobey was on a school sponsored trip, so she gets a yellow slip," she was telling Marissa. She looked up and smiled at Norie, as she brushed back a wisp of dark auburn hair that had curled its way out of her French braid. "And what can I do for you?"

"I just need an insurance form," Norie said.

Ms. Race handed her one and said to Marissa, "You handle Tobey, and I'll get the next one. Can I help you?"

Her eyes were on the kid behind Norie. We stepped aside, and Norie leaned in to Marissa who was filling out my slip. "Hey," she said. "Did you hear Cheyenne got ragged on by some kids about being at the flagpole?"

Marissa shook her head. Her dark eyes looked hurt. "That's awful," she said.

"It's disgusting. I want to talk to her. Can you get her schedule?"

"Sure," Marissa said. "I can get everybody's schedule if you want."

"Everybody," I said. "You mean, like all the girls who were at the pole?"

"Sure," she said.

"Why—" I started to say.

But Norie cut me off. "That's a rad idea," she said. "We need to get everybody back together and give Cheyenne some support. Otherwise, we're going to lose her."

" 'We?' " I said. I wasn't quite sure what we were talking about.

"We can't just show up at the pole and make this statement that we're Christians and then throw each other to the wolves," Norie said, as if I should have figured that out for myself already.

"I wouldn't exactly call them wolves—" I started again.

Norie sliced me off with a wave of her hand this time. "What about Friday for lunch? I could do a memo on my computer,

Marissa could get me everybody's schedules, and I could deliver them. Where should we meet?"

She looked at me. My head was like a bowl of oatmeal.

"Flagpole?" Marissa said.

"Nah," Norie said. "We've got stuff to talk about. We don't want to be out there with the buzzards."

"Vultures," I muttered.

"Yeah," Norie said. "I'll ask around, see if any of the others have suggestions. Anyway, be expecting a notice tomorrow."

"All right, Marissa, we have another customer," Ms. Race said.

I tucked my absence slip into my pocket and started off.

"Thanks, Marissa," Norie said. And to me she whispered, "This is going to be so rad."

"Yeah," I said. In my head I was reviewing everything I had to do Friday and wondering how I was going to fit five more people into my life.

Then Damon hurried by, going in the direction of his locker, and I decided I needed something—anything—over by the five hundred lockers.

CHAPTER THREE

I PROBABLY COULD HAVE TALKED TO DAMON, TOO, IF Coach Gatney hadn't appeared out of the mob of people in the halls and said, "Hey, L'Orange, I have to go to the office. Can you get to class a little early? Get the little chickies started?"

"Yes ma'am," I said. I gave one last, longing look toward locker 505, although all I saw was somebody's environmental science book sailing by, and took off for the gym.

The little vultures were in rare form that day. Emily asked me if I'd prayed for a boyfriend for her yet. Jennifer and Hayley were sticking their bangs straight up in the air behind Angelica's back and then laughing like they were David Letterman or something. By the time I pushed them out on the volleyball court and got a game started, they had obviously decided I wasn't going to be any fun to harass. They gave Angelica their full attention.

"Hey, Pedro-ette!" Emily called to her as the other team was setting up to serve. "Don't eat it this time. It isn't a taco!"

Angelica turned around to look at Emily, eyes confused, just as the girl on the other team sent the ball hurtling over the net. It caught Angelica right on the back of the head. I blew the whistle and pointed to the serving team.

"No duh!" Hayley said to me.

"Watch the ball, Beaner!" Jennifer said.

"Watch your language, Potty Mouth," I said.

Jennifer looked around innocently. "What? What did I say?"

The other team served the ball, and I stared Jennifer down. Next thing I knew a bunch of sneakers squealed, and Angelica was sprawled on the floor. I ran over to her.

"Have a nice trip?" Hayley said. She looked to Emily and Jennifer for supporting laughter.

"Are you okay?" I said to Angelica.

She nodded, nearly swiping me with the bulkhead-bangs, and scrambled up. I looked around the court, but nobody was making eye contact. I had a weird feeling.

"Okay," I said. "Whose ball is it? I didn't see."

"Theirs," Emily said. "Thanks to her." She eyed Angelica.

"How was she supposed to get it?" I said. "She was on the floor. Where were you?"

I didn't wait for her to answer. I pointed to the other side of the court and trotted off to the sidelines. Out of the corner of my eye, I could see Coach Gatney coming in the double doors. With any luck, the vultures wouldn't see her, and they would get caught in the act of being themselves. I gave the whistle a toot, and the girl with the ball served.

This time I kept my eyes glued to Angelica. She was standing with both knees bent, staring at the approaching volleyball like it was the Hale-Bopp comet. With her hands already up in the air and all that concentration, there was no way she was going to miss it as it sailed right toward her.

Then this leg shot across the floor right behind her, attached to Emily who was sliding on her rear end like somebody had hauled off and knocked her down—except that she had a Barney-sized grin on her face, and she aimed her leg right for Angelica's heel. Just as the ball reached Angelica's fingertips, Emily collided with her, and Angelica took a dive backwards. Emily rolled out of the way, and Angelica fell with a resounding thud to the gym floor.

I didn't even get the whistle into my mouth before Coach Gatney was suddenly there, hands on hips and already yelling. "What's going on?" she screeched at them. "This is volleyball, not rugby!"

Everybody on that side of the court looked at Coach Gatney like the dead had just arisen. Emily recovered remarkably fast.

"This little wench tripped me!" she said.

I laughed out loud. "Right!" I said. "Sorry, Emily, but I saw the whole thing. You slid all the way up here on your fanny and knocked her feet right out from under her."

"Like I would really do that!" Emily said.

She scooped in her two cohorts with her eyes. Hayley and Jennifer looked equally indignant.

"That was the second time Angelica fell," I said to Coach Gatney. "I didn't see it the first time, but I watched this time."

"Anybody else see what happened?" Coach Gatney said. Her bark echoed emptily in the gym. Everybody just kind of shrugged and surveyed the ceiling. I bored my eyes into the three vultures.

"Did you feel somebody trip you?" Coach said to Angelica.

Angelica's eyes swelled, and I could almost hear her swallowing. Coach Gatney sniffed.

"All right," she said. "It's Tobey's word against yours, Emily. I have no reason to doubt her word, but I'll be looking for reasons not to trust yours. You watch your step."

She gave me a sharp nod and walked backward off the court, the way those PE types always do. But as I turned around to go off, I could feel the girls' eyes drilling holes in my back.

And you know, it didn't bother me. Standing up for people was getting to be my trademark. It was a no-brainer that nobody else was going to do it.

I put my whistle up to my lips and smiled at Emily before I blew it. She scratched her nose with her thumb.

I heard about nothing else the entire day. It was all over my second-period English class before I even got there. Norie came up to me and said, "I heard you busted a sophomore in your PE class."

"How did you hear about it?" I said.

"Jennifer Oakman's brother's girlfriend has the locker next to mine."

"Oh," I said. "That explains everything."

"Yeah," she said. "Who needs a cell phone, right? Here." She thrust a folded piece of paper into my hand.

"What's this?" I said.

"The memo about lunch Friday."

I stared at her. "Already?"

"I did it first period. I was supposed to be in the library doing research for an article on child abuse, but I wanted to do this first. We have to get Cheyenne some help. She's dying in this jungle."

I nodded, although I wasn't sure I was getting it. I was kind of glad when Mr. Lowe reminded us all that he was the teacher and he would like to start class.

Anyway, by the end of the day, everybody and his brother had either heard that I "saved some Mexican chick's fanny" or that I "busted Emily Yates's," depending on who told them. And the story grew, too. By the time I got to track practice after school, rumor had it that Emily Yates's father was probably going to drag me into court, seeing how he was an attorney.

I was laughing so hard when little Zena Thomas, a freshman, told me that, I didn't notice the presence beside me. He had to nudge me before I even looked up.

Into those eyes—the blue, gray, gold ones.

"The way I heard it," Damon said, "her old man's the district attorney, and he's already got a warrant out for your arrest."

I gave a really unattractive snort.

"That's what I thought," he said. "Rough day for you?"

"No," I said. I ran my finger casually under my nose, just to be sure I hadn't blown anything disgusting out of it. "Actually, it kind of cracks me up. You do the right thing like you're supposed to, and everybody thinks you're like this hero or something."

"Or a traitor," Damon said. "Depends on who you talk to."

He grinned, and I grinned back, and all the Angelicas and Emilys and vultures and rumors in the world faded off. Man, I had it bad.

"Um, Tobey?" said a voice at my elbow.

It was Angelica, looking timid and nervous. She was flicking her fuchsia-painted fingernails at about ninety miles an hour.

"Hi," I said. "Are you okay?"

"I'm fine," she said. "I didn't fall that hard."

"That's cool," I said.

I kept smiling at her, hoping my eyes were betraying my thoughts: *Please go away, honey, so I can flirt with this guy.*

She smiled back for another interminable fifteen seconds before she said, "Well, I just wanted to thank you—you know, for standing up for me like that."

I shrugged. "It's okay."

"No, really, people don't do that most of the time."

"Yeah, well, they ought to. Nobody deserves to be tripped on the volleyball court."

"But still, like I told you the other day, you're so brave."

Damon nudged me playfully in the side. "Hey, you hear that?" he said. "Somebody besides me thinks you're brave."

I, of course, grinned stupidly. "That makes all two of you," I said. "I get the feeling just about everybody else thinks I'm some kind of informant for the PE department."

"That doesn't seem to bother you much," Damon said.

No, nothing much is bothering me right at this moment, I wanted to say to him. *Except that little Angelica won't move on!*

Not only did she not move on, but three other people moved in. Utley, our team captain whose first name I never did know, and Kevin and Pam.

"Nah, nobody thinks you're a narc or anything," Utley said. He hitched up his shorts, which were forever falling down.

"I don't," Pam said. "I'm glad you told on Emily. I can't stand that girl. Of course, I hate freshmen anyway."

"I didn't do it because I couldn't stand her—" I started to say.

But Kevin had to get his opinion in there. "Thing is, see, if you turned in somebody everybody liked, that would be a whole other thing, see, but since Emily Yates is a—"

"Watch it," Utley said. "Tobey doesn't cuss."

"Yeah, well, you know what I'm sayin'," Kevin said. "A lot of other people have wanted to do that. They just didn't have the guts."

"All right, Tobey," Damon said, patting me on the back. "You have guts."

"Yeah," I said.

We exchanged grins as Coach Mayno yelled something about were we going to do warmup today or just stand around flapping our lips.

I started to go out on the grass behind the rest of our little crowd, but Damon caught my arm. When I looked up at him, he had half a smile going.

"For what it's worth," he said, "I like girls with guts."

I'll admit it, I ran better that day than I probably ever had. If I really wanted to get cheesy, I'd say my heart had wings or something. Seriously, even though Coach took us out across the desert, past where they were building the new houses, in a head wind, I had all this air, which is saying something at forty-five hundred feet. And my legs didn't cramp up, which is also saying something, considering that out there, you're either going up, or you're going down. I stayed right behind the first clump of boys on the whole run—or more specifically, right where I could see Damon. And I was grinning the entire time.

I wasn't completely off in Cinderella Land, however. I did turn around once or twice to check on Angelica. I don't know, I guess I was feeling sort of responsible for her all of a sudden.

It was weird—she stayed right in the middle of the pack. Not that that is weird in itself. But Damon had told me she was getting special coaching from Mr. Mayno. Running the way she was, sort of with an okay time and not incredible form, she wasn't exactly good enough to warrant special attention, but she wasn't bad enough to require remedial work either.

I glanced over at little Zena, who was about four-foot-eleven, weighed not an ounce over ninety pounds, and was running beside me on the way back to the school like a baby gazelle. *If I were going to give a freshman special attention*, I thought, *I'd be giving it to her.*

But then, I wasn't the coach, nor did I want to be the coach.

I had enough going on in my head at that point. And most of it was good. Very, very good. In fact, it made me feel magnanimous.

"So, Zena," I said between pants, "you and Angelica are the only freshmen on the varsity team. Nice going."

She grinned a really big smile for such a tiny face. "My friend Victoria made it, too, but she quit the first week."

"That's right, huh? What happened? I thought she was all excited."

"Excited" was actually an understatement. I remembered Victoria now. She had been all over the place like a Labrador puppy. She had this long braid that she whipped around. That thing could kill you.

Zena was looking at me intently. She had rich blue eyes, and they were really studying me.

"What?" I said. "Did I say something wrong?"

"Oh, no!" she said. "I just don't want you to think anything bad about Victoria."

"Why would I? Cross-country isn't for everybody." We straggled onto the track for our cool-down walk. "Coach Mayno can be tough."

As if on cue, he snapped out just then, "All right, people, you looked like a bunch of turtles out there. My grandmother runs faster than that. You're going to have to hustle if you don't want to embarrass yourselves up at South Tahoe."

"When is it?" Utley said, spraying spit over everybody in front of him.

"The captain doesn't know when the first meet is," Coach Mayno said. He flashed a smile over the pack as he walked backward in front of us down the track. "Can anybody save Utley's behind, or do we all run another four laps?"

"No, man!" Kevin moaned. "Somebody's gotta know!"

"When is it, Tobey?" Pam said. "Please tell me you have it."

"A week from Saturday," I said.

"You're a goddess," Kevin said.

"Watch it now," Coach Mayno said as he spun around. "Let's not insult Tobey's religious integrity."

"What'd I say?" Kevin said.

"Figure it out while you take two laps. Come on, everybody, let's hit it!"

Coach Mayno took off, and we followed at a jog, most of us groaning all the way. Pam trotted up to Zena and me and nodded toward Coach. "He's such a jerk sometimes," she said. "But it's like we take it because he's so cool."

"I guess so," I said. I was craning my neck to get a glimpse of Damon.

"What about you, Zena?" Pam said, bouncing her ponytail in the freshman's direction. "Don't you think Coach Mayno's a babe, you know, for his age?"

"He's not my type," Zena said. Then she looked up from the track like she had startled herself. "That's nothing bad about him," she said hurriedly. She shoved her bob behind her ears. "He's a good coach and all that—"

"Relax," Pam said. She chuckled. "You freshmen really need to learn to lighten up. Especially that one."

I followed her gaze to the side of the track. Angelica was standing there, bent over at the waist and clutching her knees.

"She looks like she's hyperventilating," I said. I had this maternal urge.

I broke out of the pack and ran over to her. I got there the same time Coach Mayno did.

"What's going on?" he said.

"She just all of a sudden stopped running," I said.

"Why don't you let her answer, Tobe?" he said. He leaned over Angelica while I blinked.

Okay, just trying to help. I didn't mean to be pushy.

"You okay, Angel?" Coach Mayno said.

The head of thick, black, curly hair shook.

"What?" he said.

"No. I think I'm sick."

"Do you want me to get her some water?" I said.

"No, you know what?" Coach said. "I want you to go on back and finish your laps. I got this handled."

I felt kind of stung, and I dragged my feet getting back into the lane. Behind me, I heard her say, "I really need to go home. I can't stay after today."

"You'll be all right," he said to her. "Sit down."

She was there when the rest of us went back to the locker rooms, and Coach Mayno was with her. I was still feeling like I'd had my hand slapped.

Good thing Damon called that night, and I had a reason to forget all about it. He asked me out.

CHAPTER FOUR

FRIDAY WAS LIKE RIDING THE BUMPER CARS. SO MUCH was going on, I'd start out in one direction but bump into something else I was supposed to be doing and start off the other way. I was driving like Ernie Irvin and then—wham!—something else would come up.

The day started off with Dad playing mental bumper cars with me in the kitchen before I even got out the door. Mom was packing my lunch, he was reading the *Reno Gazette-Journal* at the table, and I was trying to gulp down a bowl of Cheerios and study for one of Mr. Lowe's killer vocabulary tests.

Dad put down the paper to look for another section and said, "Now, who's this boy you want to go out with tomorrow night?"

"Damon Douglas," I said. I had a sinking feeling, and I put down my spoon. "I thought I was going out with him. I thought you guys said it was okay."

"Oh, it is—I think," Mom said from the counter.

"It's all right for you to date," Dad said. He crackled open the Local section. "You're sixteen, and you've been responsible about going out with your friends."

He stopped as if that were the end of the explanation. It wasn't as far as I was concerned.

"I heard a 'but' in there," I said.

"But," Dad said, "your mother and I haven't met this boy. You know we like to meet your friends before you go out with them. I thought that was a given."

I started to panic. "But he's a Christian!" I said. "Isn't that all you need to know?"

Mom smiled this mother-sly smile. "Why don't you want us to meet him, Tobey? Does he have a pierced nose or something?"

"No!" I said. "I don't care if you meet him—I mean, I want you to meet him—but I hate that it's like this test or something. If you guys don't happen to like him, I can't go out with him?"

My father's eyebrows went up to the middle of his scalp.

"Is it my imagination?" Mom said. "Or are you taking a tone with me?"

"Sorry," I said tightly. "I just thought this was all settled. I mean, why can't you trust my judgment?"

"What's she got her panties in a bunch about?" Fletcher said from the family room.

"Go to school," I said.

"I can't until you take me," he said.

I gave my parents a pleading look.

"Go start the car, Fletcher," Dad said to him. "She'll be right there. And do not back it out of the garage."

Fletcher jammed out of the room, and Mom handed me my lunch bag.

"Look, Tobey," Dad said, "I'm sure if you like this boy . . ."

"Damon."

"I'm sure if you like him, he'll be just fine. Only let us do our parent thing, okay? This is in our contract." He went back to the *Gazette-Journal*.

"I don't remember signing any contract," I mumbled as I got in the car.

Fletcher's eyes gleamed, even in the darkness of the garage. "Cool," he said.

"What?" I said.

"The parents in your face for a change. I get sick of being the only one."

"You're the only one who blows it," I said.

We batted that around all the way to school—all of about a

two-minute drive. Then I dismissed it the minute we pulled Lazarus into the parking lot. Lazarus was the name of my red Honda Civic, so named because he had been brought back from the dead many times. Roxy and Gabe were sitting on Gabe's car waiting for me.

"Did you forget about judicial board before school?" Gabe said.

"No," I said. "I'm on my way. Do you mind if I get my backpack out of the car?"

"Tell me it has the agenda for the class meeting in it," Roxy said. "And don't tell me if it doesn't, or I'll have to go in the bathroom and puke."

"Somebody needs to switch to decaf," Fletcher said. He ambled off toward the building. The three of us passed him in overdrive.

That's the way the rest of the day was. First we had judicial board in the conference room in the office. Ms. Race served us orange juice and donuts, and I found out she was the principal's new secretary. I wanted to ask her where she bought her great ethnic-looking clothes, but Mrs. Quebbeman, our adviser, called the meeting to order.

Mrs. Quebbeman was also my counselor, which I never could figure out. I always thought she should have been a CPA or something, the way she loved to shuffle folders around and quote you statistics. She had this sensible short haircut—gray hair, of course—and she always wore loafers and was brisk and efficient. She was great at scheduling and telling me what my chances were of actually becoming a nurse or a landscape artist or a whatever, but I couldn't imagine actually going to her with a problem.

We spent forty-five minutes that day talking about how we would run the election for homecoming queen. Well, thirty minutes arguing first. I stayed quiet until Pam called Gabe a chauvinist pig, and then I cut in and said could we knock off the name-calling and talk like civilized people. The warning bell rang right when we took the final vote to let juniors be nominated.

I walked Pam to class trying to explain to her that Gabe was just a harmless control weenie—so I was late for PE. But we didn't dress out because the period was short so class meetings could be held. I spent the half-hour of PE filling out a bus request for Coach Mayno.

"Hey, Tobe," he said while I was writing. "I'm sorry I snapped at you the other day at practice."

"It's okay," I said. "I get all protective of Angelica, too."

"What does that mean?" he said.

My head came up from the page. His voice had a funky edge to it, and his eyes had the same. It faded when he grinned at me.

"There I go again," he said. "I heard Utley and those guys saying she was a kiss-up because she trains overtime—I just get a little peeved."

"I don't think she's a kiss-up," I said.

"I know." He reached over and touched my cheek. "You're too good, Tobe. I wish I had a whole team full of Tobeys."

I felt better. After making the necessary six copies of the list for him, I booked through a vocabulary test so I could sprint to the theater to set up for the junior class meeting. Mr. Ott, our adviser, was already there, but he was pretty much useless. All the poor, pudgy, half-bald man ever did was pace and rub his hands together and ask me if I needed anything.

"No sir, we've got it together," I said. I glanced behind him at Roxy, the class secretary, who was dragging her fingers through all that red hair and bulging her eyes at me like I was two tacos short of a six-pack.

"Don't ever admit to him we aren't totally ready for a meeting," I'd told her a million times. "He'll have a coronary. Just pretend we know what we're doing."

Actually, we did. But you don't run a meeting of 350 kids without stressing out some. We made it through the whole agenda—setting up a fund-raiser for prom, appointing a prom committee, and assigning a bunch of people to start on the homecoming float—and Mr. Ott only paced once, when Norie got up and said, "Some of the journalism staff might be coming up to you asking you to answer a questionnaire about gender fairness in the classroom. Would you guys please, like, cut them some slack and either answer it or just say no?" When nobody threw anything at her or yelled an obscenity, Mr. Ott calmed down.

I, on the other hand, had a huge sweat ring in each armpit by the time we were through. As I was gathering up all my folders off the podium, I was hoping Mom had packed two juice cans in my lunch because I was about to die of thirst from talking so much. Somebody tapped on the podium and made me jump a foot.

"Hey, L'Orange," Norie said. "Thanks for letting me make that announcement."

"No problem," I said.

"You're coming to the meeting, right?"

I looked at her blankly.

"Flagpole Girls," she said. "You didn't forget—lunch—on the patio behind the art room where they fire the ceramics?"

"Oh, right," I said. I tried to save face with a laugh. "I have so much going on today, I had to stop and think."

"Okay, get there as soon as you can." She rapped the podium with her knuckles and marched off. She always seemed to be marching somewhere.

"I have to go to my locker first to get my lunch," I called after her.

"Don't get your lunch; let me take you to Port of Subs."

I turned around. Damon was at my elbow. My heart thudded.

"Oh, man," I said. "I'm sorry. I already have plans."

He gave the half-smile. "Who is he?"

"No—she—them!" I rolled my eyes.

"Uh-huh," he said. "I'm with ya."

"No, it's the girls I met at the flagpole the other day." I watched his eyes. They actually looked disappointed. I wanted to yell after Norie, "Sorry, can't make it. Got a better offer!"

Impulsively, I grabbed Damon's wrist. "Why don't you come with me? It's us Christians—it isn't like a private club or anything."

Damon shook his head. "I think I'll pass," he said. "No offense, but it kind of sounds like a girl thing."

"It sounds like that," I said. "It isn't, really . . ."

But I stopped. I was getting a flash of *his* getting a flash of
Brianna and the other beauties. Call me insecure, but I hadn't
even been out with the guy yet. I didn't want to lose before we
left the starting line.

"You might feel kind of lame being the only guy," I said.

He gave my arm a squeeze and let go. "No sweat," he said.
"I'm seeing you tomorrow night, right?"

I nodded like a geek.

"Pick you up at seven."

"You might want to come a little early," I said. "My parents
want to meet you. It's no big deal, you know, but—"

"I hear you," he said. "I won't cuss. I won't bring my ciga-
rettes in."

I must have looked stricken because he laughed this kind of
husky little chuckle thing. "I don't smoke," he said. "I was just
messing with your head."

Mess with it all you want, I thought as he walked off up the
aisle. *Man, I have got it bad.*

The halls were starting to clear by that time. We had five minutes to get to our lockers and out of the hallways before they
locked them up. It was King High's way of keeping food out of
the building or something. I had to run to my locker, and of
course my lock wouldn't open the first time. Mr. Holden, the
principal, was pacing the hall behind me saying, "Hurry up,
folks. We're about to lock down." I flung open my locker and
threw my folders in there, snatched up my lunch, and saw a
piece of paper float to the ground.

I didn't recognize it, but it had to have come from my locker.
It was folded weird, like somebody had stuffed it through the
little vent things.

I crammed it into my jeans pocket and fled for the double
doors just as Mr. Holden was shutting them.

"Where you headed, Tobey?" he said. He had salt-and-pepper

hair and a nice smile. I'd always kind of liked him. I grinned back.

"Art room," I said.

"Is there anything you aren't involved in?" he said.

I didn't explain. I took off for the ceramics patio and arrived just as Norie was clearing her throat. Everybody else was there.

"We thought you ditched us," Cheyenne said.

"Never happen," Norie said.

I squeezed onto a bench between Shannon and Brianna and worked at catching my breath.

"Since we only have forty-six minutes," Norie said, "which is the next thing I want to attack in the newspaper, you can't even start to digest in forty-six minutes. Anyway, since we don't have much time we probably ought to get right down to it. Cheyenne, how's it going?"

Cheyenne shook her bangs out of her eyes and looked at us dolefully. "Awful," she said. "Before, everybody just ignored me. Now they go after me in math class every single day. 'Hey, Jesus Freak, can you walk on water yet?'"

"Tell them, 'Not yet,'" I said. "Tell them you're still working on turning water into wine." I stopped in the middle of un-Velcroing my lunch bag and laughed. "No, don't tell them that. They'll all show up at your house with their flasks."

"Is that what you would say?" Marissa said to me. She was halfway nibbling on a cheese sandwich and twisting a piece of her hair around her finger.

"Sure," I said. "Or something like that. You just can't let people get to you."

Brianna straightened way up on the bench next to me. "Well, that's fine for you," she said. "Everything you do, you about get a standing ovation. It's the new trend the next day."

"Get serious!" I said.

But her big black eyes were dead serious. She folded her hands around her knees as if she were trying to keep her feet from kicking me.

"It doesn't have anything to do with who I am," I said,

eyeing her toes. "Anybody can do it. You just know what's right, and you stand up for it. People might rag on you for a while, but if you're doing what Jesus would do, you just do it and sooner or later people stop bugging you about it and it's fine."

Brianna locked her arms across her chest. "I just don't think that's going to be much help to Cheyenne. I don't know about the rest of you."

I looked around at the rest of them. Cheyenne looked as if she were about to cry, and Marissa wasn't much different. Shannon was examining her palms like she could have found a better answer there. I didn't even want to look at Norie.

But Norie didn't jump down my throat or break out pad and pencil. She just leaned forward, the usual baggy T-shirt hanging down over her knees.

"I have an idea," she said. "My dad—" she made an exaggeratedly proper face "—the thoracic surgeon—are you impressed?—is a recovering alcoholic. He's been sober for ten years, blah, blah. Anyway, he's big on AA, you know, the whole Twelve-Step program."

"Your point is?" Brianna said, shooting up a sophisticated eyebrow.

"Yeah, I usually have trouble getting to it. My point is, we could use the AA approach here."

"I don't drink," Cheyenne said.

"What are you, the Queen of the Non-Sequitur?" Norie said. "Never mind, it doesn't have anything to do with drinking, it has to do with how we help each other. Instead of trying to fix somebody . . ." She looked directly at me. ". . . we just tell our own story and how we handled it and let other people take it as they want to. We don't give our opinions of what somebody said, we just pray for each other."

"I can get to that," Brianna said.

She looked around at the rest of us. They all looked a little more hopeful. I felt like flying out of there, finding Damon at the Port of Subs, and having him assure me I wasn't this little

Christian snob I'd just basically been told I was. But I nodded and popped open my juice can.

"Okay, so we know Tobey's story. She told everybody to bug off."

"I didn't!" I said. "I just told them what we were doing, and they asked me a lot of questions like 'Will you pray for a guy for me?' " I shrugged uneasily. "I just said what I believed, and then I dropped it. Really, it doesn't bother me."

No one looked comforted by that. Marissa raised her hand.

"Yikes, this isn't class," Norie said. "You don't have to do that. Just talk."

Marissa fiddled with her bag of cookies and then stuck them in her lap and stared at them. "Nobody said anything to me except this one girl in the bathroom."

"What did she say?" Shannon asked.

"She goes, 'I would have been too embarrassed to stand out there and pray in front of everybody.' I just told her it wasn't embarrassing because you guys were all so neat." She wiggled around and picked up her cookies and put them down again.

"Whoa," Norie said. "I feel, like, honored or something."

Brianna nodded thoughtfully. "I like that answer," she said. "Who else?"

"My friends are so P.C.," Norie said.

Cheyenne wrinkled her nose. "What's P.C.?"

"Politically correct. All they wanted to know was whether we were violating the First Amendment. I straightened them out, and they shut up." She shrugged one shoulder. "I don't think that'll work for everybody."

It got quiet. I felt as if I should say something. I had this awful sense of failure, like I'd let them all down. I looked at Cheyenne. "I'll pray," I said. "I'll pray that something one of us said will help you."

She smiled her little-girl smile at me. "It already does," she said. She looked at Marissa. "What you said—I like that. It's like you guys are my pack. I feel safer with a pack."

"What are we, wolves?" Norie said

"I don't know about wolves," Marissa said. "But I'll say this."

And then, of course, she didn't, until Brianna said, "Say it, girl!"

"No offense to the rest of you," Marissa said, "because I don't know all of you, but I wouldn't have come today if I hadn't known Tobey was coming. What you said is true, Brianna. If she does it, then it'll turn out to be the cool thing to do."

I could feel myself squirming. First I'd felt like a complete loser. Now I was up on some pedestal I didn't belong on.

Brianna poked me in the side with her elbow. "Aren't you gonna take a bow or something?"

I shook my head. Then she blew me away by putting her arm around me. "You don't have to be all modest," she said. "If you got it, girl, flaunt it."

"I'm not sure I've got it," I said.

But I felt better somehow, especially after we held hands again and prayed for Cheyenne. She was beaming like a little kid who just saw the birthday cake coming. I couldn't be sorry I came when I saw that.

The first warning bell rang, and Brianna said, "Everybody take your garbage with you. I promised Ms. Squires we wouldn't trash the place if she let us use it."

I had already closed up my lunch bag, so I jammed my sandwich bag into my jeans pocket. My fingers hit the note I'd crammed in there earlier, and I pulled it out.

"Hey, you guys," Norie said. "Do you want to make this an every-Friday thing?'

"Yes," Cheyenne said. "That would be rad!"

I'm not sure what everybody else said. I just kind of nodded like a mummy. I was still numb from the note in jagged handwriting that I'd just read:

You better be careful who you stand up for. Angelica Benitez is a tramp.

CHAPTER
FIVE

SO, NEXT FRIDAY. SAME PLACE." NORIE JABBED ME IN THE ribs. "L'Orange, are you coming?"

Still moving like R2-D2, I stuffed the note in my backpack and said, "Sure."

I started to follow Shannon and Brianna out, but Norie nodded me back. "Look," she said, voice lowered, "I didn't mean to make it sound like you were being, like, patronizing or anything. It's just the rest of us aren't as far along as you are, you know, spiritually. Somebody starts firing out clichés at me and doesn't tell me what I'm supposed to do with them, and I'm out of here."

"Don't worry about it," I said.

"I'm not worried about it." She grinned this sort of square smile that pretty much matched the rest of her. "I'm just warning you that I intend to pick your brain. If anybody actually lives what they believe, it's you. The way I look at it, you have, like, this obligation to show the rest of us how it's done."

She marched out of there, immediately yelling to somebody about interviewing them for her child abuse piece. I stood there like a robot in the doorway so people had to shove past and glare at me to get in.

Obligation? That didn't sound so good to me. Being a Christian had always been something I just did. In our house it was as natural as eating and sleeping and fighting over the remote.

Norie and the rest of them made it sound like it was supposed to be hard.

And they were expecting me to teach them how to do it.

I talked to Damon about Angelica on our date the next night. Not right away, of course.

After Fletcher yelled from the garage, "Hey, who do we know with a blue truck?" and I met Damon at the door, the first fifteen minutes of our date were spent in my living room. My father came out of his study right off the front entrance hall, trying to look even taller than his six-foot-two and wearing this what-are-your-intentions-boy expression. My mother hurried in from her craft room, pulling straight pins out of her mouth and holding a half-made teddy bear.

"You must be Damon," Mom said, sticking out her hand.

"No, Mom, it's the paper boy." Fletcher passed through, grunted at Damon, and disappeared into the kitchen.

"The rest of us are a little more civilized than Fletcher," Mom said. "Do you want to sit down . . . have some iced tea?"

"We probably ought to get to the movie," I said as I edged toward the front door.

So we stood up for fifteen minutes while Dad interrogated Damon. He asked him a bunch of questions about what his dad did, where they went to church, and how long they had lived in Reno. I was half-expecting Dad to request a urine sample, but Damon didn't look as if he minded all that much. He nodded a lot and said "Yes sir," and every time Mom smiled—which was every two seconds—he gave her the full treatment, both sides of his mouth.

By the time Dad finally said, "Well, you kiddos have a good time. Be in by eleven-thirty," I had sweat rings the size of tortillas. I practically ran to Damon's truck. He kept smiling until we were buckled in and had pulled away because both my parents were standing on the front porch waving. Then he burst out laughing.

"What?" I said.

"You were a crackup," he said.

"Me?"

"That whole ordeal was right up there with having a root canal for you, wasn't it?"

"No!"

He cut me one of those half-smiles.

"Okay—yes. The only thing missing was the naked light bulb. I am so sorry."

"For what?" Damon said. "They were just being parents. That's why you turned out so good."

"Do your parents do that every time you go out with somebody?"

"Yeah," he said. "We have to go over to my house right now so they can check you out."

"Seriously?"

He grinned, full throttle. "Nah, I'm just messing with your head."

"Don't do that!" I said. "I'm so gullible!"

"No," he said. "You're honest. Which is cool."

Frankly, I'd have believed anything he told me.

We had a blast at the movies. I couldn't tell you what we saw. I mean, I watched it, and it was good. But right now all I can remember is us sharing a tub of popcorn big enough to bathe in and picking out our favorite colors of Starbursts, and his saying, "Let's go see that," after every preview.

Afterward we walked around Virginia Lake. It was one of the few really peaceful places in Reno. Nicknamed The Biggest Little City in the World, Reno was long on clanging slot machines, even in the grocery stores, glaring neon showgirls on signs, and people in big Elvis and Marilyn heads handing you free drink coupons on the sidewalk. It was very short on peaceful.

But Virginia Lake was at the edge of downtown, where runners and senior citizens and about a thousand ducks hung out during the day, and hardly anybody went at night. It was one of my favorite places to run and think. That night, it just became my favorite place, period. It couldn't have been more romantic if it had come out of a Danielle Steele novel. The moonlight rippled across the lake, and the ducks sounded like they were muttering sweet things to us under their breaths as we passed, and the night air caressed our skin. We must have strolled around the water five times while we ate Frosties from Wendy's and talked. And talked. And talked.

I told him my entire life story, which took all of about seven seconds. Besides moving from Kentucky when I was six and living in Reno from first grade on, there wasn't much to tell, although Damon acted as if every little scrap I told him was material for CNN.

"So you helped lead a major youth conference when you were a sophomore?"

"It wasn't that big of a conference . . ."

"You actually ask yourself 'what would Jesus do' every time you make a decision?"

"I learned it from this book I read. A lot of people do that . . ."

"You really have an 'outie' belly button?"

"Yes—and don't plan on ever seeing it because I don't do bikinis."

At that point he stopped on the little arched bridge we were crossing and held up both hands. The smile was gone. "Whoa," he said. "Time out."

"What?" I said.

"I wasn't asking for a showing, okay? I want you to know I'm not into the whole pressure-girls-to-sleep-with-you thing."

Somehow we had made a quantum leap from navels to sex. I just stood there, blinking stupidly.

"What I'm saying is I don't believe in sex before marriage," he said. "I just thought I ought to make that clear."

I grinned at him. "Well, okay. Thanks."

He grinned back—the half-smile. All I could do was stand there and think how blue-black his hair looked, all wavy under the moonlight. Then he picked up my hand and tucked it inside his. "It's still early," he said. "Want to go to Kmart?"

Yet another quantum leap: from True Love Waits to discount stores.

"Kmart?" I said.

"Yeah," he said. "What else is there to do in a town where you have to be twenty-one to do everything?"

"O-kay," I said slowly. "What did you plan to do at Kmart?"

He dug into his pocket and pulled out a wad of bills. "We each take two bucks," he said. "In fifteen minutes we have to buy each other two things with it. And one of them has to be blue."

I know I was staring at him like an idiot, but that didn't seem to bother him. In fact, nothing seemed to bother Damon. It was one of the things I was finding so . . . refreshing about him.

"Okay," I said. "Let's go for it!"

The Kmart was open twenty-four hours a day, although I'd never been to it at 10:30 at night. It was amazing how many people were in there with loaded shopping carts. It was the most fun I'd ever had in there at any hour.

I cruised the aisles with my little two dollars in my fist, looking for cool stuff for Damon. It was amazing; I'd only known him, what, a week, and already I knew what was totally Damon and what wasn't.

I rejected the plastic water pistol—too violent—and the dashboard hula girl—too crude. I finally settled on a box of crayons that colored fluorescent and a toy truck you could practically fit in one of your molars. Blue, of course.

Damon met me out front with his little bag, and he made me sit on the horsy-ride thing while I opened it. There weren't too many toddlers screaming for a ride at that time of night.

I pulled out a pacifier first, and he chuckled in that way he had that really got to me. "That's for you to put in your mouth while your parents are cross-examining me," he said.

I popped it in right then and dug for the second item. It was a little girl's butterfly ring. Blue.

I stuck it on my pinkie and admired it.

"Butterfly's the symbol for transformation," Damon said. "I'm kind of watching you come out of a cocoon, right before my eyes. Pretty cheesy, huh?"

"No!" I said, spitting out the pacifier. "I love it."

"Okay," he said. "But don't tell your dad I gave you a ring on our first date."

Our first date? I wanted to say to him. *Does that mean there's going to be a second?*

Instead I said, "Open yours."

He pulled out the crayons.

"You color everything," I said. "Stuff that was just kind of ordinary before."

"Wow," he said. His voice was soft, and I suddenly felt shy. I motioned to the bag in spastic fashion. "Look at the other one."

"It better be blue," he said. And then he grinned. "My truck!"

"It had a baby," I said. "What's your big truck's name?"

"Its name?"

"Yeah."

"It doesn't have a name."

"It has to have a name. How can you call it in the parking lot when you forget where you've parked it?"

"I'm not even going to ask you if you do that," Damon said.

"I do. My car's name is Lazarus."

Damon examined the miniature pickup and said, "L'Blue."

"L'Blue?"

"Yeah. Your name's L'Orange. His is L'Blue."

"Cool," I said. "And this is Baby L'Blue."

Damon rolled the toy truck up my arm. "He likes that. He's gonna give you a kiss. And then so am I."

The truck touched my cheek, and Damon's lips did, too—soft and gentle and, I don't know, reverent. We were still smiling at each other when something behind him caught my eye.

I sat up straight on the horse.

"What's wrong?" he said.

"Nothing," I said.

I didn't want to go into a long explanation of what was happening about twenty feet from us. In the first place, I didn't want them to hear me. In the second place, I wasn't sure exactly what I was seeing.

It was Angelica. I could have ID'd the hair from a mile off, although I had to look twice at the clothes. She was wearing baggy black jeans belted so far down on her hips I was surprised they didn't go ahead and fall off. Her belly button definitely wasn't an outie. She was also falling out of a black sports bra covered uselessly with a red blouse you could see right through.

But it wasn't even that that got me. It was the headlock the guy with the wrestler's body and the tank shirt had her in. I wasn't sure if he was hurting her or messing around. From the way she was squirming to get away from him—but without making a sound—it was hard to tell.

Then she broke out from under his arm and started to run. He had her by the wrist before she could go two steps and was yanking her back.

"Where you goin', baby?" he said way louder than he had to, since he had her face a half-inch from his mouth.

She still didn't utter a peep. I'd have been screaming my head off. His face split open—I'm not sure if it was supposed to be a smile—and he plastered his mouth right on hers. It was the longest kiss I'd ever seen anyplace but on a screen.

I guess you could call it a kiss. It looked more like he was trying to perform a tonsillectomy on her with his tongue. He held her by the back of the neck with one hand and planted the other one on her belt and jerked her closer to him—if that was possible.

And the whole time, she didn't move, not even to pull away. I didn't move either as I sat there on the horsy ride gaping.

Damon followed my gaze over his shoulder, and then held out his hand to me.

"Come on," he said. "Let's go."

I was more than happy to escape to the truck. I was numb. Damon didn't say anything until we were well out of the parking lot.

"Was that Angelica?" he said.

"Yeah," I said.

"Nice boyfriend," he said.

"I don't think that's her boyfriend. I mean, she didn't look like she was having fun." I looked at the side of Damon's face and swallowed. "Do you think Angelica's a tramp?"

"Excuse me?" he said.

I immediately felt idiotic. "Never mind," I said.

"No, come on—that obviously got to you. What's up?"

We stopped at a stoplight, and I hugged my arms around myself. "Somebody put a note in my locker yesterday. It said, 'Be careful who you stand up for. Angelica Benitez is a tramp.'"

"Do you know who did it?"

"I just assumed it was Emily or one of them," I said. "You know, just trying to be mean."

"But now you're thinking maybe it was true."

I looked at him sharply as he put the truck in gear to go up the hill.

"What difference would that make?" I said. "Even if she were a tramp, she doesn't deserve to be tripped on the volleyball court."

"Then why do you ask?"

I shook my head. "I don't even know. That whole thing back there was just kind of ugly. I was hoping you'd tell me I didn't even see it."

"Okay, you didn't even see it."

"Yes, I did."

Damon pulled the truck into my driveway, turned off the ignition, and looked at me, smiling the half-smile. "You don't do denial too well, do you?"

"No," I said.

"Okay, you saw Angelica being molested in front of Kmart by a guy she evidently knew. She obviously wasn't out with him because he put a gun to her head. I mean, she acted like she was there of her own free will. Can you do anything about it?"

"No," I said.

He slid his arm across the back of the seat. "Then maybe you should forget it." He touched my shoulder with the tip of his finger. "I had a blast tonight."

"Me, too," I said.

"Want to do it again?"

"Yeah," I said.

I guess it just didn't take that much for me to forget about Angelica.

CHAPTER
SIX

THE NEXT WEEK WAS SO FULL I DIDN'T HAVE MUCH chance to think about Angelica anyway. Besides Damon calling every night, we ate lunch together every day, and we got Cokes after every track practice and went to Virginia Lake in L'Blue. Sigh. Besides all that, every teacher decided to give a test, and Mr. Ott gave me a pile of paperwork to fill out about what the junior class was doing for homecoming week, which was still a month away. Then there was Roxy. She pulled me into dark corners every chance she got. Her first question was always, "So what's going on with Damon?"

"I think we're officially going out," I told her one day in the room in the chemistry lab where they keep the beakers and stuff. We were supposed to be washing test tubes. I was washing them. Roxy was leaning against the counter raking her hair, interrogating me, and waiting for them to dry—so I could put them away.

She grabbed my hand and examined the little blue butterfly ring on my pinkie. "Is this from him?" she said.

"Yeah."

Her lips twitched. "He spares no expense, I see."

I yanked my hand away from her and made a face. "It was kind of a joke thing. Besides, he gives me a lot more than things. We really connect."

Her hazel eyes got round and serious. "I am so happy for you. I mean, if this is what you really want."

I stared at her. "When did that become important?" I said. "To hear you tell it, if I didn't get a steady boyfriend by the end of the semester, I was going to be retarded socially for the rest of my life."

She blinked at me. "I know I never said that," she said. "I don't even know what that means."

"Forget it," I said. I popped some soap bubbles at her.

"So, do you still think he's cool?" she said.

"Yeah," I said. "Why wouldn't I?"

She scooped her hair back into a temporary bun and leaned her elbows on the counter. Now she was into territory where she was the expert. "Okay, you wouldn't know this because you haven't ever actually had, like, a relationship. But sometimes guys don't turn out to be what you thought they were at the beginning."

"I'm pretty perceptive, Rox."

"And some of them are pretty sly. You have to watch it."

I plunked the last test tube into the drainer and scowled at her. "What is this? First you tell me to practically throw myself at the guy. Now that we're dating, you're telling me he might be a stalker or something!"

"No, listen, forget I said anything," Roxy said. "You're happy; who cares?" She peered at the row of tubes. "Are these dry yet?"

For once, I took Roxy's advice. I forgot she said anything.

Anyway, on top of all that, Mrs. Quebbeman reminded me I was going to be out of school all day Friday to attend a leadership conference in Carson City. Not only did that mean I had a ton of classwork to do ahead of time, but it made two people very unhappy.

One was Norie. She handed me my notice about the Flagpole Girls meeting in English, and I told her I couldn't be there.

"Aw, man," she said. "That is a drag. We'll be totally lost."

"Look, I'm not some paragon of virtue," I said.

"Ooh, nice phrase," she said. "Can I use that?"

"Yeah—I don't know what for."

"I'll think of something." She finished jotting it down and looked hard at me. She seemed to do everything hard. "You'll be there next week, won't you? I mean, I meant what I said the other day—I really want to know how you do it."

"Sure," I said. I didn't know whether to be flattered or bugged. It didn't matter. Coach Mayno drove all thoughts of the Flagpole Girls right out of my head.

"You're going to miss a practice the day before a meet?" he said when I gave him my pre-excused absence form. There was no teasing twinkle in his blue eyes.

"Yes sir," I said. "It was on my thing I filled out for you at the beginning of the year."

"I never pay any attention to those things, you know that," he said. His mouth was in a tight line. "Who do I talk to to get you out of it?"

"Mrs. Quebbeman," I said. "But I don't think it'll do any good."

"Yeah, she's a hard-nose," he muttered. "Woman needs to go out and party. All right, I'll excuse you." He gave my shoulder a squeeze. "But only because it's you, you hear? Don't spread it around or I'll have every Bozo on the team asking if he can go to the dentist during practice or something."

"So I can still run in the meet at Tahoe?" I said.

"Yes, and you had better run those sweet buns of yours off or you'll pay for it next week." He ran his hand across my hair and grinned. "Now get out there and run—you have to do two practices in one."

As I was putting my form in my locker, I couldn't shake off a weird feeling. I can only say weird, because I couldn't identify it. Something Coach had said to me jarred me, like it wasn't something he should have said. I couldn't put my finger on it. I just felt like I wanted to put on a looser shirt or something. Weird.

The next day was the leadership conference. I really like those things. They do a lot of let's-get-everybody-jazzed stuff, and even though I know that's what they're doing, I get jazzed anyway. I was bouncing around in my seat in the school van all the way back through Washoe Valley, with all these ideas going nuts in my head.

"Would you chill?" Pam said to me. "You can't change the world by being junior class president, you know."

"I know. I just got some really rad ideas today is all."

She patted my leg. "Just wait until next year when you get senioritis," she said. "You'll wonder where all this enthusiasm went."

But it was still there when we returned to King High. In fact, when I saw Coach Mayno's car in the parking lot—about the only one there—I decided to surprise him and suit up and run some, even though practice was over.

"You are a sicko," Pam said to me as I grabbed my backpack and headed for the gym.

"Oh well," I said, grinning at her over my shoulder. "What can I tell you? I have to pick up my running clothes for tomorrow anyway."

It was the last completely confident thing I was going to say for about a month.

The gym was silent when I went in. I threw my head back and yelled into it, "Coach May-no, guess who's he-ere!"

He didn't answer, even when I banged on the coaches' office door.

"Yoo-hoo!" I hollered. "Coach May-no, I'm ready to run! Are you impressed?"

The hall seemed to suddenly crack open as the girls' locker room door swung in. Coach Mayno stepped out, keys in his hand. He locked it behind him.

I could feel my energy fizzling out, and I didn't know why.

"Hey, Tobe," he said. "What are you doing here? I thought you were out learning how to lead the world."

"I was," I said. "I saw your car still here when we got back so I thought I'd make up practice." Something made me add, "But I don't have to if that doesn't work for you." I don't know what it was. Maybe the flicker in his eyes. Or the big smile on his face when there wasn't really anything in particular to smile about.

"Actually, it doesn't work, Tobe. I was just on my way out."

He took my arm like he was an usher at a wedding and started to guide me down the hall. He was so firm about it, I was almost afraid to stop. But I did and said, "Since I'm here, can you let me into the locker room? I totally forgot to take my stuff home to wash it for the meet tomorrow."

His smile turned to plastic right there in front of me. "What would you have done if I hadn't been here to open it?" he said.

"I'd have been smelly and wrinkled tomorrow," I said. "And you would have been mad."

Right then there was nothing I believed more. His eyes took on kind of a cold glint, and the smile, plastic or otherwise, disappeared. He gave my arm a hard squeeze and let go. It felt as though his fingers were still wrapped around it.

"Okay," he said. He went toward the door with the keys. "But don't disturb Angelica."

"Angelica?" I said.

"She hurt her ankle today. I was in there dealing with it."

"Will she be able to run tomorrow?" I said.

"She'll be fine," he said.

He pushed open the door, and I started to go in, but he barred the doorway with his arm.

"Angelica," he called into the locker room, "Tobey's just going to come in to pick up her stuff. Okay?"

There was a faint, "Okay."

"You get home and ice down that ankle," he said. "And stay off it tonight."

There was no answer. Coach didn't seem to expect one. "Hurry and get your stuff," he said to me. "I'll come back and lock this later."

The smile reappeared, and he twinkled his eyes at me and pinched my cheek. I wasn't sure if I had imagined his being way ticked off because I'd shown up. But I couldn't help watching him walk away, strutting like he always did. I had that weird feeling again.

"Hurry up, Tobe," he said over his shoulder. "I do have another life, you know."

I blew into the locker room. Angelica was standing up in front of her locker, staring vacantly into it as if she had never seen it before. It was the first time I'd been alone with her since Saturday night, but right now she didn't look at all like the girl in the jeans-down-to-you-know-where who was being swallowed in front of Kmart.

"Hi," I said. "What happened to your ankle?"

She didn't look at me. "Nothing," she said.

"Coach Mayno said you hurt it. Did you twist it or something?"

I craned my neck to look at it, but she pulled it up behind her other leg like a flamingo. "No," she said. "I really have to go."

She snatched a wad of clothes out of her locker, stuffed it under her arm, and headed for the door. "Thanks for asking though," she said and then let it swing closed behind her.

I didn't say anything. All I could think was that she wasn't limping.

Then suddenly I wanted to get out of there. I felt as if I were in somebody's house when they weren't home.

I dug out my shorts, socks, and T-shirt and plopped my backpack on the bench to open it so I could shove them in. Right below the bench, on the floor, was a piece of white clothing.

"Bummer," I muttered to myself. "Angelica left something." I knew it couldn't have belonged to anybody else. Coach Gatney made a clean sweep of the place at the end of every day and put anything left lying around into the bulging lost-and-found box. "I run a tight ship," she always said.

And if she didn't, the janitor did. I'd heard he was famous for taking dropped stuff home. I'd better get whatever it was for Angelica.

Leaning over, I picked it up. Then I held it there, in mid-air, for what was probably a good thirty seconds. I couldn't stop staring at the pair of men's briefs I was holding in my hand.

The minute it really registered, I threw them away from me and jammed my hands behind my back. I was still staring at them, trying to get myself to move, to get out of there, to do anything to wipe out the scene that was fast filling up my mind. The scene I'd almost walked in on.

I sank down on the bench and stared at the underwear with my hand plastered over my mouth. *No way*, I thought. *No way they were . . .* I scrunched my eyes shut. *No, those don't belong to Coach Mayno. He wasn't in here—without them—with Angelica. No, this is stupid.*

I stood up and crammed my stuff into my backpack. I didn't even bother to buckle it. I just wanted out that door.

I was almost there when I stopped and looked back at the briefs, lying guiltily on the floor. What was going to happen when the janitor came in? Would he take them home, or turn them in? There would be so much trouble.

I listened at the door. No footsteps coming down the hall. Using my index finger and my thumb—only the tips of them—I picked up the underwear and tossed it in the trash can. Then I slung my backpack over my shoulder and jerked open the door. I ran down the hall and all the way to my car, although I don't think I needed to. Coach Mayno didn't even stick his head out the door as I flew by.

My mother was in her craft room when I got home. With a show coming up in Sacramento next week, she was thigh-deep in teddy bears, bunny rabbits, and homemade dolls, but she still called out, "I'm in here, Tobey. Come tell me about your day."

That was standard procedure, usually followed by some kind of incredible mother-made snack. Today I'd have done just about anything not to have to go in there. I knew I was wearing what I hadn't seen all over my face.

But it was easier to try to make it through a conversation than to explain why I didn't want to talk. I dumped my backpack in my room and reluctantly dragged back to the craft room. She smiled at me over a mound of fake fur. "Hey, darlin'. How was the conference?"

Funny, I could barely remember I'd been at a conference—the same conference I was so psyched about less than an hour ago. "Fine," I said.

"Did you learn anything neat?" she said. "You always seem to get so much out of those things."

She twirled the wheeled chair around to hunt for her scissors. Her back was to me. I sagged against the doorframe.

Should I tell her? I thought frantically. *Do I tell anybody? What do I do?*

Do you always think what Jesus would do every time you make a decision? Damon had asked me.

I bet Jesus never saw anything like this.

I swallowed hard. I hadn't really seen anything. But there was no shaking what I hadn't seen out of my head. It was clinging like a shadow.

I looked at my mother, her silky, sand-colored head bent over a toy she was making for some little child. She smelled clean, like she always did, and only had nice things to say to me, like she always did. Suddenly I felt dirty being there with her. Like I had been a party to something nasty, and I couldn't bring myself to tell her about it.

"Are you all right, darlin'?" she said.

I jiggled back to find her watching me, big, pale blue eyes mother-soft.

"Yes ma'am," I said. "I'm just wiped out. I think I'll take a nap."

"You need to rest up before your meet tomorrow," she said. "You sure you don't mind that Daddy and I aren't driving up to Tahoe for it?"

"No," I said.

And I didn't mind. I wanted to keep my face away from their perceptive ones until I figured out what to do.

So I stayed in my room most of the evening, and I slipped out early the next morning to park my car in the compound at school. I was no closer to knowing. In fact, I had almost decided forgetting about it sounded really good.

But that became totally absurd the minute I saw Coach Mayno, strutting around with his clipboard, pounding everybody on the back, and asking if each person had eaten a decent breakfast and gotten a good night's sleep.

I tried to avoid him, but Damon dragged me right up to him. "Hey, Coach," he said, "we're here."

"I've already checked you both off." Coach Mayno stuck the clipboard in the back of his sweatpants and nudged Damon with his shoulder. "So," he said, "are you two an item?"

Damon actually blushed—I'm not kidding—and grinned like the president had stopped to give him special attention. They were so close to bonding, I felt nauseous.

But when I saw Angelica, I didn't know what to feel. She had abandoned the taco-shell bangs that morning. Her hair looked really soft all pulled up into a curly ponytail. She wasn't wearing any makeup, and she looked young and gentle. Kind of vulnerable.

She also wasn't limping, and she looked right over everybody's heads as she moved down the aisle to the back of the bus and sat by herself. I watched her, and then I couldn't look at her anymore. It just jammed everything up in my head.

Damon and I sat together, but everybody was babbling about the race, so I could avoid answering any questions. I stared out the window as we made our way up Mt. Rose Highway. Normally, I would have been going on ad nauseam about how beautiful it was up here, what with the Sierras all dotted with big ol' fluffy pine trees and our first glimpse of sapphire-blue Lake Tahoe, and how even though I'd seen it a thousand times it always took my breath away—blah, blah.

But I wasn't thinking about anything beautiful when Damon nudged me with his elbow and said, "Do you always get this way before a meet?"

"Huh?" I said.

"Is this some kind of prerace ritual, your shutting out the rest of the world and looking like somebody died?" He picked up my hand. "Tell me it's that and not your deciding to dump me."

"No!" I said.

And then I felt like I was going to cry, something I rarely do. Great. I squeezed his hand, really tight. "It isn't you," I whispered. "Can we talk about it later?"

"Sure," he said.

His blue-gray-gold eyes turned so soft and sympathetic, I almost did start to bawl. But he held my hand all the way up to South Tahoe High School, and that helped. At least I could concentrate during the race on something besides a pair of men's underwear lying under a bench in the girls' locker room.

But off and on during the day, I'd have to think about what I didn't want to think about. We were warming up out on the football field at South Tahoe High with the Sierras and the ski resorts right there. I was feeling almost decent, and I'd just dropped into a long stretch when I felt somebody looking at me. I glanced up in time to see Angelica dart her eyes away. And I remembered.

The same thing happened when we were getting into formation for the girls' race. I was toward the back because I don't really hit my stride until about the second mile and then it's easy for me to pass people who are tired. Angelica was mid-pack, and it struck me that all the extra coaching she was receiving hadn't improved her running that much. Only maybe she wasn't getting extra coaching.

During the day, when we were standing around waiting to receive our first-place trophy and while we were eating lunch in Incline Village on the way home and Coach was calling out our individual times, she started to look at people again, and she smiled once or twice. When she passed us going to her seat on the bus, she even looked at me without glancing away immediately. I don't know, maybe I was imagining things, but I thought deep in her eyes she looked absolutely terrified.

Damon leaned against me. "Do you have to do a postrace ritual, too?" he said.

I peeled my eyes away from Angelica. "It wasn't the race," I said.

"Then what?"

He took my hand again and buried it between his two big ones. It felt safe.

"Can I ask you a question?" I said.

"Anything."

I said in a whisper, "If you thought somebody was . . . involved—"

"Involved."

"You know, sexually, with somebody way older than them, but you didn't know for sure—"

"You mean, like abuse?"

I looked down at our hands. "Is that what you would call it?"

"How much older?" he said.

I already had it figured up. "About twenty years."

"Whoa." Damon's voice was sharp. I looked up at him. He seemed to have aged ten years himself. He said, "I'd tell somebody."

He said it so seriously I felt anxiety prickles up and down my arms.

"Even if you only suspected?" I said. "If you didn't really know?"

"Then I'd ask—her. Is it a her?"

"I don't want to say," I said. "I don't want to say anything. I don't want to ask!"

Damon gripped my hand hard with both of his and looked right into my eyes. "Tobey," he said, "you pretty much have to, don't you? I mean, if you even think somebody's being abused? You have to convince her she's in trouble. And the guy ought to be, like, thrown in jail or something."

"I can't," I said. My voice sounded flat.

His eyes widened. "What do you mean, you can't? Tobe, if anybody can, it's you. That's all anybody says when I tell them I'm going out with you. How you can do anything, and it's still cool. People look up to you. This girl is probably dying for somebody like you to help her."

"I don't know if she is or not," I said. "I don't know anything."

I leaned my head back against the seat, but he took my chin in his hand and tilted my face up close to his.

"It's the right thing. Nobody should get away with abusing a girl, even if she doesn't realize she's being abused, okay?" He looked at me long and hard—and then soft.

"Okay," I said.

He pulled my head down onto his shoulder, and I left it there.

I don't know if at that moment I was sure about talking to Angelica. But I was dead sure I was falling in love with Damon Douglas.

CHAPTER SEVEN

I STILL COULDN'T TALK TO MY MOM ABOUT ANGELICA. When I got home from the track meet, she was so excited about the trip she and Dad were taking she was dashing around the house like a little middle-school freak. Which was actually kind of cute, and definitely okay since I didn't know if I could put the whole thing into words. She still gets flustered when somebody says the word "sex" on a TV sitcom. If I said, "Mom, I think the track coach and a freshman are having an affair," we would probably have to do CPR.

I did think about talking to my dad. He might be a little out of it sometimes, but he does pastoral counseling. It occurred to me for the first time in my life that there probably wasn't anything he hadn't heard before.

Damon told me later that night when we were walking around Virginia Lake he thought talking to Dad was a good idea, too. But when I got home, Dad was already asleep. I even stood beside my parents' bed, staring at him, watching his reddish, bushy eyebrows go up and down when he breathed and willing him to wake up. He just snored and turned over.

I gave up the idea on Sunday. In the first place, Fletcher and I had both learned from about the time we were weaned that we didn't broach any subject—from iffy grades to permission for anything—until after Dad's two services on Sunday. He might be sitting at the breakfast table with us, but he had no idea whether he was eating pancakes or Fletcher's old Nikes, and he sure didn't know any of the rest of us were there.

That morning my mom was rambling on about how they had to leave for Sacramento the minute church was out, but he didn't hear a word. Forget asking him for advice.

In a way, he kind of gave me some anyway in his sermon. It's incredible I even heard it, after what else happened at church.

I was leaving Sunday school, jacking my jaws with people I never see during the week. One of them, Wendy Dunbar, sidled up to me and out of this little hole she made out of the side of her mouth said, "That guy over there is staring at you."

"Get over yourself!" I said.

"Fine, don't believe me," she said. "He's way cute—I'll take him for myself."

What are you going to do when somebody says something like that? Of course I looked. And there was Damon, leaning up against the wall in the hall with his arms crossed, smiling half a smile. His eyes were dancing around.

I totally blocked out Wendy and the rest of them and plowed through everybody, squealing, "What are you doing here?"

"I was planning to go to church here," he said. "Unless you have some rule—"

"No!" I said. "Why didn't you tell me you were coming?"

"Because I wanted to see you get all flustered and make a fool out of yourself in front of your friends."

He nodded toward the knot of girls who were at that moment staring openly at the two of us. When I looked up, they all started to examine their cuticles.

"Well, come on," I said. "Let's get a seat."

We sat in my usual spot in the church, where I'd been sitting since I was a kid. My mom always sang in the choir and put Fletcher and me right down in front so Dad could keep an eye on us when he preached his sermon. By the time I was about ten, I had figured out he probably didn't even know we were there, but it worked. We never threw spitballs or anything. When

Fletcher figured it out, he moved back a couple of rows. This Sunday he grunted as I passed with Damon in tow.

"No PDA!" he hissed at me.

I ignored him. I ignored everything. As we sat down in the pew, I realized I was shaking. I don't think it was so much my being head-over-Reeboks for Damon. It was just having my guy come to church with me—to me that was big.

As soon as we got settled, I grabbed Damon's hand and gave him this big ol' smile. He grinned back at me, one corner of his mouth at a time. The gold and the gray and the blue in his eyes all melted together, and I could see he had really brushed all that black wavy hair and . . .

Okay, I won't overdo it. I just know he had never looked more incredible to me.

That's why it was a miracle I heard the sermon. I probably wouldn't have if I hadn't felt my dad's eyes on me the minute he stepped into the pulpit. Ten years I'd been sitting in that spot, and we had never made eye contact. That day he rested his hands on the sides of the pulpit like he always does and looked out over the congregation with his brown eyes behind his glasses and—chink—we locked gazes.

His eyebrows shot up, and when my dad's eyebrows do anything, you notice since they're like two more heads of hair. His entire forehead rose to the occasion, which is something since his hairline goes back a little farther every year, and his face lost some of its ruddy color. For an awful moment I thought he was going to say, "Tobey, what's he doing here? What are his intentions?"

He got his act together and went on with the sermon. But I didn't dare take my eyes off him because his kept coming back to us like some kind of protective male bird's. I even slipped my hand away from Damon's and folded it in my lap. I could feel Damon's shoulders jiggling as he laughed at me.

God does things in weird ways. If Damon hadn't come and Dad hadn't seen us and I hadn't been so intent on paying attention like a dutiful daughter, I might not have really heard the sermon. And I might not have made up my mind about Angelica.

I didn't know all that at the time. All I knew was Dad was talking about Eli insisting that Samuel tell him everything God said to him. That couldn't have been easy for Sam, Dad explained, what with Eli being such an old grump and all.

I was wondering what Damon was thinking about my father using the very hip phrase, "an old grump," when Dad said something that stuck in my head like Velcro. "So in chapter three, we read, 'The Lord was with Samuel, and he let none of his words fall to the ground.'"

I don't know what it was about those words, but they made a dive right for me, as if my dad had opened up my head, seen what I needed to hear, and sent them in my direction.

"None of his words fell to the ground," Dad said. "Whether they were what old grouchy Eli wanted to hear or not, God didn't let them go to waste. Now that's a thought we can all take to heart from time to time."

Right then was the time for me. I found myself leaning forward in the pew and thinking about them. And curling up in my room after Mom and Dad left that afternoon and thinking about them. And pulling out an old diary one of my aunts had given me for Christmas when I was twelve and writing them down and thinking about them. They were all I had to hang on to, all that made me decide Monday morning when I was brushing my teeth that I should talk to Angelica.

My words won't fall to the ground, I silently told my self-in-the-mirror. *God will be there, and they'll come out, and Angelica will get it, and it'll all turn out right.*

Angelica wasn't even an "old grump," so what was I worried about?

I spit in the sink and started to plan. I was going to get Coach Gatney's permission to take Angelica aside during class first period and talk to her.

It would have been perfect, if she had been in school.

I looked around during roll call, but I didn't see her stiff little shield of hair.

"Where's Angelica Benitez?" I said.

Emily Yates looked up from the vulture circle and said, "Who cares?"

I bristled, even more than usual. "I do," I said. "Is she sick or something? Does anybody know?"

"Good grief, just mark her absent," Hayley said, freckled lips curling. "Don't make an issue out of it."

She looked at Jennifer, who, of course, rolled her eyes. I truly wanted to smack them both, and Emily, too. For once, I guess I didn't do such a great job of hiding my feelings. Emily bulged out her eyes and went "Oooh," and Jennifer and Hayley shrank back like they were afraid of me and nervously laughed. A couple of the girls around them tittered.

Half of me felt like an idiot for letting them see they were getting to me. The other half of me wanted to really lay into them. Emily seemed to be voting for the second half.

"Why are you always defending Angelica?" she said. "You'd think she was your sister or something."

"No, señorita," Hayley said through her nose in the worst Spanish accent north of Tijuana. She pointed at me. "Wrong color."

"Yeah," Jennifer said to me. "You're not a spic."

Before I could even jump on that one, Emily cut in. "Besides, you're not a slut either."

I jerked toward her with more violence than I would have if she had called *me* one. The whole gym seemed to suck in its breath. I dropped my clipboard. "What?" I said. "What did you say?"

"Everybody knows she's a total tramp," Hayley said. "You've probably never seen her with her boyfriend." Her chin came up defiantly, but her freckles were standing out like bas-relief. I knew she thought I was about to come at her with fingernails and teeth.

But all the wind had just been knocked right out of me. I *had* seen Angelica with her boyfriend—and the vision of it was like a big, shadowy doubt on my nice, clear decision.

Coach Gatney, bless her heart, came into the gym just then. I leaned over and picked up my clipboard.

"You through with attendance, L'Orange?" she said.

"Yes ma'am," I said. "May I just go put it into the computer now?"

She waved me off, and I escaped like there was something after me. There was. My own confusion. I sat in the coaches' office in front of the Mac with thoughts duking it out in my head.

I did see her in front of Kmart with that guy.

Oh, come on, anybody could see she wasn't enjoying that.

So? She was there.

What difference does that make? Coach Mayno's a teacher. He's twenty years older—

I stopped with my hands frozen on the keys. Did that make a difference? What if Angelica was . . . doing whatever it was she was doing with Coach because she wanted to? Was that still abuse? Was it any of my business then?

I stabbed my elbows down on the desk on either side of the keyboard and sank my forehead onto my hands. What would Jesus do? What in the Sam Hill would He do?

I don't have enough information—I can't decide this.

"Hey, Tobe, you okay?"

The voice went up my spine like a shock from a bad wire. Before I could pull my head up, a hand came down on my neck— and massaged it.

"You all right?" Coach Mayno said.

I could barely nod. It was as if his touch were paralyzing.

"You ought to go to bed nights," he said, still massaging. "And sleep."

He laughed. A sort of aren't-I-just-a-riot laugh. When he finally let go, I scrambled out of the chair like a squirrel. I didn't look at him as I dove for the file cabinet.

"You're stressed out," he said. "You have nine million things going on again today?"

"Yes sir," I said. I fumbled for the right folder to put the attendance sheet in, but I couldn't focus.

Coach Mayno scraped the chair across the floor. "Sit down," he said. "I'll give you a quick shoulder rub."

My fingers fused to a file folder. I couldn't even open my mouth.

Instead, the door opened. It was Mr. Holden.

"He found you, Tobe," Coach Mayno said without missing a beat. "What did you do this time?"

"Hi, Tobey," Mr. Holden said. "You're off the hook—not that you've ever been on it. I'm looking for Coach." He smiled his nice smile at Coach Mayno. "You have a minute?"

"Hey, are you ready for me to smoke you on the golf course Sunday?" Coach Mayno said as they left together. I stood there staring at the chair that was still in the middle of the room.

Three days ago, I would have sat in the chair and let Coach Mayno give me a backrub without a second thought. Three minutes ago, I'd have done it, too—because how in the world would I have said no to a teacher?

I shoved the chair under the desk and felt like a jar of jelly. Man, I needed more information. And I needed it fast.

I didn't know where I was going to get it until I headed off to English the next period, and Norie was marching into the classroom just ahead of me. I grabbed her by the backpack and pulled her out into the hall.

She swatted at me until she saw who it was. Then she launched into conversation before I could even get out a word. "Hey, we missed you Friday," she said. "I mean, we prayed and all, but most of us are still like these Christian rookies, except for Shannon, and most of the time she's, like, paralyzed from the neck up. What the heck is the matter with you?"

She brought her square face close to mine and dug at me with those needly brown eyes. "Are you in some kind of major trouble or something?" she said.

I nodded numbly.

"What's going on?" Norie said. "I've never seen you look creeped out before."

The bell rang, and Mr. Lowe poked his head out the door. "Are you ladies joining us today?" he said.

"Can we have a minute?" Norie said.

He scanned us both and to my surprise said, "Sure."

Norie waited until the door clicked shut before she resumed her scrutiny of my face. "What's up?" she said.

I took a breath. "I just need to know—you're doing that article on child abuse. Do you know anything about . . . sexual abuse?"

She didn't bat an eye. "You mean of a minor by an adult?"

"Yeah."

"Some. Mostly I've studied incest—some pedophile stuff."

"What's a pedophile?"

"Somebody who abuses other people's kids—for kicks. He's got a fixation. Having sex with minors is like his hobby—no, more like part of his career."

I felt as if I were going to throw up. That was more than I really wanted to know. She set down her backpack and ran a hand through her hair.

"Why don't you ask me a specific question?" she said. "Otherwise, I could probably go on for days and make you sick or something."

"Okay," I said. "What I want to know is, if some guy is like, you know, messing with some girl who's, like, twenty years younger than him, and she's a minor—"

"That's sexual abuse. He's molesting her."

"Even if she might be . . . agreeing to it?"

"Yeah—only that's kind of hard to define. There's agreeing to it because she's afraid not to, and there's agreeing to it because, for some gross reason, it does something for her psyche."

"You mean, because she just does that kind of thing all the time, like with guys her own age?"

Norie craned her neck at me, and her eyes gleamed intensely. "The question is, is she getting it on with this adult because she's some kind of nympho—which I doubt—or is she barin' it and sharin' it with other guys because this dude, who's supposed to be a grownup, has made her feel dirty. A lot of girls who have been sexually abused start hating themselves, and they just self-destruct—you know, do drugs or start sleeping around."

I sagged against the wall. Norie narrowed her eyes at me.

"You're not talking about yourself, are you?" she said. "I mean, that just doesn't fit."

I shook my head. All I could think of was Angelica, the way she had looked last Friday in the locker room—like she just wanted to get away from me. That was bigger in my mind than the picture of her in front of Kmart.

"L'Orange?" Norie said. "You okay?"

It was pointless to say yes. I probably looked as nauseated as I felt.

"I don't know," I said.

"Can I help?" she said.

"I don't know that either. I might get back to you."

She nodded, still watching me, as she picked up her backpack. "Well, in the meantime," she said, "I'll be praying for you, and Whoever She Is. Any way you look at it, this is a drag for both of you."

"Thanks," I said. I watched her go into the room, with my mouth hanging open.

Norie Vandenberger, who until today had always been pretty much like a case of chiggers for me, was going to pray for me. Huh.

All day I thought about what she said. I was in the middle of "A lot of girls who have been sexually abused start hating themselves" during lunch when Damon poked a banana in my side and said, "Give me all your thoughts or I'll shoot."

I gave him a lame laugh.

"You still thinking about your friend?" he said.

"Yeah," I said.

"Have you talked to her yet?"

"No," I said.

"Are you going to?"

I started to shrug. But then I couldn't—because I knew what I had to do. "Yeah," I said. "First chance I get."

CHAPTER EIGHT

THE CHANCE CAME SOONER THAN I EXPECTED
Angelica showed up at practice after school.

She avoided me in the locker room, and my heart kind of hurt for her. I wanted to yell at her, "Don't be ashamed, Angelica. I understand!"

Instead, I hung around until everybody was dressed and gone. I waited by the potty stall for her to come out. She about jumped out of her sweatsocks when she saw me.

"Can we talk for a minute?" I said.

She shook her head until even the stiff part of her hair waggled. "No," she said. "Coach will get mad if we're late."

She made for the door, and I tailed her.

"All I wanted to ask," I said when we were in the hall, "is whether you want to go out for a Coke after practice."

She stopped and looked at me. She was quivering on the edge of one of those baby smiles. I hadn't seen that in a week or so.

"With you?" she said.

I about cried. She looked hopeful—and innocent.

"Yes, with me," I said.

She ducked her head. "Will Damon be coming?"

"Nah, this is a girl thing," I said.

"Well, thanks a lot."

I looked up, stunned. Damon was not six feet away. Coach

Mayno was next to him. I couldn't read their faces. I just felt, well, paralyzed again.

"I'm not invited, huh?" Damon said. He was smiling. It was okay. I took a deep breath and forced myself to grin back.

"Not this time," I said. "It's just going to be Angelica and me."

Beside me, I could feel her body starching. I grabbed her arm and tucked it into mine and brushed past the male contingent. I didn't look at Coach Mayno as I said, "We have to warm up now."

Outside, Angelica looked up at me with awe on her face. "Wow," she said.

"What?"

"Doesn't it scare you to blow off Damon like that?"

"I wasn't blowing him off," I said. "We're just going out. He doesn't own me. No guy owns you."

Her shiny black eyes went round and again she whispered, "Wow." I realized she had never considered that concept. If I hadn't been sure before, I was now. I had to talk to her.

I was rehearsing what I was going to say in my head during the run on the small back roads of the housing development up McCarran Boulevard when Damon slowed down to let me catch up to him.

Zena was, of course, running beside me like we were Siamese twins. She had taken to doing that every day, which was fine, except at times like this, when I wished her little friend who had dropped out—what was her name? Victoria?—was still around for her to pal around with.

"Hey, Shorty," Damon said to her, "I bet you can't keep up with the guys."

Zena looked ahead at Utley and Kevin and some of the other guys and then looked quizzically at me. "Should I?" she said.

Damon poked me.

"Yeah," I said. "Go for it."

Damon waited until she was on Utley's heels before he said, "How come you're going out with Angelica after practice instead of me?"

I stole a look at him. "Does that bother you?" I said.

"Oh no. It's just, you and I almost always go. I just wondered if I messed up or something."

I laughed out loud, probably the first time I had laughed in days.

"What?" he said.

"No, you didn't mess up. You couldn't mess up if you tried. I just need to talk to Angelica."

"About wh—"

Damon almost came to a stop. I looked back over my shoulder for Coach Mayno and grabbed Damon's shirt to drag him on.

"Is she—is Angelica the one?" Damon said.

"Shh. Yes!" I hissed at him. "Please don't say anything to anybody, okay?"

"I'm not going to—only—"

He concentrated on running for a minute. I kept looking over at him, watching him figure something out right on his face.

"What?" I said.

"That guy we saw Angelica with, he wasn't an adult. He couldn't have been over seventeen."

"It's not him," I said. I stared straight ahead of me. This was going to be a whole lot harder than I'd thought. He was becoming one of Coach Mayno's favorites. Damon was going to be way disappointed if he found out about this.

"Her dad?" Damon said. "Man, that's disgusting, isn't it?"

"Yeah," I said. I felt sick to my stomach for the thirtieth time that day. "Come on," I said. "I'll race ya."

Hard or not, I knew I was going to go through with talking to Angelica. I barely got wet in the shower, and I threw on my clothes before anybody else was even thinking about it.

"I'll meet you out at my car, Angelica," I called to her as I left the locker room. "It's the red Honda."

But as I was dumping my stuff into the backseat, she came running across the parking lot without her backpack. And she didn't have the baby smile on her face.

I said, "Go ahead and get in. His name's Lazarus—he's friendly."

"I can't come," she said.

I looked at her over the top of the car. Unmistakable tears were in her voice.

"What's up?" I said.

But before she even said it, I knew. And it made me sick.

"Coach says I need to stay to work with him," she said. She wouldn't meet my eyes. "He says I can't run in the next meet if I don't improve. I have to stay."

She threw in a "sorry" I could barely hear and fled back across the parking lot like a frightened little baby bunny. I stood there and watched her, and I felt every bit as low as Coach Mayno for not going after her.

When she disappeared into the gym, I slumped down into the front seat of the car and flung arms and head on the steering wheel. I closed my eyes really tight, but I could still see it. I could see Angelica going into the locker room. I could see Coach Mayno letting himself in. I could see him—

But I couldn't watch my own imagination.

I got out of the car and walked, head bent down in the wind, toward the front of the building with only my car keys in my hand. I could feel the pacifier on my key ring and I clung to it.

I wish Damon were still here, I thought. *Man, I hope Norie is.*

I wasn't even sure I knew where the journalism room was, so I went up and down every hall, peering into the little windows on the doors. It was after four o'clock, so most of them were dark, including the one with the *King's Herald* sign on the door. I could feel myself wilting.

If I could just talk to her, maybe get some more information, I wouldn't feel so scared. I'd really felt strong about it after I'd talked to her that morning. Maybe I should go home and call her at her house.

Still feeling as if I'd been forcibly drained, I clutched my keys and went toward the front door. I heard heels clicking on the tiles behind me.

"Hi there," a female voice said.

I turned around to a splash of flowing turquoise batiste. It was Ms. Race.

"It's Tobey, right?" she said.

"Yes ma'am," I said. Any other time I would have been impressed that she remembered my name.

She caught up to me and fell into step. Her earrings danced happily against the sides of her face. They were wooden Christian fish, obviously hand-painted. Any other time I'd have told her I liked them, asked her where she bought them. But this wasn't any other time. I couldn't say anything.

"Are you all right?" she said.

I must have looked startled, because she winced a little. "I don't mean to be nosy," she said. "You just look so upset, and usually you walk around here with a glow about you."

"Oh," I said. "Thanks."

"Sure," she said. She opened the door for me, and we both stepped outside. The desert wind blasted us with sand, and she scrunched up her eyes. "I'm going to run to my car," she said. "You want to do the sprint thing with me, or should I say goodbye here?"

"You go ahead," I said woodenly. "My car's the other way."

"Okay," she said. She started down the steps at a trot, and then looked back at me. "You take care now," she said.

I couldn't even answer her. I wasn't the one who needed someone caring about her. Angelica was the one.

Unable to shake that thought, I charged, head down, through the wind to the car. Angelica's neediness mingled with the insistent clanging of the flag rope and was screaming in my head as I ran.

I knew I couldn't leave her there alone. I wasn't sure what I planned to do as I turned with the gale ripping at my clothes. I think I was praying one of those "Help me, Father, please, help me" prayers.

The outside gym door was still unlocked, and I pried it open against the wind and leaned on it once I was inside. Okay—what to do?

I couldn't just storm into the locker room. It was probably locked anyway, and besides, it wasn't Coach Mayno I wanted to see. I really never wanted to see him again. In fact, the mere thought of him was steadily making me madder. I could feel it doing a number on my shoulder blades.

So what was I going to do? What happened to words that didn't fall to the ground? I hadn't even had a chance to say any yet.

My hands squeezed behind me on the door bar.

That was it.

I had to say the words. I had to talk to her. I'd just camp out here until she came out. Someplace where Coach wouldn't see me. Meanwhile, I'd pray that I'd somehow get to her in time.

I didn't know in time for what. I didn't even want to think about it. I was beginning to feel really naive. Even Norie had used terms I didn't have a clue to and didn't think I wanted to know.

I occupied my mind with finding a place to park myself. I squeezed into a little indentation in the wall outside the locker room, about the size of two phone booths, where the water fountain was. If Coach did come out that door, if he was even in the locker room, he wouldn't see me. Then I could duck in there, grab Angelica, and run.

Okay, I know now that plan was lame. But I was so torn up, I wasn't even thinking straight. I just tucked my little self in under the water fountain and prayed. It was the most secure I'd felt all day.

I must have been there five minutes, when I heard a door open and then close inside the locker room. And I heard somebody—a girl—crying.

I came to conclusions at 220 megahertz. That was the door from the locker room to the coaches' office. Coach had left the locker room. He was gone, and now Angelica could cry.

I couldn't sit there under the water fountain any longer. I wriggled out and went to the door and listened. She was crying in big sobs, the way you do when you're by yourself and you have to let it all out before it eats you. It made my chest hurt, and I curled my fingers around the door handle.

The door came open.

Just a little bit, maybe an inch. I stopped it before it opened any farther. But it was enough to hear Angelica loud and clear.

"Please, no," she said. It was the voice of a little girl, begging. "You said we wouldn't go this far again. Please."

Another voice answered her, the voice of a grown man, scolding. "You just need to stop crying and relax," he said. "I'm not going to hurt you—you know that."

"Please, no" was all she could sob.

Coach Mayno was saying something else, but by then I let the door close. I didn't know if it made any noise or not, or if the sound of my feet tearing down the hall or my keys jangling in my hand echoed against the walls. I just knew I had to get out of there.

How I got home I still don't know. There must have been an angel driving Lazarus because I couldn't have done it. All I knew was that I had to get to my room so I could cry. But when I got there, no tears would come. I could only shake—and try not to throw up.

I wasn't successful. I went in the bathroom and upchucked everything I'd eaten all day, in big painful chokes. Then I sat there with my head on the toilet seat, sweating like I'd just run the mile in five.

For a while all I could think was, If I felt this bad, how must Angelica feel?

She didn't want to be there. She kept telling him no. *Please, no.*

I shuddered and closed my eyes. Right. Like that was really going to shut out anything. There was no choice now. I had to do something.

The question was, what?

The house was empty of anybody I could ask. I'd have killed at that moment to hear my mother's sewing machine whirring in the craft room or my father's computer keys clacking in his study. But all I heard was the bass on Fletcher's stereo in the next room.

I had to talk to somebody before I went totally out of my mind. I mean it, the anxiety was racing through me like a laser, erasing every rational thought the minute it managed to creep in. I wiped out my mouth with a washcloth, grabbed the portable phone in the hall, and took it in my room. My fingers were shaking as I dialed Damon's number.

"Hi, this is Damon. I'm out. Leave a message—or send money. Either way, wait for the beep."

I couldn't even talk to the machine. I hung up and panicked. Whoever it was who said Tobey L'Orange didn't freak was looney tunes herself.

I started to poke buttons again, but before I finished Roxy's number I pushed the off button. She wasn't going to know what to do. Gabe? Forget it. Somebody at church? Wendy Dunbar maybe?

Realization slapped me in the face. I was the leader. When I needed help, there wasn't one other person my age I could call who knew any better than I did.

And who were my adults? My parents, who weren't there. Mr. Lowe, Mrs. Quebbeman, Mr. Ott. Like I could really talk about sexual abuse to any of them.

Then it hit me. I snatched up the phone and practically squeezed it to death as I carried it out to the hall to the phone book. I sat down in the middle of the floor and smacked the pages aside until I got to the V's. *Vandenberger*. Please, please, please, let there only be one.

There were three. George. Michael. Quinton, M.D.

Norie had said her father was a thoracic surgeon.

I punched at the buttons in a frenzy. A bright, sharp voice answered. "Vandenberger residence, this is Norie speaking."

"Thank God," I said.

There was only a fraction of a silence before Norie said, "Is that you, L'Orange?"

I think that's when I started to cry. "You have to help me," I said. "Please, there's nobody else."

"Man, you are stressed. Okay, first of all, try to calm down. I can barely understand a thing you're saying. Take some deep breaths. Close your eyes and just breathe."

I tried. Sobs were coming out of my nose, for Pete's sake. But I did what she said, still clutching the phone as if it were a lifeline.

"Okay," she said. "Talk to me—and you don't have to do it ninety miles an hour. I got all night."

"Okay," I said. And then once again I said, "Okay, okay."

She waited.

"I heard something I wasn't supposed to hear," I said finally.

"Does this have something to do with your friend who's being sexually abused?" she said.

I nodded.

"I'll take that as a yes," Norie said. "Okay, what did you hear? Can you talk about it?"

"I wasn't eavesdropping or anything—"

"Who cares!"

"I just opened the door, and I heard her begging him—not to—"

"Look, I know you're a clone for the Virgin Mary, but you have to tell me what you heard if I'm going to be able to help."

I blurted it out so maybe I wouldn't have to hear it. "She said, 'Please, no—you said we wouldn't go this far.' She was crying so hard."

"Wow. Okay—did he say anything?"

"Yeah."

"Do you want multiple choice?"

"No. He said, 'You just need to stop crying and relax. I'm not going to hurt you.'"

"Jackal," Norie said. Her voice was harsh and mad, and it gave me strength somehow. She had all the anger I couldn't get myself to feel.

"Did he say anything else?" she said.

"Yeah. She said no again, all crying, and then he said, 'Lie down—'"

I stopped. I couldn't tell her the "Angel" part. I didn't know what we were doing yet, whether we were telling or what.

"She definitely didn't want to be there," Norie said. "And she's too scared to kick him where it counts and get out. I'd like to have the pleasure." She grunted. "Sorry. I just get so ticked I want to throw up."

"I already did," I said. "I just don't know what to do now. My parents aren't home. They won't be back till Wednesday morning."

"That could be all right," Norie said. "I'm no expert on this, okay, but from what I've read and the people I've interviewed, the best thing to do is get the girl to report it to the right people. Unless it's her father, in which case she should talk to her mother. Is it her father?"

I started to cry again. "No," I said. "But I bet she thought he was like one—I did."

I bit my lip. Norie let out a soft, "Whoa."

"You know this guy?" she said.

"Yeah. I don't want to say any more about him though, okay?"

"I'm not asking you to. I just want to say this. If he's a pro, you have to be careful."

"What do you mean?"

"About yourself. Don't be alone with this guy. Don't let any girl be alone with him, if you can help it, until your friend talks."

"No way!" I said. "He's not gonna—"

"Just don't trust him is all I'm saying." Norie sighed. "Sorry. I bet you want to go throw up again, huh?"

"Yeah," I said.

"Okay, look—what are you going to do right now?"

"I could call her—"

"No, I'm talking about for you. You can't go busting into her house in the shape you're in. You have to plan stuff for the rest of the evening so this won't totally creep you out."

"I don't know," I said. I felt like a helpless little kid.

"You want to pray?" she said. "We could, like, do the God-thing here on the phone."

Suddenly that was the only thing that sounded even remotely comforting to me. I took the phone back in my room and shut the door. It was dark in there, but I didn't turn on the light. I stretched out on the floor under my window and stared out. "Okay," I said. "Let's pray."

We must have been on the phone for an hour. Fletcher banged on the door once, yelling that he was starving to death. He went away and I eventually smelled mozzarella baking. He must have found the frozen pizza. The rest of the time, Norie and I were with God like I've never been with Him before. She talked to Him like He was on a third line, going "Uh-huh," and saying, "I love you, Tobey."

"God," she said when we were about to hang up, "we know You're going to help L'Orange. We're asking You to give her the guts, the words, the compassion. She's so wrung out, she needs everything, and at this point, You're the only one who can give it to her. We're counting on You—big-time."

"Amen," I said.

"Are you cool for the moment?" Norie said.

"Yeah—for the moment. Maybe for the night. I don't know about tomorrow."

"My dad, you know, the Twelve-Stepper—"

"Yeah."

"He's always saying, 'One day at a time.' I think that definitely applies here."

"Could we just make one plan for tomorrow though?" I said.

"Like what?"

"Like, could we call a Flagpole Girls meeting?"

"I'm all over it," she said.

And that was the only reason I slept that night.

CHAPTER
NINE

I DON'T KNOW HOW SHE DID IT, BUT BY SECOND-PERIOD English, Norie reported to me she had contacted the Flagpolers, and we were all going to meet on the art patio at lunch. Brianna was supposed to work on Ms. Squires to get permission.

"Hang in there," Norie said to me. "You don't look too hagged out."

"You're the only one who thinks that," I said. "I didn't feel like doing my hair this morning so I just shoved it back with this headband. Emily Yates told me first period it made me look like I was twelve."

"Did you tell her she looks like a thirty-year-old divorcée?" Norie said. And then she shook her head. "Of course you didn't. You have a terminal case of nice. But you can't be nice about this thing, okay? You know that."

I did know that, which was why I'd smiled at Angelica all through PE like a toothpaste model—and why I couldn't wait for the Flagpole meeting. But when I walked into the hallway outside the art room at lunchtime, the five of them were standing there looking frustrated. Norie's square face was red.

"I can't help it," Brianna was saying. "Ms. Squires is absent. The substitute said she wasn't going to be responsible for an unauthorized meeting out there with all that dangerous equipment."

"And these subs wonder why they can't get a real gig," Norie said.

Cheyenne giggled nervously.

"Now what?" Marissa said.

"Ladies, we're clearing the halls now." Ms. Race floated toward us. I didn't even notice what she was wearing. I was too busy gnawing on my fingernails.

"Who is this woman?" Norie muttered to us.

Nobody got to answer before Ms. Race stopped just outside our little circle. "Is everything all right, girls?" she said. "You look upset."

I know Norie started to say, "We're fine, thanks," but Cheyenne said, "We were supposed to have a meeting in there, but the teacher's absent."

"What kind of meeting?" Ms. Race ran her crinkly blue eyes over the clipboard she was carrying. "I don't see one on the schedule."

Norie glared at Cheyenne, who cowered behind Shannon. Ms. Race looked at me as if she were confused.

"It's just personal," I managed to say. "We kind of wanted some privacy."

"Ah," Ms. Race said. She looked down the hall at the last of the kids fleeing to Round Table Pizza for their forty-six minutes. "I think I have a place for you. Follow me."

Cheyenne bounded after her like a puppy, and Marissa and Shannon followed at a more sedate pace. Brianna looked doubtfully at Norie and me. Norie was tailing Ms. Race with her eyes.

"What's up with her?" she said.

"If she tells Mr. Holden we're holding an unauthorized meeting, we're history," Brianna said.

I don't know if it was my basic weenie state of mind at that point or the memory of Ms. Race telling me the day before to "take care," but I said, "She's pretty nice. I think she just wants to help."

"That would be a first around here," Norie said. But she shrugged. "I guess we don't have much choice. I wonder what cell she's going to put us in."

"Do you trust anybody?" Brianna said to her, as we followed the group toward the office.

"You guys," Norie said.

The "cell" Ms. Race had in mind was a supply room, which was deserted during lunchtime.

"Nobody should bother you in here," she said, as she ushered us in. "I don't think I have to tell you not to bother anything. This looks like a neat group."

She smiled at us and closed the door behind her as she left.

"I like her," Marissa said.

"Fabulous," Norie said. "You two can do lunch sometime. Right now we need to get started. L'Orange has something heavy she needs prayer for."

"Are you okay?" Shannon said to me. Her almost transparent eyebrows were knitted together.

"Are you sick?" Cheyenne said. "I had a cold last week—"

"Cheyenne," Norie barked at her. "Sit." She pointed to a box of copy paper, and Cheyenne dropped onto it. Norie nodded for me to sit next to herself, and Marissa was on my other side. That felt good to me.

When we were finally settled amid the shelves crammed with staples and paper clips and everybody but me had her lunch spread out, Norie said, "A girl is being sexually abused by an older guy—like, way older—against her will. L'Orange has to convince her to turn the dude in."

"Ouch," Brianna said. "It bites to be you, doesn't it?"

"Yeah," I said. "It definitely does."

"You can do it, Tobey," Cheyenne said. "You can do anything!"

All the energy was suddenly sucked out of me. I threw my face into my hands. "Please," I said, "I can't do anything! I don't know if I can do this at all!"

"I hear you, girl," Brianna said.

"Me too," Marissa said. She slid a warm, brown hand on top of mine. "I never feel like I can do anything."

I grabbed her hand and squeezed. Norie took my other one.

"Let's pray," she said. And then she laughed. "I'm really getting into this."

Amid the smell of new paper and felt-tip markers, we prayed.

"Lord, be there for Tobey. Don't let her be alone."

"Don't let it be hard."

"Help her do right for You."

"And for the girl."

"And bust the chops of the guy who's hurting her, Lord. Break him down. Make him know this isn't right."

"Let Tobey know we'll be praying for her all day, even at the very minute when she sits down with the girl. Let her know she has the power of the Spirit."

When we lifted our heads, Brianna said, "When are you going to do it?"

"This afternoon," I said. I was choosing my words carefully. Nobody could know. It was Angelica's secret.

"What time?" Shannon said. "I want to be praying."

"About four o'clock," I said. "I'll probably take her someplace—probably Taco Bell."

I snagged my teeth over my lip. Brianna caught it.

"The way you said that—is this girl Hispanic?"

"I really don't want to say, you guys," I said.

"I'm not trying to guess her identity," Brianna said. "But if she is Latino, don't expect a lot of support for her around here. Am I right, Marissa?"

Marissa was looking miserably down at the bag of chips in her lap. She nodded.

"What difference does it make what race she is?" I said.

"It shouldn't make any difference." Brianna hugged her knees as if she were trying to keep herself in control. "But it does. People have stereotyped ideas, and they just plug them in. Ten to one, people are going to say Hispanic girls are tramps anyway—she must have asked for it."

"People?" I said. "What people? This isn't anybody else's business."

Brianna looked at me across the circle. There was wisdom far beyond her seventeen years in her eyes. "They'll make it their business, honey. Trust me," she said.

"But you know what?" Norie said briskly. "One thing at a time. First Tobey has to convince the girl to turn this guy in. That's enough to think about for today."

The warning bell rang, and we all hustled around picking up chip bags and soda cans. Marissa leaned down beside me. "Brianna's right," she said. "This could be really hard on your friend if it gets out."

I looked at her in surprise. Her usually barely audible voice was firm.

"If she needs somebody to talk to about it," Marissa said, "you can call me." She tucked a piece of paper into my hand. "That's my phone number."

"Are we exchanging phone numbers?" Norie said from the doorway. "Rad. Why don't all of you give me yours, and I'll make up a master list and get it out?"

She was still mapping the logistics as she marched out. It made me laugh, and I needed to laugh. But it was going to be the last time for a while.

Right then, though, I was feeling brave again. I think it was from what my dad would have called "being prayed up." Anyway, I at least had my head cleared enough to come up with a plan.

It was raining, which happens all of about five times a year in Nevada—must have been God. That meant we would do stretches and stuff in the theater lobby for our whole practice instead of running. It also meant Coach Mayno had no reason to keep Angelica for extra work afterward. Still, I waited until I was sure he could hear me, and I said to her, "I'm ready to take that rain check for a Coke this afternoon." Before she could say anything—although not before she glanced over at him—I charged in with, "If you're going to stay after, I'll just wait in the locker room until you're done."

It was all I could do not to look at him to see his reaction. That would have been way too obvious, and I was already feeling as if I was walking around with a sign on my back that said, "I know something you don't know I know."

Angelica's face went into her baby smile. "Okay," she said. "If you're sure you don't mind waiting."

"She doesn't have to wait, Angelica."

We both looked at Coach Mayno. He kept his eyes on his clipboard where he was checking off our names. "Weather's too bad to work outside," he said. "Go do your thing."

She smiled happily at me, just like a little girl. I wanted to belt him right there. As we started our workout, that bothered me. My attitude toward Coach Mayno had done a complete flip. He used to be my bud. He was always teasing me and joking around and squeezing the back of my neck—

I froze in the middle of a hurdler's stretch. *If he's a pro, you've got to be careful,* Norie had said to me.

Images slithered into my mind. Coach Mayno holding my head down on the desk while he gave me a hard time. Coach Mayno curling his fingers around my arm. Coach Mayno brushing my cheek with his hand. Coach Mayno referring to "those sweet buns" of mine. I jerked out of the stretch and stood up.

"What's going on, Tobe?" Coach Mayno called across the lobby.

"I have to go to the rest room," I said.

"What do you think, people?" he said. "Should I let her go?"

I didn't wait for the vote. I jumped over three kids and made it to the bathroom just in time to lose my lunch. And then I stood there in the stall and shook.

It could have been me, was all I could think. *It could have been me.*

I think that made me even more determined to leave the school that day with Angelica. I stayed right in her space through the rest of warmup and on the laps around the gym.

I was so preoccupied, Damon had to snap his fingers in my face to get my attention. "Hey," he said. His voice didn't have its usual husky chuckle in it.

"Hi," I said. I felt dumb. I should have at least told him today was the day. He had a right to be miffed with me for ignoring him.

"What happened to you at lunch?" he said.

Lunch. Dang. "I'm sorry," I said. "I had Flagpole Girls today." I glanced warily at Angelica, who was at my heels. "It was important."

"You could have said something," he said. "What's going on?"

"Can we talk about it later?" I said.

He gave me a long look from under his eyelashes before he stared straight ahead. "Do I have a choice?"

"Well, yeah," I said. My head was starting to spin. What was up with this?

"Okay, then no," Damon said. "I don't want to talk about it later. I just want to know if we're on or we're off, and I'd like to know now."

I almost tripped. "What?" I said. "You think we're off because I missed a lunch?"

"You didn't call me last night."

"I tried. You weren't home."

"You didn't leave a message. I tried to call you for an hour, and your line was busy."

"I was—" But I stopped. Why was I defending myself over something this stupid when I had a thing that was way bigger hanging over my head?

I got closer to him and leaned my head in. "You were right," I said. "You don't have a choice. I can't talk about this right now."

I gave a loaded glance back at Angelica. His eyes flickered and followed. I expected an I-get-it to cross his face. He just twitched the corners of his mouth.

"Later," he said. "I'll come by at six-thirty. Then we can talk."

"Sure," I said, though he hadn't waited to hear my answer. He was already sprinting around the next corner.

I watched him for about half a minute, and then I shook my head. I couldn't worry about him just then. Angelica had to be taken care of first.

I was right at her elbow when we went in to change. I did

everything but take a shower with her. When she and I walked past the coaches' office on our way out, I could feel Coach Mayno's eyes boring through my back. I didn't care.

We were pulling out of the parking lot when another car drove up beside us—a Nissan truck—and Fletcher leaned halfway out the passenger window to yell to me, "Don't forget I'm going over to Ricky's for dinner."

"Oh yeah," I said. "What time are you coming home?"

He wiggled his neck all defensively. "Nine! That's my curfew on school nights!"

"Okay," I said. "Don't have a coronary. I'll see you at nine."

The Nissan fishtailed out, spraying the Honda's windshield with dirty water. I rolled my eyes at Angelica as I turned on the windshield washer and pulled out of the parking lot.

"Do you have any brothers?" I said.

She shook her head. "It's just my mother and me."

"That must be nice. Are you two close?"

She looked shyly down at her fingernails. "I don't see her much. She works as a maid at the El Dorado. But she's a saint. I don't know what I would do without Mama."

That stabbed me somewhere. Every time I turned around there was another dimension to this thing. Now it was her mother, who was probably going to absolutely die when she found out what had happened to all she had in the world.

Suddenly I couldn't imagine doing this in the middle of a fast-food restaurant. Fletcher had just provided a much better meeting place.

"Want to go to my house where we can listen to music and have something decent to eat?" I said.

She glowed. I felt like a jerk. I knew what I was going to say would wipe that glow right off her sweet little face.

CHAPTER TEN

THE MINUTE ANGELICA SAT DOWN ON THE MAROON leather L-sofa in our family room, she picked up one of the pillows and hugged it to her chest. "This is a beautiful house," she said. Her big ol' dark eyes scanned the place as if she were looking at the Hearst Castle.

I went to the other side of the island between the kitchen and the family room. Ducking my head into a cabinet, I checked to see if Fletcher had eaten every chip on the premises.

"Thanks," I said. "It would look better if my mom were here. She does everything but iron the curtains every day." I stood up with half a bag of Doritos and grinned at her. "She would make you nachos. From me you're just getting chips and a jar of salsa."

"That's okay," she said, wide-eyed. "You don't have to do anything, really. I could just have a glass of water."

"After that practice, I think we both need something stronger than water," I said. "Coke okay?"

"Whatever you're having," she said.

By the time I dumped everything onto the table that fit into the L of the sofa, she had finished taking in the family room and was squeezing the pillow to her so hard I expected it to shout for air.

She's so fragile, I thought.

I wasn't sure I could go through with this. But I knew I had to for that very reason: She was so delicate she just might shatter.

I sat cross-legged on the couch and picked up my own pillow to hug. Angelica clutched her Coke can and sipped at it, but the chips and salsa went untouched. I took a deep breath and did what Norie had advised. "Just plunge right in," she had said to me. "Don't beat around the bush, or she'll see what's coming and bolt out of there. Don't give her a chance."

"I feel as if I'm setting a trap for her," I had said.

"No," Norie had said. "You're letting her out of one."

"So," I said now, "are you glad you didn't have to stay after for extra practice today?"

"Yes," she said. "This is more fun."

"Anything would be more fun." I squeezed the pillow. "Angelica, I think I know what's been . . . what Coach Mayno has been doing to you when you guys are alone. I accidentally heard you yesterday in the locker room."

She looked down into the opening on her Coke can as if she wished she could disappear into it. Her face turned pasty beige.

I went on as if I was picking my way on stones across the Truckee River. "I know you didn't want to—"

"He says I did."

I stared at her. Of all the reactions I'd imagined in the last twenty-four hours—Angelica crying hysterically or running off with me chasing her or shaking her head and denying the whole thing—this response had never entered my mind. She was talking about it as if we were discussing the salsa.

Until I looked at her closer. Her eyes had stopped focusing, and she was sitting unnaturally still. I wanted her to talk some more so I'd know she was still alive. My heart was starting to pound, and I was moving from underarm sweat rings to sweat lakes.

"Coach Mayno said you wanted to?" I said.

She gave a numb nod. "The first day he told me to stay after practice. He came in the locker room when I was in my underwear. I held my blouse up in front of me, and he laughed."

"He laughed?" I said.

"He said it was okay; I didn't have to pretend to be modest. He said he knew I wanted him as much as he wanted me. He had seen it in the way I smiled at him the first day." She stared at the top of the coffee table, her face as stiff as her little wall of bangs. "I don't know what I did to make him think that."

"You didn't do anything!" I said.

"He says I did. He says he's always liked us Mexican girls because we're naturally sexy."

"Coach Mayno said that?"

"It's okay if you don't believe me," she said. "That's why I never told anybody. He says nobody would believe me."

I tossed the pillow aside and moved toward her. "I can't believe he told you that!" I said. "I know you're telling the truth."

"Why?" she said. "Because you heard us?"

I heard the slightest hint of bitterness in her voice. It pushed me back against the sofa. Would I have believed her if she had come to me with this story out of the blue? Would I be able to picture Coach Mayno walking in on her when she was half-naked and telling her he thought she was sexy? My Coach Mayno, who was like a dad and a bud and a role model all in one?

I wasn't sure I would have, and the thought made me nauseous again. But the tight way Angelica was sitting across from me on my couch, like there was nothing she could do but keep being abused by somebody we had all trusted—

"No," I said. "Not just because I heard it. Why would you make something like that up?"

For the first time, she showed some emotion. Her hand started to shake so hard the Coke splashed out of the pop-top hole. I took the can from her and set it on the table and grabbed both of her hands. "I want to help you," I said. "I don't want you to have to keep doing this."

She held on to my hands like they were the only thing that was keeping her from falling off a cliff. "I don't want to keep doing it," she said. "I hate it. It's terrible. He whispers things to me that make me feel so dirty."

Please don't start giving me the details, I thought. *I'll be sick; I know it.* But I nodded and held on to her hands.

"He calls it making love, but it isn't. It can't be! It hurts and it's scary and it makes me feel like a—" She looked at me, blinking fast and fighting with her face. "I don't want to cuss in front of you. He makes me feel like I'm a prostitute. I could go out and be one of those women in a trailer out in Lyon County now—I know what it feels like."

Then she pulled her hands away from me and slapped them against her face and cried into them like I've never heard anybody cry before. They were frightening, violent sobs, and they shook her until I thought she would break. My heart was all the way up in my throat as I slid over next to her and put my arms around her. I fought not to vomit.

She must have cried without talking for a good fifteen minutes. The only sounds were her gasping sobs and the wind slapping the rain against the windows. It was the longest quarter hour of my life, but at least it gave me time to think about what to say next. I definitely didn't want to hear any more of the story. I wanted her to tell it to somebody who could do something about it.

When she finally went from major sobs to minor hiccups, I brought her a box of Kleenex and a glass of water and sat down on the table facing her. "The only way this is ever going to end," I said, "is if you tell somebody who can make it stop."

Her eyes by this time were bright red and almost swollen shut. But there was hope in them, too.

"Who do I tell?" she said.

"Have you told your mother?"

She looked as if she were going to panic. "No! I can't tell her. It would break her heart!"

"She's going to want to protect people," Norie had told me. "Try to get around that."

"Okay," I said. "What about your boyfriend?"

"I don't have a boyfriend."

I let that one pass. "Some other adult you trust?" I said.

Angelica sadly shook her head. I knew exactly how she felt. She clutched at my hands again. They were like a pair of Popsicles. "You said you could help," she said.

"That's what I'm trying to do," I said.

"Can't you talk to him?"

I felt like somebody had just poked me in the rear end with a cattle prod. "You mean Coach Mayno?" I said.

She nodded. "He respects you."

"Right," I said. "He offered to give me a back massage in the coaches' office the other day." I shuddered. "I'm never going near him alone again."

That was probably the most reassuring thing I'd said to her all afternoon. Her face broke into that sweet baby smile that made my chest ache. I got up and went for the phone.

"Who are you calling?" she said. Her eyes were anxious.

"A friend of mine who can tell us who to go to," I said. "Don't worry, I won't tell her your name or anything. She's totally cool."

Angelica sank back into the couch, looking small and vulnerable. "I trust you," she said. "I think it's going to be all right now."

I wished I were as sure as I took the phone into the hallway. Norie answered on the first ring.

"Were you sitting right next to the phone?" I said.

"Yes," she said. "I thought you would never call. I've been going nuts. How's the girl doing?"

"She says she'll talk to somebody."

"Yes!"

"Okay, so who? She says she can't tell her mother, and she doesn't have any other adults she can trust. Man, I wish my parents were home. What about yours?"

"We could do that. My dad's a doctor so I'm sure he knows the drill, but if you want to do this the really legal way, you need to call . . . let's see, I have the number right here. I called some of my sources."

I had this image of Norie with a pencil behind her ear, calling up a list on her computer. It was comforting somehow. I stopped sweating a little.

"Okay, you call the Division of Welfare. They have an office here in Washoe County. Ask for a child protection worker. Now, warn your friend that she'll have to talk to a bunch of people, including a doctor, but they'll probably all be pretty cool. The people I interviewed down there were neat. Anyway, here's the number . . ."

I scribbled it down. It was the first time I realized how bad I was shaking.

"How are you holding up, L'Orange?" she said.

"I'm fine," I said.

"You are the worst liar," she said.

I pulled the phone even closer to my ear. "This is so creepy. I feel like somebody else, you know?"

"You're like in shock," Norie said. "You probably ought to stay in it."

"I forgot to pray," I said.

"Don't worry about that. We're all doing it for you. Make the call and get her down there before she chickens out."

I peeked in at Angelica after I hung up. She was drinking her Coke, although it could have been gasoline for all she knew, and jiggling both knees like she had to go to the bathroom. I decided to make the call first, then tell her.

The woman I talked to sounded busy. But when I started to fill her in, she cut me off and said, "How soon can you get her here?"

"Fifteen minutes," I said.

"Do it," she said. "What's her name?"

My lips turned to wood. For the first time, it was going beyond the three people who knew—Coach Mayno, Angelica, and me. As soon as I said it, it wasn't going to be a secret anymore.

"Ma'am?" she said. "Her name?"

"Angelica," I said. "Angelica Benitez."

As I hung up the phone, I had this feeling I'd just turned some corner or something. The hallway, the family room, the couch looked different to me. Especially since it registered that Damon was sitting there, hair damp, shirt speckled with raindrops.

"Hi," I said.

"I'm early," he said. "Sorry. I saw your car out there—I didn't know—"

He looked at Angelica, who had gone back into her shocked little shell and was staring into her Coke can. Then he looked back at me. The soft, caring eyes I loved so much were back.

"Are you okay?" he said.

I shook my head.

He glanced nervously at Angelica who still wouldn't look at him. I slid in next to her.

"Angelica," I said. "I think Damon can help us. Do you mind if I tell him some?"

She looked up at me sharply and searched my face, the way babies do when they're deciding whether to smile at you or start screaming their heads off. She opted for a soggy smile. "Whatever you think," she said.

That's when I realized she was leaning on me for everything now. I had to have Damon in my corner, or I might not be able to do this.

"Angelica's being sexually abused," I said carefully. "She's decided she wants to tell the officials, and I'm going to take her down to the Division of Welfare. I know it's going to be all right," I said quickly, "but we're both pretty shook up."

Damon nodded in that way he had that made him look mature and wise. The insecure boyfriend I'd been running laps with that afternoon had disappeared. "You guys want me to take you?" he said. "You don't look like you could drive to Safeway, much less downtown."

"Would you?" I said. I refrained from getting down and kissing his feet. I just followed him gratefully out the door with Angelica clinging to my hand.

The child-protection worker was short and cheerful and had one of those take-charge personalities that made it easy for me to let go of Angelica when she said, "I'll need to talk to Angelica alone first. You guys can wait out here."

It also made it easy for me to sink into one of the orange plastic chairs and start bawling. Damon put his arm around me and kept saying, "It's going to be okay now, Tobey."

I really thought it was. That wasn't why I was leaving a trail of snot and mascara all over his sleeve. I was crying because I finally felt like it was over.

It's amazing how wrong you can be. I started finding that out in about the next five minutes.

"You're really torn up about this," Damon said when I stopped blubbering and was blowing my nose. "She must have told you a pretty disgusting story."

"She didn't give me any of the details, thank heaven," I said. "Just that it happened is disgusting enough."

"Was she, like, raped?"

"In a way, yeah. He didn't force her physically. Just mentally—because of who he is."

"Who is he?"

It felt like I'd just run into a wall. Duh—there were people who were going to find out, and it was going to mess them up the way it had me. I looked at Damon, who was waiting with his wonderful, trusting, gold, blue, and gray eyes. I sure didn't want him to hear this from anybody else.

I touched his hand. "It's Coach Mayno," I said.

It took a minute for it to sink in. It didn't take that long for him to yank his hand away from me and look at me as if I'd just told him Christmas was being canceled.

"No way," he said.

I should have expected that. I mean, I'd already admitted to myself that if I hadn't heard them, I might not have believed it either.

"Yes way," I said. "I accidentally heard them from outside the locker room yesterday—after I found a pair of men's underwear in there the week before, when they had just been in there and I surprised them by showing up—"

Damon covered his ears. He actually put his hands right over them and shook his head. "I don't want to hear this," he said.

"I know," I said. "I've spent the last day throwing up."

"And she's in there telling this to some social worker?" Damon said.

I nodded. "That's what we brought her over here for. I told you that."

"Yeah, but I thought it was her uncle or her mother's boyfriend or something."

"What difference does it make?" I said. I was starting to feel anxiety ripples up and down my arms. Damon's face was turning stony on me again.

"Are you going to, like, testify against him?" Damon said.

I blinked. "Testify?"

"Yeah. Are you going to be her witness?"

"What are you saying?"

"In court or whatever. Are you going to stand up and say you heard him . . . doing whatever it was you heard him doing."

"In court?" I said.

"Good grief, Tobey," he said. "Do you live in some kind of Christian vacuum? When you charge somebody with child molestation, there's usually a trial. You know, lawyers, judges, juries—"

"Tobey?"

I peeled my eyes away from Damon and looked at the woman who had taken Angelica in. She was leaning in the doorway, motioning me over with her head. I went to her, saying, "Yes ma'am?" But my mind was still back there with Damon, hearing words like "trial" and "witness." And seeing his exasperated expression.

"I'm going to need to call Angelica's mother and ask her to come in here," she said. "We need a parent's permission to pursue this. Angelica's still pretty shaken up though. Would you mind sitting with her until I can get back to her?"

"Sure," I said.

I glanced toward Damon before I followed her into the office. His chair was empty.

CHAPTER
ELEVEN

ANGELICA WAS CURLED UP ON A COUCH IN A LITTLE
waiting room, clutching a plastic cup of water. At least her face
was calmer. She smiled when she saw me.

"I like Kathleen," she said. "She totally understood."

"Is that the lady you were talking to—Kathleen?" I said.

She nodded. "Once I got going, I wasn't embarrassed anymore. It was good to get it all out. I feel like you do when you've
just thrown up, you know what I mean?"

"Yeah," I said. I wished I felt better. Right then, I was ready
to heave again. "What did she say? I mean, about what happens
next?"

"She has to tell Mama. I hate that, but Kathleen said it would
be okay. And she said I'll have to see a doctor. Somebody will
probably come talk to you." She looked at me sideways. "Is that
okay?"

"Of course," I said. "We're in this together."

I felt that way. I really did. But Damon had scared me with all
that stuff about courtrooms and district attorneys. Maybe he had
just watched too many episodes of *Law and Order*. I wanted to
ask Angelica if Kathleen had mentioned any of that to her. But
another look at her curled up on the couch like a little girl who
had just awakened from a bad dream, and I couldn't.

We sat there until the parking lot lights came on and fizzled against the raindrops. Rain was also drooling down the windows. I wavered back and forth between reassuring Angelica and silently reassuring myself. Finally, Kathleen poked her head in.

"Your mother is here, Angelica," she said. "Tobey, you can go ahead home now. If an arrest is made, the police will definitely want to question you. You're what's called an 'outcry witness.' Anyway, you'll want to alert your parents. They don't usually like surprises."

I stood there like C3PO as Angelica hugged me and Kathleen thanked me. The door to her office closed behind them.

I don't like surprises either! I wanted to scream after them. *Arrest? Police?*

Suddenly I knew if Damon were standing there he would have said I must have been in—what had he called it?—some kind of Christian vacuum.

Damon.

I tore out of the waiting room into the reception area with my arms already flexed up to hug him. But his chair was empty. So was the hallway, the elevator, and the parking space I could see from the window. No Damon. No steely blue Chevy S-10.

I went to the receptionist who was obviously packing up for the day.

"Did you see a guy—cute—dark, wavy hair?" I said.

She frowned for a second and then nodded. "Oh, yeah, Damon somebody? Are you Tabby?"

"Tobey," I said.

"Right. He said to tell you he had to go."

"Home?" I said stupidly.

"He didn't give me a destination," she said. "He just said to give you the message."

"That's all? He didn't say if he was coming back or for me to call him?"

She just shook her head. Her mind was already calling it a day.

I drifted away from the counter with a head of lead. He had just left me here? What the heck?

Everybody was closing up shop and giving me we-hope-you're-on-your-way-out looks. I didn't have time to figure out Damon. I had to find a way home.

There was a pay phone by the front door. Only because God loves me did I have a quarter in my jeans pocket. My hands were sweating as I poked out Norie's number.

"I'm on my way," she said. "You sound awful."

"Thanks," I said. "Just hurry."

I've never been so glad to see a vehicle as I was Norie's dark green Jeep. It splashed into the parking lot where I was standing in the end-of-the-storm drizzle. Glad doesn't even describe how I felt when Marissa hopped out of the passenger seat to let me in.

"She was over praying with me when you called," Norie said as I climbed into the back. "I didn't think you would mind."

"I love it," I said. "I am so glad to see you guys. This whole thing is like a bad dream."

"No, it's definitely real," Norie said. "But you did it. You can just veg now."

"No," I said. "The police are going to question me. And Damon says if there's a trial—"

"Damon? He knows about all this?"

"He's the one who drove us over," I said.

She looked at me quizzically in the rearview mirror.

"He left me there," I said, in a voice I didn't even recognize. "I'm sure there's a really good reason. I'm just so confused . . ."

I pulled my knees up to my chest and willed myself not to throw up. Marissa reached around to pat my ankle. "What can we do for you?" she said in that soft voice of hers.

"I just need people around me," I said. "I don't know why. I just don't want to be by myself."

"That can be arranged," Norie said. "Would your parents mind if you had about five girls over while they're not home?"

"Not these five girls, no," I said. "They wouldn't mind."

"Good," she said. "You have that phone list I just gave you, Marissa?"

"Got it right here."

"Okay, we'll start calling as soon as we get to your house. How many phone lines do you have?"

"Two," I said. "One in my dad's study."

"Ah, the simple life," Norie said. "We have four."

They used my lowly two phone lines, and within half an hour everybody was there except Cheyenne, who said "they" wouldn't let her out on a school night.

"Poor baby was in tears," Norie told the rest of us as we snuggled in on the family room couch and passed the microwave popcorn.

"I think we're the only friends she has so far," Brianna said. "I've been calling her every night, just to be sure those little jerks in her math class are staying off her case."

"That's why I can never get through," Shannon said. "Her line's always busy."

I sank back into the couch. "You guys call her and stuff?"

"She's really pretty cool," Marissa said. "We went to the mall Saturday. Neither one of us bought anything, but I never had so much fun without spending any money."

"I feel lousy," I said. "I never even see her at school."

"You've had a couple of other things to think about," Norie said. "Which is why we're here. What do you need? Prayer? Talk? A food fight?"

"Not in this house, girl," Brianna said, gazing around our family room. "In our place, salsa on the carpet could only be an improvement."

"Mine, too," Marissa said. "Now, Norie, I imagine you in a big two-story with all this art hanging on the walls."

"Originals," Norie said. "That's all my father will buy. He's such a snob."

Brianna nudged Marissa. "You're the interior decorator. What about Shannon's house?"

Marissa looked nervously at Shannon. "Is this okay?"

"Well—yeah," Shannon said. She smiled her thin, willowy smile. "I totally trust you guys."

I didn't listen to Marissa's vision of Shannon's home life.

Shannon's words were echoing in my ears. "I totally trust you guys." How many times in the last few days had I heard that from this group? I didn't even know these girls, and yet I'd trusted them with the most awful secret I'd ever been privy to. They were the ones I wanted with me when I was so scared all I could seem to do was throw up. Even at that, I wasn't as close to them as they already were to each other. I had this deep longing to be part of what they were building right there around me.

"You guys," I said, "could we do that hold-hands-and-pray thing?"

"No doubt," Norie said. "Everybody grab on."

We did, and we were deep in the throes of each other and God when I heard the front door creak open. I didn't look up. I knew it must be nine, and Fletcher would be coming in. He would probably get one glimpse of us and crawl to his room.

When we finally did say amen and look up, my parents were standing next to the couch. I stepped on two people getting to my mother, and as soon as her arms went around me, I started to cry.

"I think this is our cue to cut out," Norie said.

"Don't run off, ladies," I heard Dad say. "We like to meet Tobey's friends."

I smeared the tears off my face as I pulled away from Mom and started the introductions. Both my parents nodded, but I could tell they were baffled.

"These are the girls I met at See You at the Pole," I said. "We've started kind of hanging out."

"Like we have a choice," Norie said. "We're all Jesus has at King High."

My mother liked that, I could tell. She also took in Norie's T-shirt, which I noticed for the first time read, "Girls who think they're equal to men lack ambition." Mom's lips twitched.

My father didn't seem to notice any of that. He had a concerned look that went all the way up to his ruddy hairline. "That was some pretty intense praying," he said. "I could feel it the minute we walked in the door. I thought somebody had died." He looked a little startled. "No one did, I hope?"

"Not exactly," Norie said. "Why don't we go so you guys can talk?"

The last thing I wanted was for them to leave, but the hugs and the hand squeezes and the whispered "I'll be praying for you's" got me through it. When the last one disappeared out the door, my mother already had the coffee table cleared, and Dad was in his chair, waiting.

"What's up, sugar?" he said.

He hadn't called me that for years. I suddenly wanted to crawl into his lap. But this wasn't a bedtime story I was about to tell him. I perched on the edge of the sofa, with my mother at my elbow, and told them the whole thing. Names. Details. What Kathleen had said to expect. I even mentioned what Damon had said.

"I hope you're not mad at me for doing this without you here," I said. "I know it might be a hassle with the police coming over and all—"

"Don't you even think about being sorry," Dad said. "I'm just glad the storm drove us home earlier than we had planned so we could be here for you."

I stared at him. His face was a study in compassion as he leaned forward in his chair. "You did the right thing, and I'm proud of you. That took a lot of courage."

"I don't think it was courage," I said. "All I could do almost was throw up."

"Really? Seriously?" Mom said. She looked as if she were ready to go for the Pepto-Bismol.

"Yeah. I couldn't have done it without those girls. I don't get it exactly . . . I have all these other friends, but these girls were the ones who helped me."

"It's a God-thing," Dad said. "He sure provided for you when we weren't here. That is glorious to me."

Glorious. Nobody says "glorious." That's what I would have thought two weeks before. But right then, I didn't care how unhip my father was. I did climb into his lap.

I woke up when he tried to stand up with me in his arms. My

mother was in her bathrobe beside us, giggling. "She kind of hangs over, Grant," she was whispering.

"I can walk," I said. "I'm a big girl."

But he held on to my arm as he set my feet on the floor. "You're going to have to be," he said.

"Yeah," I said sleepily. "I have to be there for Angelica. Marissa and Brianna said people might give her a hard time if the word gets out."

"Oh, sugar," Dad said. "I don't think Angelica is the only one who's going to have a hard time."

At first I thought he was wrong. Nobody said a word about it the next morning, and I really didn't expect them to. Angelica and I were the only ones at school who knew. I hadn't used names with any of the Flagpole Girls, not even with Norie.

There was Damon, of course . . .

But I tried not to think about Damon. He would have an explanation for ditching me at the Division of Welfare. If I didn't think about it too much, I could keep believing that.

Besides, even if somebody does say something hateful to me, I thought at the end of first period as I was changing my clothes, *it would be worth it*. Angelica looked more relaxed than I'd seen her . . . well, since I'd met her. There was more of the sweet-baby smile and less of turning herself away so she wouldn't have to look at people. I wasn't sure, but I thought her hair even looked softer.

We both left the locker room at the same time. "You okay?" I whispered to her.

She nodded, and I know she was about to smile when her whole expression froze as if someone had thrown a glass of ice water in her face. I looked up to see Coach Mayno coming around the corner. She must have felt him coming, like some kind of evil presence. The thought made me shiver.

"Just keep looking right at me," I said under my breath. "Don't let him catch your eye."

She nodded obediently and stared right at my nose. I laughed out loud as if she had just said something hilarious. We must have looked like the typical pair of giggly high school girls conspiring in the hall.

"You want to hold down the noise, Tobe?" Coach Mayno said as he breezed by us. "People are trying to study here."

He flashed a smile over his shoulder. And then he winked at me.

When I looked back at Angelica, her eyes were closed, and I thought she was going to pass out.

"He winked," she whispered. "He always winks."

"He won't be winking much longer," I whispered back.

"Do you think he knows yet?" she said.

I shook my head. "He wouldn't be winking—or smiling."

Suddenly that terrified pinch appeared around her eyes again. "I'm afraid of what he might say to me when he finds out I told," she said.

"Don't worry about that," I said. "It's out of our hands now, remember? We have a whole bunch of people who are going to handle everything." I grabbed her wrist. "Come on, I'll walk you to class."

I was almost late for second period, and Norie was waiting for me in the doorway practically panting. "I've been going crazy!" she hissed to me.

She dragged me out into the hallway, glancing furtively over her shoulder as if the CIA were trailing us. "Have they talked to you yet?" she said.

"Who?" I said.

"The police."

"No, did you think they were going to come to my house at eleven o'clock at night?"

"They're here."

"Where?"

"Here—here on campus. I had to go to the office last period, and they were just going into Mr. Holden's office."

"So?"

I knew I was answering like a robot, but it hadn't hit me yet.

"So I just want to make sure you're ready for this. Don't let them talk you out of anything, okay? You stick to your guns. If they harass you, you can call that child protection worker."

"Kathleen," I said.

"Right."

I went for the door, but she stopped me once more. "It's weird to me that they've come to question you at school."

"Maybe it's not even about this. Policemen come here all the time."

"Nah, this is too much of a coincidence. I wonder if Mr. Holden will even let them take you out of class for this—I mean, if he has a choice. You know how uptight they all are around here about losing precious classtime."

"I guess they're doing it here because he works here," I said.

As soon as I said it, I wanted to bite off my tongue. As it was, I tried to shoulder my way into the classroom and pretend I hadn't said it, but it wasn't lost on Norie.

"Whoa," I heard her gasp. "It's a teacher."

The bell rang just as I was sinking into my desk under Mr. Lowe's you-were-almost-late-again frown. I barely connected my buns to the seat when a girl came in with a pink slip, and Mr. Lowe waved it at me.

"For you, Tobey," he said. "Get back as fast as you can. We're starting Emily Dickinson today."

"Oooh—life's desire—you don't want to miss that, Tobey," Gabe said to me. His green eyes sparkled as he grinned at me.

"You aren't in trouble are you, Tobe?" Roxy hissed to me from the desk by the door. "Write me a note when you get back."

I smiled at all of them, and I decided Norie and the rest of the girls must be praying for me. I didn't feel nervous. Not until somebody dove out of the boys' bathroom at the end of the hall and verged on tackling me.

"Damon!" I said. "What happened to you last night?"

He didn't answer right away but pulled me over to his locker and opened it. He didn't take anything out or put anything in. He just left the door hanging, as if he wanted to hide behind it.

"I had to go," he said. "My parents didn't know where I was. Look, Tobey, did you get called to the office?"

I looked him full in the face. His skin looked like paste, and his eyes were jumpy. You would have thought he was some kind of fugitive from justice.

"Yes," I said. "I think it's the police. They're supposed to question me about the thing with Angelica."

"It's them," he said. "I was down at the office when Mr. Holden sent for you."

I tried to giggle. "Does everybody in this school spend the day down at the office?"

Damon shook that off with his head. "What are you going to tell them?"

My giggle and my smile faded. "The truth," I said. "What else can I do?"

"But are you sure it's the truth?"

My insides started to cave with relief. So that's what this was about. "I'm sorry," I said. "It's hard for me, too—the way I've always felt about Coach—but it is the truth. I know what I heard, and it fits with what Angelica has told me."

"I just don't—I can't believe it."

"I know." I fidgeted with the pink slip. "I have to go. Will you meet me for lunch, and we'll talk about it?"

"Just one more thing," he said.

"No, really," I said. "Later. I don't think I ought to keep the police sitting there waiting on me, you know?"

I backed off a few steps and then took off at as much of a run as I could get away with in the halls.

"Tobey, wait!" he whispered after me.

But I didn't. I had had zero experience with the police. I wasn't taking any chances on ticking them off right from the start.

I shouldn't have worried. The two officers who questioned me in the conference room were great. One of them was a big ol' bear who kept nodding and saying "uh-huh" like he thought it would make me feel better. The other one was a woman, and I could see the anger sparking in her eyes as I told the story. She looked as if she wanted to say, "That jerk!"

When I was done, they asked me to step outside for a few

minutes. They went into Mr. Holden's office. Ms. Race was at her desk, and she smiled at me over her computer terminal. It was a how-are-you-holding-up smile. She knew.

I looked around the office where the secretaries, with their professionally manicured nails, were crisply answering phones and flipping through files. Pretty soon, they were all probably going to know.

I'd seen Coach Mayno come through there flashing his dazzler of a smile at all of them, and I'd seen the way they all smiled back and joked with him. He had told me more than once that he pretty much had them wrapped around his little finger when it came to secretarial favors like making his copies and filling out his forms. This was going to be a blow for them. I really hated that.

After a few minutes, Mr. Holden and the police officers came out. They picked up the vice principal from her office and went off down the hall. Any other time, I'd have hummed the theme from *Dragnet* to myself. But they looked so ominous, so official, so full of serious purpose, I suddenly didn't want to sit there by myself anymore. I went over to Ms. Race's desk.

"Do you know what's going on?" I said.

She looked at me for a second and fiddled with one of her dangling earrings. Then she clicked a few keys on her computer and pushed herself away from the desk.

"Want a soda, Tobey?" she said. "I have some bottled water, too."

"Water, please," I said.

"Why don't you wait for me in Mr. H.'s office? I'll be right in."

Now I was nervous. Office people didn't invite you in and serve you refreshments, especially not in the principal's suite.

When she came in with two waters and a couple of glasses, I said, "Shouldn't I be getting back to class?"

"Mr. Holden wants you to wait here," she said. "He needs to chat with you a little more after they're done."

"Done doing what?" I said.

She filled our glasses before she answered. "Arresting Coach Mayno."

I dug my nails into Mr. Holden's couch. "Will kids see it?"

"I don't know. I doubt it. They'll probably be discreet, but I think they have to make the arrest as soon as they have the information they need."

I stared at the glass she tried to hand me. "And I gave it to them," I said.

She set the glass on the table and gently touched my arm. "I wouldn't think of it that way," she said. "You didn't get him in trouble—he got himself in trouble. You did what you had to do."

I took a sip out of the glass. "I think I'm going to be glad when this whole thing is over."

Ms. Race didn't nod like I expected her to. She flipped her braid back over her shoulder and fiddled with her earring again. "I don't know if it's my place to say this," she said. "I probably wouldn't if I didn't know what kind of girl you are. But, Tobey—" She touched my arm again. "—I think it's only beginning."

CHAPTER TWELVE

I DIDN'T HAVE A CHANCE TO ASK MS. RACE WHAT THAT was supposed to mean. Mr. Holden came in then, and she slipped out. But the minute he opened his mouth, I knew what it meant.

It began. Mr. Holden sank into the love seat opposite me and folded one lean leg onto the other knee. He ran his hand wearily across his salt-and-pepper hair. There was no nice smile.

"Tobey," he said, "the police have arrested Coach Mayno. They just took one of our best teachers off in the backseat of a patrol car in handcuffs. The only good thing I can say about it is no students were out there watching."

I sat there blinking at him. The only good thing? What about Angelica Benitez not having to worry about his forcing sex on her ever again?

But I didn't say that. The lines on his face were so grim, I knew every word would definitely "fall to the floor."

"Can you tell me something, Tobey?" he said.

"Yes sir?"

"Can you tell me why you didn't bring the girl in to see some-one here before you went to the authorities?"

My head went into a confused stutter. "I just thought it was the legal thing—you know, the right way—"

"It was perfectly legal, but I'm not sure it was right."

I just shook my head. "I don't understand, sir," I said.

He leaned forward on his knees, cupping his nose with both hands. "We could have confronted Coach Mayno right here and perhaps avoided an unnecessary arrest. Now, no matter how this turns out, his reputation is stained. In cases like this, people will assume he's guilty just because he's been charged."

"But he is guilty!" I said. "Didn't the police tell you? I heard him in the locker room forcing himself on her!"

"They told me what you said you thought you heard—"

"I did hear it!"

"May I finish?" His voice was stern. It cut me clean and sharp. "I reminded the officers that you didn't see anything. All you really know is what you inferred."

"They arrested him," I said. "It was enough for them!"

"It was enough for the district attorney who already had the warrant for his arrest ready to go. They called him, he sent over the necessary paperwork, and it's done. On your word, Tobey."

"What about Angelica's word?" I said. I didn't care now whether my words fell on the floor or not. They were coming out in a sputter I couldn't control—that I didn't want to control.

"Her accusation certainly warrants investigation," Mr. Holden said. "But it's purely her word against his."

"But why would she lie?"

He looked at me long and hard—so hard I didn't recognize him as the pleasant Mr. Holden who was always nice to me in the halls. "What I'm about to say doesn't go out of this room, Tobey. Can I count on you for that?"

I nodded.

"The Hispanic portion of our student body has been grumbling about discrimination for a year now. I haven't taken any action on it because I've seen no evidence of it. That doesn't set well with them." He pressed his lips together as if that were it.

I gaped at him for a stunned thirty seconds. "You mean, you think Angelica made this up just to prove there's prejudice against Hispanics?" I said.

"Made it up—or set it up," he said.

"But she wouldn't do that!" I said. "I know she wouldn't. In the first place, she didn't know I was out there listening—"

"I'm sure she didn't do it all on her own. She was so frightened in here this morning, I sent her home after her interview with the police."

I wanted to bolt out of there and go find her and hold her. Frightened? If she had any idea that they doubted her word, she was probably hysterical.

"I think I know you, Tobey," Mr. Holden said. "I told you that day this summer when you came in to set up the praying around the flag exercise, I'm impressed that you stand by your convictions. But I think this time your idealism may have carried you away. You have to think before you point your finger, think about whose lives are being affected."

"I did think," I said to him. "I was thinking about Angelica's life. And mine. And all the other girls he touches everyday."

Mr. Holden's eyebrows shot up like a pair of arrowheads. "I will not have you starting a witch hunt in this school."

"Witch hunt?" I said. "I didn't mean that kind of touching! It's just that we all trusted Coach Mayno, and now—"

"And now he may never be trusted again, even if the charges are dropped or his case goes to court, heaven forbid, and he's acquitted. The damage has already been done, Tobey. But if you had come to me in the first place, it might have been avoided."

As if from someplace far away, the bell rang. It had an unreal quality to it because I'd forgotten I was at school, a place where people were supposed to protect you. This couldn't be King High School because I suddenly felt very unsafe. I felt terrified.

Mr. Holden glanced at his watch. "I have lunch duty," he said. "Ms. Race will give you a pass for tomorrow to get back into the classes you've missed."

He got up and looked down at me, hands on hips. Disappointment was on his face. Harsh disappointment. Its bitter energy followed me out of the office to Ms. Race's desk. She had my pass ready, but she kept hold of my hand as she pressed it into my palm.

"Tobey," she said, "if you need a friend to talk to—anytime—I'm here."

"Thanks," I said.

But I knew I wouldn't need to take her up on that. I had plenty of friends—and I was going to find one of them right now, because I needed a hug.

I didn't really recognize anybody's face as I squeezed through the mob of people all trying to get someplace for lunch. I was surprised I even found my locker. I was even more surprised that Damon wasn't there.

"Tobey, what the heck, dude! You were gone for three periods!" It was Roxy, red hair flying in ten directions, face full of questions.

"What's going on?" she said.

I sagged against the bank of lockers. It was clear I couldn't tell her now—not after all the things Mr. Holden had said. I needed Damon.

"Have you seen Damon?" I said.

"Yeah," she said. "I just saw him go out the front door. Is this about him? Tell me what's happening!"

"Out the front door—you mean, like he was leaving campus?"

"I guess so. He had his car keys in his hand when he waved to me." Her eyes drooped. "Did you guys have a fight, Tobe? I'm sorry . . ." She chattered on.

I watched her mouth move, but I didn't hear a thing she said. I could only stand there and wish a fight with Damon was what was wrong.

"I knew this was going to happen with him," she was saying. "I would have told you, except—"

"I have to go," I said.

"Where? Do you want to go to Jack-in-the-Box with Gabe and everybody?"

"I'm going to the journalism room," I said.

"Journalism? What for? Are you being interviewed?"

I didn't even answer her. I'd answered enough questions for one morning.

The journalism room was empty. So, it seemed, was the rest of the school. It matched my insides, actually. Bleak-hearted and vacant-headed, I wandered outside. It was kind of windy, the way it is about three-fourths of the time in Reno. Hardly anybody was out there, either, except for the group of alternative types who always gathered across the street to smoke and sit in their cars. The only living being in the schoolyard itself was a lone cottonwood across the front walkway. I went over to the tree and slid down the trunk. It was only when I had my backside on the grass that I realized somebody else was there, too. It was Cheyenne.

"Wow," she said.

Her beautiful lips were in an awed *"O."* I looked around us for some miracle I'd missed.

"What?" I said.

"I was just sitting here praying for you," she said. "And then you just, like, show up. Wow."

"You are a piece of work, Cheyenne," I said woodenly.

"No," she said. "It was God. I know it. That kind of stuff happens all the time. Like I had this dream that I was in a mall with a bunch of people, only I didn't know any of them, but I was having, like, this really good time, and then the next day—the next day—Marissa comes up to me and asks if I want to go to the mall Saturday—"

"I heard you guys had a blast," I cut in. I wasn't sure I could follow any more of her monologue.

"Anyway," she said, "I was praying for you. Norie told me what's been happening." Her mouth went into an *O* again. "You are so brave."

I couldn't help it. I rolled my eyes.

She rolled hers, too. "I know—I'm not supposed to say that. But I really do think you are; so I don't get why I can't tell you that."

I wanted to hug her. "Tell me that anytime you want," I said. "I think I need to hear it."

"There she is!" somebody said.

I looked back toward the front steps. Utley, Kevin, and

Pam were all headed into the building. Kevin was pointing at me.

I waved, but none of them waved back. They went into a huddle, gesturing with their hands and jerking with their heads. It was like watching a movie with the sound off, except for the clanging of the flagpole rope in the background. With a jerk, Pam stomped away from them, taking the steps up two at a time, ponytail flipping. Kevin and Utley looked at each other and headed in my direction.

"Do you want me to go?" Cheyenne said.

"No," I said. "Why would I?"

"Because they look mad," she said.

She was right. When they got to me, Kevin's narrow face was honed down like an ax head, and Utley was doing some kind of agitated tribal dance thing. He hitched at his pants and let Kevin do the talking.

"You really messed things up," Kevin said.

"What?" I said.

"Coach Mayno. Dude in my art class was out having a cigarette when the cops drove off with Coach."

My head was doing a thousand revolutions per minute. Okay, somebody saw him. But how did they connect it to me?

Utley shoved his hands deep into his baggy pockets. "We found out if you hadn't opened your mouth, Coach wouldn't be downtown gettin' fingerprinted."

"See, now you've messed up the whole team," Kevin said. "He'll be out for the rest of the season. It takes three or four months to get to court. See, I know, 'cause my uncle's a deputy DA."

"Plus, if he can't make bail, he'll sit in county jail the whole time," Utley put in.

"Yeah, but that ain't gonna happen. We've already started taking up a collection." Kevin chopped his face at me. "You oughta put in about five hundred bucks."

"Pam wouldn't even come over here to talk to you," Utley said. "She says it makes her sick that you'd believe that little Mexican slut over Coach Mayno."

Kevin shook his head. "See, it doesn't surprise me that much. I heard you started hanging out with a bunch of lesbos. They're the type who's always accusing every guy that looks at them of being a rapist—"

"Shut up!"

I felt my whole body wrench as Cheyenne shot to her feet. Her face was magenta, and her little fists were shot puts at her sides.

"Just stop it!" she shouted at them. "She isn't a lesbian! She's a Christian, and she just did what was right! Leave her alone!" She spat out the words as if they were little bullets and as if she would fire again if they gave her half a reason.

"Back off, ya little psycho," Kevin said. He took a step toward Cheyenne, and she took one right back at him, chin thrust forward and rear thrust backward. Utley grabbed Kevin's shoulder.

"It ain't worth it," he said. "Come on, the chick's wiggin' out."

It wasn't until they had disappeared around the corner of the building that I realized I hadn't said a word after my initial "What?"

Cheyenne watched them vanish before she sat back down and leaned right into my face. "Are you all right?" she said.

"No," I said. I was still in a daze.

"Those jerks." Cheyenne scowled so deeply her eyes almost disappeared under her eyebrows. "Is it un-Christian to hate them?"

I couldn't help smiling, although the casual passerby would most likely have thought it was a grimace. "Probably," I said. "My father would say we should pray for them."

"Somebody else is going to have to do it then," Cheyenne said. "I'm praying for you. And I'm telling everybody you did the right thing; I don't care what they say." She shrugged. "They all think I'm a dork anyway, so who cares, right?"

I wasn't sure I could agree. I'm telling everybody, she had said. She was going to have to—because now everybody was going to know.

And I still couldn't figure out how.

However it happened, it happened fast. The word spread like a case of poison oak. By the time I got to fifth-period American history, half the class was whispering and looking at me as if they thought I didn't see them looking at me. A quarter of the class was staring with open hostility, and the other fourth was crowded around my desk waiting to interrogate me. I could have kissed her feet when Marissa arrived from the office with another pink slip for me.

She waited for me out in the hall. "Are you all right?" she said. Her black eyes were soft with concern. "I heard in the lunchroom that a bunch of kids from the track team were planning to beat you up."

My eyes must have bulged from my head because she said quickly, "But you know how rumors go around here."

"Yeah," I said. "But I don't get how they even found out. You guys didn't even know the names. I didn't even tell you it was a teacher."

Marissa shrugged and rubbed my arm.

"And what does Mr. Holden want now? He's already had me in his office for three hours."

"It isn't Mr. Holden," she said. "It's Mrs. Quebbeman."

That was a relief. I didn't think I could take anymore you've-ruined-a-man's-life speeches.

As I moved off toward the counseling suite, Marissa whispered to me, "Don't forget, we're all praying for you. You don't have to worry about a thing."

I wanted to believe that. But as I sat down in Mrs. Quebbeman's office, and she closed the door, I could feel the room going cold. Even the pictures of her kids all over the desk seemed to be taunting me with "Tattletale!" I expected them to stick out their tongues.

Knock it off, I told myself. *You're freaking out!*

"How are you doing, Tobey?" Mrs. Quebbeman said. She looked at me briefly over her half-glasses, with her short, crispy gray hair poking out at harried angles, and then went back to the file folders she was shuffling through.

"I've been better," I said. "I guess you've heard."

"I wish I'd heard a little sooner," she said, still focusing on the folders. "I think I could have helped. That's what I'm here for."

I wanted to groan aloud.

"But you're okay?" she said. "You're bearing up all right now that the word is out?"

"So far," I said. "I mean, what's anybody going to do? I told the truth. They can't nail me for that."

It was as if she didn't hear me. She pulled one slim folder out of the stack with an "aha!" and opened it on the desk. "This is what I was looking for," she said. She read from it silently, her colorless lips moving, and nodded. All I could do was stare at her—and wish I were someplace else. That she could care less "how I was doing" was totally apparent.

"Okay, listen," she said. "I don't want you to feel as if you're in a trap. Everything in school is a learning experience, and we learn from our mistakes."

I nodded, but I know my face was vacant. What the Sam Hill was she talking about?

"We had a girl here about, let's see . . ." She consulted the file. "Six years ago. She thought she saw two of our teachers parked in a car at night in the faculty parking lot—necking." She looked pointedly over her glasses. "They were both married to other people. Anyway, she started telling other kids, and before you know it we had a scandal here that made Monica Lewinsky look small-time. The school district was brought in, and it looked for a while as if both teachers were going to lose their jobs—and both of them had kids and mortgages and every other thing. It was a mess."

Mrs. Quebbeman took off her glasses and smiled into the past. "Fortunately, I was able to talk to the girl and help her to realize she really wasn't sure at all whom she had seen in that car. But she was so far into it, she felt there was no way out. Well, we found one, and in a few weeks it all blew over." She put the file folder back on the stack and smacked them all smartly on the desktop, as if that were the end of that discussion.

I was still staring at her.

"All I'm saying, Tobey, is, if you want to recant, I can help you do it with a minimum of embarrassment. But come to me. We take care of our own here."

Right! I wanted to scream at her. *I really feel taken care of right now—uh-huh!*

"I think I need to get back to class," I said.

She nodded crisply and initialed my pink slip. As she handed it back to me, she said, "Obviously, Coach Mayno won't be at track practice this afternoon. I'm planning to come down to meet with the team and answer any questions. I can try to field any attacks on you, but they're going to happen. You know that. Coach Mayno is very popular."

My heart thudded to my kneecaps.

"Do I have to be there?" I said.

"Oh, I think it would be in your best interest to be there," she said. She tilted her head at me. "If you run from their questions, they're going to wonder if you have the answers."

She gave her eyebrows a significant twitch, as if she weren't sure herself that I had any answers, and went back to her folders. I stormed out of the office with smoke coming out my ears. For the first time during the whole incident, I was so angry I wanted somebody to come up and say something to me so I could punch them out. The only problem was, when I get angry, I want to cry—big ol' hot tears that burn all the way down to my chest.

I spent the next two periods hiding behind my books and holding back the tears. All I wanted to do was cry in Damon's arms.

Except it became abundantly clear the minute I stepped into the gym after school that Damon wanted no part of my arms— or anything else about me.

CHAPTER THIRTEEN

MRS. QUEBBEMAN HAD THE WHOLE TEAM SITTING IN A clump on the gym floor, and she was perched on the bottom row of the bleachers facing them like some large, carnivorous bird. Damon was on the far side of the group, next to Utley.

He looked up—right at me—when I walked in. I charged toward him, and he turned his head sharply like he had just been slapped and whispered to Utley.

Utley lifted his chin toward me, and his eyes went right through mine and, I'm sure, out the back of my head. I came to a stop so abruptly my shoes squealed on the floor.

That seemed to be everybody's cue to stop chittering and to stare at me. A hush louder than a roomful of accusing screams fell over the place. I dropped to the floor just outside the circle and stared down at my socks.

"Come on now, Tobey," Mrs. Quebbeman said. "We aren't going to do that. We're here to get everything out in the open. Come over and be part of the team."

Somebody gave a derisive snicker. I tried not to believe it was Damon and moved about an inch forward. Mrs. Quebbeman gave me this knowing look—like she even had a clue about what I was feeling—and swept her eyes over the group.

"I'm here to dispel rumors, first of all," she said. "It always amazes me how students get information none of us on the staff could possibly be privy to, which means that information is usually false." Her face slipped into a condescending smile. "Let me give you the real facts."

I chanced a glance to the other side of the group. Pam and Kevin were rolling their eyes at each other. Damon was studying his shoelaces. Utley was keeping up a whispered running commentary into his ear. I felt like a stranger.

"Angela Benitez has charged Coach Mayno with sexual abuse. There was enough corroborating evidence for the police to arrest him. He has been formally charged with child molestation in the third degree, and he has been released on bail."

A hand shot up—Pam's. "Will he be back at school while he's on bail?"

"That is up to the school board," Mrs. Quebbeman said. "Mr. Holden has told me that Coach Mayno is taking a few days off to wait for their decision. If they do decide to suspend him until the trial, he will be out for several months."

An angry murmur rifled its way through the team, and I knew it was aimed at me. I blinked up at the ceiling. Like I wasn't mad because the season was going to be all messed up? Like this all wasn't affecting me, too?

If they would only give me a chance to explain. A lot of them were my friends—they were closer to me than they were to Coach Mayno. I closed my eyes and felt a prayer up to God. *Please just let them listen to me. Let them understand.*

"I have a question," somebody said.

It was Kevin, waving his arm like a kindergarten kid.

"Go ahead," Mrs. Quebbeman said. "That's what we're here for."

"What was the 'carbureting evidence'?" Kevin looked right at me out of his hatchet face. I stared back.

"That's 'corroborating,'" Mrs. Quebbeman said. It was her turn to look at me. "Do you mind, Tobey?"

What if I had minded? Handling it like that, she might as well have just told them. I shrugged and tried not to wish she would be boiled in oil.

"Tobey was a witness to the abuse," she said—in a voice that was suddenly reluctant to speak.

"Gross!" some sophomore boy in the back said. "You mean you saw them gettin' it on?"

I heard somebody smack him. I wish it had been me.

"Do you want to answer that, Tobey?" Mrs. Quebbeman said.

I got up on my knees so I could see the kid, whose face was by now as shiny as his braces. Good. He deserved to be humiliated.

"In the first place," I said, "they were not 'getting it on.' He was forcing himself on her. There's a difference."

Pam flagged her hand around at me. "If he was forcing himself on her," she said, "why didn't she just scratch out his eyes and get out of there?"

"Because she was scared!" I said. "Wouldn't you be if a teacher told you to lie down on a bench in the locker room?"

A faint shimmer of a smile crossed Pam's face. She didn't answer. But a few feet away from me, I heard another girl mutter, "I'd have liked it. I think Coach Mayno's a babe."

I whipped my head around to try to see who it was. A little garden of innocent faces looked back at me, not a one of them with the guts to either admit she had said it, or tell me I was out of my mind, or crawl over and sit by me and back me up. I felt the nausea rising up in me again.

"You didn't answer the question," Utley spat out at me across the group. "Damon says you didn't actually see them."

I almost lost it on that one. Damon? He was the one who "broke the news"? And was watering down my story at the same time?

"Tobey?" Mrs. Quebbeman said. She had an I-told-you-so look on her face.

"No," I said. "I didn't see them. I heard them. I was standing outside the locker room door. I had it open a little, about to go in, and I heard them talking. She was begging him to stop, and he was telling her to stop crying and relax."

Indignant chatter rippled through. Above it all, Pam laughed, a raspy, hard laugh.

"That's all you heard?" she said. "He could have been trying to get a splinter out of her foot!"

Kevin immediately went into a reenactment of Angelica protesting while Utley, in the guise of Coach Mayno, came at her with imaginary tweezers. Next to them, Damon was laughing and nodding his head enthusiastically. I started to gag.

"He wasn't going after a splinter!" I said to the whole, stupid, howling lot of them. "I know that because Angelica told me what happened—over and over again—against her will. Why do you need any evidence at all? Why can't you just believe her?"

"Because everybody knows she's a tramp."

"She hates Coach Mayno. He made her work too hard."

"She's got some real gangster-type friends. They're always looking for some way to nail the school."

"If I'm gonna believe anybody, I'm gonna believe him."

The voices were coming out of faces I'd never seen before, from mouths I'd never heard—and wouldn't want to. My friends, my teammates, were decent, cool people. The kids who were shouting at me were like a brood of vipers. Everything in me recoiled from them. I was angry. And it was obvious I was alone in my anger.

"All right, folks," Mrs. Quebbeman sad. "I think we've all had a chance to vent. Are there any more questions?"

The din fell to a hiss as people kept whispering to each other, faces furrowed in everything from grief to outrage. One girl was even crying.

"If nobody has any questions—" Mrs. Quebbeman started to say.

A timid hand went up. "I have one."

It was Zena Thomas. Until then I hadn't even been able to see her. She had kind of been gobbled up by the crowd. Her already high-pitched voice was shrill with nervousness.

"Yes?" Mrs. Quebbeman said.

"Do you think he'll be convicted?" she said.

Everybody seemed to want to know the answer. The gym fell deadly silent.

"I couldn't even begin to answer that question," Mrs.

Quebbeman said. She looked faintly annoyed. She fooled with her hair, leaving several wiry strands standing straight up, and leaned over to pick up her bag.

"Well, then—" Zena said.

Mrs. Quebbeman looked at her impatiently. Some eye-rolling went on in the group. Zena swallowed. "If he does get convicted, what will happen?"

"You mean what will his sentence be?"

Zena nodded. She had obviously run out of steam.

"If he's convicted of child molestation in the third degree, the sentence can be anything from forty-three months in prison to two years' probation and required counseling. Since Coach Mayno has no priors, and he has been such a model citizen and teacher, I would think a judge would lean toward probation."

"Would he still be allowed to teach?"

I was amazed at Zena's persistence. And she was so still and pale. I couldn't quite tell why she was asking.

"That would be up to the school board," Mrs. Quebbeman said.

"Could we, like, go to the school board and testify for him or something?" Utley said.

"Hey, my uncle's a deputy DA," Kevin blurted out. I thought he was going to wriggle right out of his shorts. "See, we could even testify for him at his trial—you know—like do that character thing—"

"Vouch for him," Pam said. She flipped her ponytail toward the group. "I'd do that."

There were several shouts of "Me too!" and "Who do we talk to?" Mrs. Quebbeman quieted them with her hand and an aren't-they-cute smile.

"I'm sure Coach would love knowing that you're all so loyal—"

"We're not all loyal," Utley said.

Half the room stared at me. The other half concentrated on the floor. I didn't know where to look.

"Are you referring to Tobey?" Mrs. Quebbeman said. "Let's not play games now. I said we were going to get things into the open. If you still have a problem with what Tobey has done, you need to voice it now."

Utley shrugged and looked at Kevin who shrugged and looked back.

I couldn't help looking to see what Damon was doing. He was whispering excitedly into Pam's ear. She was nodding and watching Mrs. Quebbeman. Her hand flew up.

"Pam?"

"I do have a problem with it," she said.

"All right then," Mrs. Quebbeman said. "Address it to Tobey."

Pam looked at Damon, but he didn't have the guts to look back. His eyes were planted firmly on the floor again. Pam got up on her knees.

"Okay," she said to me. "I don't mean to be rude or anything. I mean, you can believe whatever you want to and that's cool. But I don't think you have the right to impose your religious beliefs on anybody else."

I know my mouth was hanging open. "And your point is?" I said.

Even Mrs. Quebbeman couldn't let that one go. "I don't follow you, Pam," she said ever so gently.

"Okay, just because she doesn't believe in sex before marriage doesn't mean she gets to tell everybody else that's what they should believe. I mean, if Coach Mayno and Angelica had a thing, who is Tobey to judge them and say that's wrong?"

"But Angelica thought it was wrong!" I said. "And don't tell me she just shouldn't have done it because he was a teacher and she felt like she didn't have any choice—and he should never have put her in that position—"

"See, I think you told her it was wrong, and then you talked her into turning him in—which, by the way, is a great way for her to stay out of trouble."

A few people seemed to be having "aha" moments. I was having an I-can't-believe-what-I'm-hearing moment.

"See, yeah," Kevin said, scooting closer to Pam. "If Angelina or whatever her name is thought it was so wrong, why didn't she just report it when it first started happening? Why did she need you?"

I felt as if I was exploding. "Because she probably knew this was going to happen!" I screamed at them. I flung my arm out over their heads. "She knew nobody would believe her, and she would get called all kinds of names and have people saying stuff behind her back—and to her face! She couldn't handle it without somebody to help her, and I don't blame her! You're all a bunch of—"

"All right, team," Mrs. Quebbeman said briskly. "I think we've gotten to the core of it. What do you say we all pack up and go home, think about all this, and if we need to have another meeting, or if any of you want to come into my office and chat with me about this privately, if you're having trouble dealing with it, you can do that. Okay?"

The gym emptied around me. All I could hear were whispers and squeaking soles. I didn't look at any of them. Eventually, when they were all gone, I saw Mrs. Quebbeman's brown loafers appear next to my knee. She squatted down beside me, smelling like stale coffee.

"How are you doing, Tobey?" she said.

"Not very well," I said to my toes.

"You didn't think this was going to be easy, did you?" she said.

There was no point in answering.

She patted my shoulder. "They're all confused and hurting," she said. "Give them a couple of days."

Give them a couple of days to do what? I wanted to say to her. *To forget about it? To forgive me? To accept me back into the fold? I don't want any of that!*

She patted me again and stood up, giving me a hand to help me up. I scrambled up on my own and squeaked my way over to my backpack. I heard her say, "Hmmm" behind me.

I guess my response didn't fit neatly into one of her file folders.

I was too mad to cry on the way home. When I slammed my

way in the front door, Mom, Dad, and Fletcher were there, and every one of them looked as livid as I felt.

Mom was squirting cheese over tortilla chips the same way she hunted down a spider with a can of Raid. Fletcher was sitting on the couch, wiggling his foot at light speed. My father was pacing. He was actually pacing. I don't think I'd ever seen anyone pace before, and he was doing it with a purple-faced vengeance.

When I came in and dropped my backpack on the floor, he paced right over to me and engulfed me in this huge hug. I could barely breathe. I started to sob.

"I know, sugar," he said into my hair. "I know. Fletcher said you've had one awful day. Bless your heart."

I could feel my mother's hands on me, too, rubbing my back. The three of us must have stood there for five minutes until Fletcher said, "I think the nachos are burning."

There was a scuffle to the kitchen, and Dad led me to the couch where I curled up and grabbed a pillow—just the way Angelica had . . . what, had it been only yesterday?

"You don't know the half of it," I said. "Mr. Holden says I should have come to him first. Mrs. Quebbeman says if I want to take back my story she'll help me. The kids on the track team say I talked Angelica into accusing him because I'm judgmental and I'm trying to force my religious beliefs on everybody else."

"Mr. Holden, the principal?" Mom said. She set the nachos on the coffee table and wiped her hands on her jeans. She and Dad exchanged looks.

"Yes ma'am," I said.

"Who's Mrs. Quebbeman?" Dad said.

"She thinks she's a counselor," Fletcher said. "I think she's a flake."

Nobody told him to watch what he said. My parents' concerned eyes were on me.

"Didn't anyone help you?" Dad said.

"Mrs. Quebbeman thought she was helping me. She gave me

a pat on the shoulder and told me all the kids were hurting and they would get over it in a day or two."

"And in the meantime, what are you supposed to do?" Mom said.

"She didn't bother to tell me that," I said.

My father stood up and started to pace again. "This is unconscionable!" he said. "I am appalled that absolutely no one there is willing to take the word of a student over a teacher. What is the matter with those people? Who are they there for?"

"Each other," Fletcher said. He said it with his mouth full of cheese and refried beans, but I understood enough to stare at him. If I wasn't mistaken, he was on my side.

"I'm serious," he said. "These kids in my sixth-period class were talking about how somebody on the track team said they were going to get you off-campus and kick your—well, beat you up—and all's Mr. Dixon said was, 'All right, let's quiet down.'" He scooped up another handful of nachos and stuffed them fiercely into his mouth. He chewed like a boxer chomping at his mouthpiece.

"Do you think they would do that?" Mom said to me. "Do you think they would try to attack you?"

"Until today I would have said you were nuts to even ask that, Mom," I said. I tried to shrug off the new onslaught of tears that was threatening at the back of my throat. "But I wouldn't put it past them now. They were looking at me during the meeting like they hated me."

"Meeting?" Dad said. He stopped pacing. "What meeting?"

"The one Mrs. Quebbeman had with the whole track team. She wanted everybody to have a chance to ask questions and vent."

"It sounds like a school-sanctioned ambush to me!"

I nodded miserably. Dad stepped over the coffee table and sat on it so that his face was an inch from mine. As Fletcher rescued the now half-empty nacho plate, Dad grabbed both my hands.

"Tobey," he said, "you do not have to do this alone. We are here for you. If you want us at these meetings, you tell them you won't say a word until you've contacted one of us. We're never farther away than a phone, you know that."

Mom sank down beside me and rubbed my arm. I, of course, started to sob again.

"I mean, it, sugar," Dad said. "You did the right thing. We're behind you—and I want you to remember that. You are not all by yourself."

It was strange, but something occurred to me right then. I was glad they had that parental contract thing.

I sagged against Mom and cried. Dad prayed. Fletcher got up and answered the phone.

"Some chick named Norie called," Fletcher said when it was quiet again. "She said they're all praying for you. You have their support—y'know, all that stuff."

He didn't roll his eyes. That meant I had his, too.

And I was going to need it in the days to come.

CHAPTER
FOURTEEN

THE SCHOOL BOARD PUT COACH MAYNO ON A LEAVE OF
absence until the trial. Coach Gatney told us that the next day at
track practice.

"I'm taking over for him," she said, in a voice that didn't invite questions.

Pam didn't recognize the tone of voice. "Until when?" she
said.

Coach Gatney lifted her sunglasses and gave Pam a look that
should have fried her. "Until whenever," Gatney said. "Now listen up, folks. I am not going to discuss the Coach Mayno case
with anyone. Don't even bother to ask me questions or express
your point of view. I'm here to keep this team together so you
people can run this season, period. Leave your opinions in your
lockers, and let's see some good work out on the track."

Pam sniffed and folded her arms across her chest. Coach
Gatney replaced her sunglasses and said, "All right, everybody
hit the deck. Let's stretch out!"

I thought I saw a little glimmer of hope—until we set out on
our run down past the industrial park, and I fell in step beside
Coach—since nobody else seemed to want to run with me.

"Thanks for what you said before," I said. "I appreciate it."

She didn't sling her arm around my neck or even give me the
gap-toothed grin. In fact, I think she winced, crinkling up all the

leathery skin on her face. "It applies to you, too, L'Orange," she said. "I'm not going to discuss this with you."

I opened my mouth, but she cut me short with a jerk of her head. "I mean it. I'm incommunicado on this case, period. Full stop." She looked out ahead of us. "Utley, let's get the lead out up there," she called. And then she trotted away from me.

I think I could have handled that—and the dart looks I was getting from the track team. I could even have gotten past the first note I found in my locker that said, *You're as much of a liar as Benitez. We don't want liars on the team.* Written in curly, girlish writing, the note ate at me. I thought it was probably from Pam. But I think I could have dealt with it, if I'd had Damon.

But I would have required a much lower IQ not to realize he was actively avoiding me. Not only did he not call me, not only did he not answer any of the notes I put in his locker, not only did he avoid me in school like I had Ebola, but also every time I did see him—which was mostly at track practice—he aligned himself with Pam, Utley, and Kevin as if they were his personal bodyguards. Protecting him.

Like I was some kind of threat to him. Like even being seen with me was going to put him into nuclear meltdown. He didn't just hate me; he was afraid of me.

You would have thought I would have one ally on the track team—Angelica. But she quit coming to practice from the day she told me her story. And she stopped coming to school after the first day the word was out. It didn't take me long to find out why.

The day after the meeting with Mrs. Quebbeman, I went to Roxy's locker at lunchtime. "Is the offer still open to go to lunch with you and Gabe and everybody?" I said.

She got really busy with one of her binders. "I don't know how much room he has in his car," she said. "I guess you could meet us at Jack-in-the-Box."

I felt the warning hackles going up on the back of my neck. "Are you avoiding me, too?" I said.

"No!" She blinked her hazel eyes at me with all innocence. When I looked right into them, she turned back to her locker.

The binder seemed to need a lot of attention. "Gabe kind of thinks you've flipped out over this Angelica Benitez thing. And since I'm riding in his car, I can't exactly bring you with me. But if you just show up, what can he say?"

"Plenty," I said. "And why shouldn't he? Everybody else is saying exactly what they think."

She looked at me nervously through a curtain of red hair. "Are people being rude to you?" she said.

"Yes, as a matter of fact they are. But don't worry about it, Roxy. I wouldn't want you to get a bad reputation, you know, for defending me or anything."

She pulled her head out of her locker. "Are you mad at me, Tobey?"

"No," I said to her. "I don't have the energy to be mad at you."

"Well—do you have somebody to have lunch with?"

"Don't worry about it," I said as I walked away. "Just don't worry about it."

I didn't know where to go then. It was like I was the brand-new kid in a hostile school. I don't know where I would have ended up if somebody hadn't leaned out a doorway and said, "Psst! Tobey, in here!"

It was Norie, hanging out the journalism door. "Hurry up," she said. "Holden'll be coming through here in a minute chasing everybody out of the halls."

I let her pull me inside the room, which was empty except for Norie and, to my surprise, Marissa. I could see the journalism sponsor—I never could remember the woman's name—through the window in her adjoining office, but Norie waved her off with shake of her black-coffee 'do.

"She doesn't care if we hang here," she said. "And so far she hasn't expressed an opinion one way or the other about the Mayno case. Around here, that probably means she's on your side."

I slumped onto a green plastic chair. "I don't see why there are even sides at all. Angelica and I told the truth, period."

"You're not sorry, are you?" Norie said. She straddled a blue version of my chair and leaned intently over the back of it at me. Her Timberland hiking boots sprawled on the floor. "No matter what anybody says, you did the right thing. I even thought that after I found out it was a coach—and I still do."

I could have kissed the toes of the Timberlands. I felt like I was going to start crying again, for about the sixtieth time.

"I'm not sorry," I said. "Especially not now. You are the first person who has stood up for us—except Cheyenne."

"Isn't she a kick?" Norie said. "She called me up last night and asked if we should start carrying weapons."

"Sweet little Christian kid," Marissa said.

I grinned, a rare occurrence lately. "What did you tell her?"

"I told her we didn't need weapons, but thanks for asking."

"I think Angelica is going to need them." Marissa said.

We both looked at her. She set down her apple and pulled her legs-in-red-tights up under her on the chair. She tugged at the bottom of her mini-jumper.

"Why?" Norie said. Her antennae were up.

"I was working in the office before school this morning, and she came in to get a note because Mr. Holden sent her home after first period yesterday." Marissa got wide-eyed. "She was just standing there in line, not even looking at anybody, and this guy—you know, like a skater or something—he yells out, 'Hey, she cut!'"

"He said that about Angelica?" I said. My hackles were going up again.

"Yeah. Of course, everybody in the whole school, practically, starts looking at her. She turns about as red as my tights, and then the guy says, 'She didn't really cut—but how does it feel to be falsely accused, you—'" Marissa stopped. "I won't say what he called her."

"So what happened?" I said. "What did she do?"

"She broke down and just started to sob. I don't think I've ever seen anybody cry that hard. At first nobody would do anything. They were just, like, all standing there looking at her. Finally Ms. Race went out and brought her into the office, and they called her mother to come get her."

"So did any of those jackals in the line show the least bit of remorse?" Norie said.

Marissa shook her head. "Three of the girls started to talk about how they were going to jump her when she got off the bus."

I started up from the chair. "Did anybody warn her? She's just a baby; they'll tear her up!"

"I asked Ms. Race about that," Marissa said. "She said they probably were going to put Angelica on homebound. The nurse said she didn't think Angelica could handle the emotional strain."

I plopped back into the chair and threw my head back. "I don't think I can either, guys. I didn't think I was going be this hero or anything, but I didn't expect everybody to turn on us. I don't know if I can take this!"

"You can, L'Orange," Norie said calmly, "because you have us, and so far that's worked, right?"

I gave her a skeptical look.

"It has worked," she said. She started to tick things off on her fingers. "We helped you work up the courage to talk to Angelica. We helped you get her to the right people. Personally, I think our prayers are what's gotten you through so far—that and the way we tell people they're full of it when they start mouthing off. At least I do."

Marissa blushed. I reached over and touched her arm. "Don't feel like you have to go in front of a firing squad for me," I said. "I know how hard it is. Just your sitting here talking to me like I'm not the devil incarnate is enough, believe me."

And for the moment it was. But I started to teeter fifth period.

Marissa came to get me out of American history again. I was beginning to wonder if I was ever going to make it through my junior year—I was never in class anymore.

"What is it this time?" I whispered to Marissa when we were out in the hall.

"Mrs. Quebbeman again," she said.

I groaned. "She's as bad as Mr. Holden, if not worse. At least he doesn't pretend like he's doing me this big favor."

"She wasn't doing that much pretending," Marissa said. She tucked her arm through mine. "She about snapped off my head, like, 'Get her down here!' "

"Oh, man," I said.

Marissa pulled her arm out of mine at the door to the counseling suite, but she held on to my hand for a second. "I'm going to start standing up for you, Tobey," she said. "You shouldn't have to go through this alone."

I'd heard that before—from my parents. I kept it wrapped around my brain like a security blanket as I stepped into Mrs. Quebbeman's office.

Her hair was almost standing on end, and her blouse had come untucked from her slacks. She was, as usual, flipping through folders—frantically this time. When I came in, she shoved them all aside and pointed to the chair. It seemed to take more effort than normal for her to pull the patronizing smile onto her face.

"I'll get right to the point, Tobey," she said, "because I know you've been missing a lot of class. I had lunch with some of the students on the judicial board."

I felt like Norie with her antennae going up. "You mean, like Gabe and Roxy?" I said.

"Do specific names matter?" she said.

It did, but I let it go. She had already answered my question.

"They're feeling a little uneasy about the upcoming election of homecoming queen."

"Is there a problem?" I said. "I could have been at the meeting—nobody told me—"

"You weren't at the meeting because the meeting was about you." She tapped her pencil on the desk. "You're strong enough that I don't have to beat around the bush with you, Tobey. They're feeling some anxiety about working with you. They think your association with handling the election is going to raise all kinds of questions. Kids might not vote, or they'll challenge the results. You know how these things can get out of hand."

"No," I said. "I don't know. What has my standing up for

Angelica got to do with the judicial board handling the home-coming queen election? I don't see the connection."

She looked at me, eyebrows raised, as if I'd just said some-thing insubordinate. I hadn't even raised my voice or used what my mother called "a tone."

"I assured them their fears were unfounded," she said. "But truthfully I don't think I was very effective in convincing them."

Gee, I thought, *what a surprise.*

"So I'm going to make a suggestion to you, Tobey," she said. She was looking at her pencil and choosing her words as if she were picking out just the right peaches in the produce section. "I am not asking you to do this, mind you, but I'm suggesting that you take matters into your own hands."

"And do what?" I said. I could hear the ice cubes in my voice.

"Avert trouble. Step down from the judicial board before the homecoming queen election proceedings get underway."

"Step down—like, resign?"

"Okay," she said.

I felt as if somebody had just slit my throat. I was suffering from a mortal wound, right there in my counselor's office. I put my hand up to my chest to be sure I was still breathing.

"I know it comes as a shock to you, Tobey. You've never been through anything like this before. I don't think you had any idea what the possible consequences might be."

I shook my head.

She put down the pencil and leaned across the desk, hands folded. "My offer is still open. You can reverse on this anytime, and I'll be there for you."

I had to struggle to speak. "Will you be there for me if I don't?" I said.

She took off her glasses and blinked at me in disbelief. "Of course, Tobey," she said. "You don't see me taking sides, do you?"

Yes! I wanted to holler at her. *I think you're as bad as every one of those—those—jackals!*

Instead, I said the next thing that crashed into my head. "I don't get this," I said. "I go to all these leadership seminars and stuff so I can be a good leader. But when I try, nobody wants that."

"Of course they want it—"

"Is leadership just being president of the cool clubs, or is it setting an example for people?"

She nodded and toyed with her pencil. "Which do you think it is?"

"I just think I should get back to class," I said. I handed her my pass.

She briskly initialed it. "You'll think about my suggestion?" she said, as she held out the pass to me.

"Sure," I said.

But I wasn't going to think about any of this by myself anymore. I went straight to the office.

One of the secretaries, the one with the shell-pink nail polish, looked up when I cleared my throat at the counter. She had let me borrow magic markers for posters and showed me how to use the copy machine before, all with a peppy little smile. Now it was as if a window shade came down over her face when she saw me.

"May I help you?" she said coolly.

"Yes ma'am. I need to use the phone please," I said. "I have to call my mother."

"If you're sick, you need to see the nurse first," she said.

I didn't know what to say.

"Hi, Tobey," came somebody else's voice.

It was Ms. Race. She had never looked more beautiful to me—face a wreath of smiles, arm held out to me from under a raw silk caftan-type thing in shades of green.

"Are you being helped?" she said.

"I need to use the phone," I said. "I really need to call my mom."

"Come use mine," she said.

She buzzed me in and put her arm around my shoulder as she led me to her desk. I could feel the heads swiveling behind us. It was a few minutes before all the fingernails started to click on the computer keys again.

Ms. Race handed me her phone and busied herself at her desk. My hands were shaking as I dialed our number. My heart sank when the answering machine came on.

At the sound of the beep, I was holding back tears. "Hi, Mom," I said. "Things aren't good at school, and I just wanted to talk to you. I guess I'll try to get back to you later."

I hung up and looked down at the phone through the film over my eyes. *Now what?* I thought.

Just then a burst of laughter came from the copy room. Both Ms. Race and I looked up. It sounded as if somebody was having a party in there.

"Hurry up, Dixon!" we heard somebody say. Well, the person shouted, if you want to get technical. "I'm covering Mayno's health class now. I have a thousand copies to make."

"Is that the biggest crock you've ever heard?" somebody else yelled over the whir of the Xerox machine.

"What? This sexual-abuse thing?"

"Yeah, it would never have gotten this far if it weren't for that L'Orange girl and her Christian crusade."

"Another one out to save the world's underdogs."

"Yeah, well, that little underdog Benitez isn't worth a man's career."

"You got that right. You done with those copies yet? Good grief, you have enough there to wallpaper the gym!"

Ms. Race stood up abruptly from her desk. "How about some more of that good bottled water, Tobey?" she said.

But her voice wasn't cheerful, and her eyes were blazing. Her face was fast turning the color of her deep auburn hair. She had heard as clearly as I had.

"No thanks," I said. I reached for the phone again. "I think I'll try my dad's office."

"Yeah," she said softly. "I wish you would."

But before I could punch out the first number, Mr. Holden's office door opened. A disgruntled-looking Mr. Ott hurried out, skin red all the way up his half-bald head. His pudgy cheeks wobbled as he marched off through the office like the Pillsbury Doughboy on a mission.

"Tobey," Mr. Holden said. "I was just going to send for you. You must have ESP." He nodded toward his door. "Would you mind stepping in for a few minutes?"

I swallowed hard. "Can we do this when my mom or dad can be here?" I said.

He actually looked hurt. "Do you think I'm going to yell at you or something?" he said.

"No," I said. "But—"

"It'll just take a second. Come on in. Ms. Race, would you hold my calls?"

He acts like it's no big deal, and then tells his secretary to hold his calls? I thought. I watched television. I knew what that meant. If I had worked there, I'd have known I was about to be fired.

I dropped onto the couch and fought back the rising tide of nausea. I put my hands on my thighs and realized I'd probably lost about five pounds in the last few days. Who could eat when everything around me was making me sick?

"I guess you saw Mr. Ott leaving my office," Mr. Holden said. He was toying with a football he took off the shelf beside the love seat.

"Yes sir," I said.

"And I'm sure, as sensitive as you are, that you noticed he was upset."

Here we go again, I thought. *I've ruined another man's life.*

"He was so upset, in fact," Mr. Holden went on, "that he gave me an ultimatum. That's not something I've come to expect from my teachers."

"No sir,'" I mumbled.

"Here's the bottom line, Tobey," he said. "Mr. Ott says either you resign as junior class president, or he resigns as adviser."

I'd thought I'd heard it all. I refused to believe I was hearing this.

But I guess I did, because I grabbed for a Kleenex from the box on the table and held it up to my mouth until I was certain I wasn't going to throw up on his carpet. In reality, I sure would have liked to.

Mr. Holden gave me a few minutes to pull myself together. He offered me every beverage in life, all of which I refused, and then he just waited until I could finally sit up straight.

"Are you all right?" he said. "Shall I continue?"

"There's more?" I said.

"I think you ought to hear Mr. Ott's reasoning," he said. "He feels that continuing to work closely with you may imply he agrees with you. He just doesn't feel as if he can do that to a colleague."

Reasoning? I thought. *That's reasoning? That's the tormented thinking of some kind of disturbed freak!*

"Now, I know Mr. Ott is upset, as we all are, yourself included—"

He didn't get to finish. The door snapped open, and green silk filled the doorway. Mr. Holden frowned up at Ms. Race. There was an I-thought-I-told-you-not-to-disturb-me threatening on his lips.

"Rev. L'Orange is here," she said, just as if Mr. Holden had been waiting for his arrival. "Shall I show him in?"

Without pausing for an answer, she ushered my father through the door and shut it behind him. I wanted to throw myself into his arms and cling. I leaned hard against him the minute he finished shaking Mr. Holden's hand and sat down beside me on the couch.

Mr. Holden abandoned the football and started clasping and unclasping his hands between his knees. My father was perfectly still.

"I'm a little surprised to see you here—do I call you Reverend or Father?"

"Grant will be fine," Dad said.

Mr. Holden couldn't seem to bring himself to say that. "There was really no need for you to come in," he said. "Tobey isn't in any kind of trouble."

"I think she's in a great deal of trouble," Dad said. "I'd call it trouble if I were being accused of being a liar, wouldn't you?"

Mr. Holden sat up straight. "I would if that were happening. But I don't see anyone calling Tobey a liar—"

"Ah, let's use the euphemism then—or perhaps the innuendo," Dad said.

He was losing me on the vocabulary, but I was feeling stronger by the second.

"You're going to have to explain," Mr. Holden said, voice wooden.

"Members of the staff here have told my daughter she can recant at any time. They've asked her to be patient with all the people she's 'hurt.' They've explained in no uncertain terms that she has destroyed a teacher's career." Dad's eyebrows were slowly meeting in the middle. "And no sooner do I arrive here, than I hear she's been asked to resign from two of her offices—all because she chose to tell the truth and stand up for someone weaker than she."

Whoa, I thought. *That news flash got out fast!*

"And I don't even think that's the worst of it, sir," Dad went on, having barely taken a breath. "The worst of it is that while her own peers are harassing her, shunning her, and threatening her, not a person of authority in this school has stepped forward to offer her any kind of protection."

"Mr. L'Orange, I assure you that Tobey is perfectly safe here."

"How can you assure me of that, sir?" Dad said. "I don't find what happened to Angelica Benitez—right here in this building—very reassuring."

"You're speaking of what allegedly happened," Mr. Holden said.

It was the wrong thing to say. My father lurched forward with his finger out, pointing directly at Mr. Holden's chest. "Sir," he said—voice ominously low, "I will not have you casting aspersions on my daughter's word. Is that clear?"

"Are you threatening me?" Mr. Holden said. He certainly looked threatened. His lips were white.

"I am simply making myself clear. We're Christians, Mr. Holden. We don't need to threaten people—not when we can simply speak the truth."

Mr. Holden didn't appear to be impressed by that. He was still catching his breath from Dad's "making himself clear."

"So what is it you want me to do?" he said tightly.

"I want you to be certain that my daughter is protected from harassment and assault by other students."

"That shouldn't be a problem."

"And I want her to be given a fair shake by the staff here."

"I think that is already being done."

"I don't."

"Very well. I will give the matter close scrutiny."

They stared each other down. Dad won. Mr. Holden shifted his eyes up to the clock. Dad stood up and folded my fingers between his as we left the office.

He didn't shake Mr. Holden's hand.

"Do you want me to take you home, sugar?" he said when he had closed the door behind us.

I smiled into his neck as I hugged him. "No, Dad," I said. "I think I'll be all right."

For the first time, I thought maybe that was really true.

Especially when Dad leaned over to Ms. Race's desk and said in a hoarse whisper, "Thanks for calling me."

"Anytime," she whispered back. "You can count on it."

CHAPTER
FIFTEEN

I WAS WAY MORE HOPEFUL AT THAT POINT. EVEN THE second hate note in my gym locker before practice didn't shatter my world.

In fact, as I read it—*Everybody's asking you to quit their organization. Do you see a pattern here? Don't make us ask you. The Cross-Country Team*—I realized the writing on this note and the other one I'd received weren't the same as the handwriting on that one I'd gotten weeks ago, about Angelica being a tramp.

I still had the other one in my backpack and I compared the two. The new ones were done in feminine curlicues—Pam's, it had to be. The old one was in jagged handwriting.

Funny. Back when I'd received the first note, I'd assumed it was probably the three vultures. But now it was clear the writing was a guy's.

I shrugged and stuck them into my backpack. It didn't matter now, and besides, I had other problems. One of them was Damon.

It hurt to see him at practice, cavorting with Utley, Kevin, and Pam—my former friends. It was like just because he didn't want to deal with me, I didn't exist. And I still didn't know why.

I'd have tried asking him, but his Secret Service agents were always clumped around him. That day, in fact, all I did was step out onto the track for sprints, and all three of them formed this wall between us with their backs to me. I'd have been socially suicidal to even consider trying to break through it to get to him. I just walked by.

As I did, I heard Pam say in a stage whisper, "You are just so much better off without her, Damon. You don't need the hassle."

I had to practically pinch myself to keep from grabbing her by that perky little ponytail and telling her what hassle was like for somebody like Angelica Benitez. As it was, I ran up Valley Wood Drive like a chased rabbit, and I didn't care if anybody ran with me. During the cool-down laps on the track, though, Zena did.

"Hi, Tobey," she said timidly.

I looked down at the top of her shiny bob. She glanced up at me kind of shyly, and I saw that her lips looked shivery. It was only the first of October and not that cold, especially when we had just run six miles.

"Are you all right?" I said.

"Wow," she said.

"What?"

"Your life must be so awful right now, but you're still thinking about other people's feelings."

"Oh yeah, I'm just incredible," I said. "Just ask Pam and Utley and those guys. The truth is, if you want to have any kind of life around here, Zena, you shouldn't hang around with me."

She shrugged. "That's okay. They never treated me that good anyway. I'm just a freshman. Everybody knows we have like this contagious disease."

Her wonderful, rich blue eyes rolled. I found myself smiling.

"It's a bummer that both the other freshmen are gone from the team so you have to suffer alone," I said. "Of course, you can hang with me because you've got nothing to lose, huh?"

"No," she said. "I can do it because I think you're right."

I'd been waiting for two days for somebody besides my family and the Flagpolers to say that. I never expected to hear it from a mousy little freshman who didn't even know me.

"What makes you so sure?" I said.

"Aren't you?"

She looked suddenly frightened, as if she had made some huge mistake.

"I wouldn't have come forward if I weren't absolutely sure," I said. "I didn't do this to get a big name for myself or make some religious statement like everybody thinks. I did it because God didn't give any man the right to force a girl to have sex. I don't care who he is or who he thinks she is, especially when she's only fourteen years old and especially when she's a minority kid who people think stupid things about—"

I know my mouth was still moving, but I got the sound to stop. The group in front of us was looking over their shoulders and giving each other stares that clearly read, "Psycho." And poor Zena looked as if she wanted to disappear through the chain-link fence.

"I'm sorry," I whispered to her. "You came over here to be nice to me, and I'm embarrassing you. You can go on if you want—I won't be mad at you or anything."

But Zena shook her head. "No, it's okay," she said, voice quavering. "I just didn't know all that. I mean—wow."

She must have said "Wow" about eighteen more times before practice was over. That was okay. At least somebody was saying something to me.

But another person spoke to me, too—just as I was heading into the girls' locker room. A voice hissed my name from the direction of the water fountain.

That water fountain was the scene of one of the worst moments of my life, and I didn't want to go anywhere near it. But Damon was beckoning to me.

I almost cried. In spite of all the stuff Pam, Utley, and Kevin were pouring into his ears, in spite of all the times he had ignored me the last few days, in spite of all that, he was now willing to talk to me.

Maybe he had to sort it out by himself first, I thought as I took slow steps toward him. Mom always said men are different that way.

"Hi," I said softly to him. "I was hoping we'd have a chance to talk."

"Yeah," he said. He was using his husky voice. "Could we go out in the hall or something?"

Or we could climb into the trash Dumpster, sit on thumbtacks— I don't care, as long as you'll talk to me! I reined myself in from saying that and just followed him out into the empty hall that led to the ROTC area.

"Want to sit?" I said.

He shook his head, still sparkly with sweat. "No, I just wanted to ask you something."

"Good," I said. "Because I want to ask you a couple of things, too."

"Whatever," he said.

That should have tipped me off. I guess I was just so hopeful I didn't want to see what was coming. I never would have guessed it in this century anyway.

"So what do you want to ask me?" I said. "You know all you ever had to do was come to me—"

"It's just . . . I've been wondering," he said. He licked his lips. "I know you've been talking to the police and all these officials, but I think it's okay for me to ask you—"

"Ask me!" I said. I heard myself laughing—too loudly. "I'm not going to bite you or anything!"

But he looked for all the world as if he were sure I was going to bare my fangs and tear his flesh off. "Okay, then, you haven't told anybody that I was the one who like drove you to the Welfare Department that night, you know, when she pointed the finger at Coach, have you?"

I've always thought anger was a hot thing. I learned in that instant that it's at its worst when it runs so cold you can hardly speak. When I did, only the very iciest words would come out. " 'She,' meaning Angelica?" I said.

"Who else?"

"You're worried that I've told somebody that you were involved?"

"That's just it—I wasn't involved! All I did was give you a ride. And the way I look at it . . ." He shrugged. "You pretty much manipulated me into doing that."

"What?" I know my veins froze at that point. I could only say, "What?" again—and then again.

"You didn't tell me the guy she was accusing was Coach Mayno until after I was already there."

"Are you saying you wouldn't have taken us if you had known?"

Damon shoved his hands into his pockets and drew a circle on the carpet with his toe. "I'd have tried to talk you out of it, and then you wouldn't be in this mess."

"I'm not in a mess. Coach Mayno is the one who's in a mess—the one he created for himself!"

He looked up at me sharply. "You're going to be in one when they decide he's not guilty. Or have you got your head stuck so far into the Bible you can't see that?"

He immediately recoiled back into himself, the way a little kid does when he has just messed up big-time, and he knows his father is about to swat him. I could feel my eyes thrusting icicles at him.

"I cannot believe you just said that!"

"Look, I'm sorry. I'm upset about this, all right?"

"You're upset?! You just implied that I'm some kind of irrational fanatic, and you're upset?"

"Well, that's the way you're acting—"

"What are you saying? You think it's wrong to do what my faith tells me I should, even if it isn't popular?"

"Just chill, Tobey, okay? I don't want to get into a big theological discussion with you. I don't feel like being preached at."

He could have slapped me in the face or stripped down to his boxers there in the hall, and I wouldn't have been more flabbergasted. This couldn't even be the same boy who had said things to me like "My parents brought me up Christian. I was taught not to put people down"; "I thought I was the only Christian on campus"; "I like girls with guts"; "You're honest, which is cool"; "Nobody should get away with abusing a girl. The guy ought to be thrown in jail."

Those words had been so much of what made me think I was

in love with him. The things he was saying now convinced me I could never be. I felt stiff and empty.

"Whoa," I said.

"What?"

"I guess I was wrong—I thought I'd finally found a neat guy who could walk the walk."

"What are you talking about, 'walk the walk'?"

"You know, you can talk the talk—which you do. You've said all the right Christian things. But when it comes right down to it, you can't take the action."

"I'd take the action if action needed to be taken." He was starting to prickle. He even ran his hand down the back of his neck. "That's the problem with you Born Agains," he said. "You see something that isn't a big deal, only you sniff out 'sin' in it, and you start digging and pretty soon, you've got a hole big enough to dump somebody's life into!"

"You're going to have to explain that one to me, Damon," I said, "because I am completely lost."

I don't know what was happening to me. It was like the ice was cracking, and I was being split in ten different directions. Part of me wanted to laugh out loud, right in his face. Part of me, I'm ashamed to say, wanted to smack him one. And part of me wanted to peel out of there and pretend none of it had ever happened. I folded my arms hard against my chest and stared at him, just to hold myself together.

"Okay," he said. "You overhear Coach Mayno and Angelica in the locker room. You get all shook up because you're a virgin—"

"Forget it," I said. "I hate the way you're talking to me, and I won't stand here and listen to it. I don't care what you have to say."

I cut out into the hall to get past him. He grabbed my arm—hard. "See, that's what I'm talking about," he said.

"Let go."

"And that, too." He gave my arm a shake before he uncurled his fingers. "You're so naive, you just make this federal case out of every little thing. Do you call what I just did to you assault? Attempted rape?"

"I thought you were a Christian."

"There's a difference between being a Christian and acting like some holier-than-thou prude."

"Is that what you think I do?" I said.

"Yeah, in this case, yeah. And all it does is give the rest of us a bad name."

I felt as if he had just belted me right across the mouth.

"I try to mind my own business," he said. "I let other people do what they want."

"Like Coach Mayno?"

"Okay—sure."

"Then you lied to me about what you believed."

"Whatever—okay, I lied. And now I'm going to hell. But just don't broadcast it over the intercom tomorrow morning during announcements, okay?"

I shuddered, hair roots to rubber soles. He looked a fraction contrite. His eyes dropped. "Okay, that was out of line." He sighed this exasperated sigh. "I wish this had never happened. It's like, everything was great between us until you started this."

"He started it!"

"See, I'm having a hard time believing he's this evil child molester. Angelica Benitez isn't exactly a child, in the first place—"

I was shaking my head hard. "You told me one time that I wasn't into denial, but you definitely are! I knew you'd be disappointed. I didn't think you'd be blind!"

"That isn't the point."

"Then what is the point?"

He grabbed me by both shoulders and pushed his face right into mine. I froze.

"You cared more about all this—about being the big savior—than you did about me." He sniffed angrily. "Maybe it's a good thing this happened so at least I knew where I fell on your priority list."

I jerked my shoulders and got myself away from him.

"Okay, go," he said.

I did.

And then he called out to my back, "You never did answer my question. Did you say anything to anybody, about what I was talking about?"

I stopped, but I didn't turn around. "No," I said.

"Well, don't, okay?"

"Fine."

I started to walk off. He stopped me again. "I don't care about anybody else, but I don't want Coach Mayno to know I had anything to do with helping her."

A hard, raspy laugh blurted from me and bounced off the sides of the cinderblock walls.

"What's so funny?" Damon said. "What are you, losing it?"

"No," I said. "It's just a riot to me that you think you had anything to do with helping Angelica. You've hurt her just as bad as Coach Mayno ever did."

"What's that supposed to mean?" He shouted after me as I broke into a run and slammed through the double doors. "Hey, what the heck's that supposed to mean? Tobey!"

Zena Thomas was just emerging from the locker room. I went right up to her. "If I give you my locker combination, will you go in there and get my stuff?" I said. "And bring it to me at my car? The red Honda?"

"I know the one," she said. "I see you and Fletcher when you get here in the mornings."

"Thanks," I said.

Then I headed for the outside door. I had to get away from everybody so I could cry.

I was basically calmed down to the hiccup phase an hour later in my family room on the couch with my head in Mom's lap, when Norie called.

"Would your parents mind if the other girls and I came over after dinner tonight?" she said.

"Tell them to come for dinner," Mom said when I asked her. "I made a pot of chili . . ."

She went on rattling off the menu, and Norie hung up so she could start making calls. Within an hour they were all there, even Cheyenne.

"I've been telling Tassie all about it," she said. "So she said we could make an exception to the rule tonight, for something this important."

I didn't ask her who Tassie was. I was learning not to interrupt Cheyenne with questions, or we would be there for days.

She wasn't the biggest surprise. After the last of the girls arrived, the doorbell rang again, and Dad let Ms. Race in. She was wearing this oversized denim jacket and flung her arms out to wrap me in them.

"Thanks for letting me come help," she said. "You've wormed your way right into my heart."

I looked at my dad over her shoulder, but he just gave me this innocent look. I was beginning to wonder why I'd ever thought he was anything but completely cool—in his own frumpy kind of way.

Mom put a huge pot of chili, a basket of cornbread muffins, and a giant salad out on the table in the kitchen with bowls and spoons and let everybody serve themselves. We gathered around the coffee table in the family room.

"Cloth napkins," I heard Brianna whisper to Marissa as she shook out one of those checkered things we use every night. "We're talking uptown, girl."

But nobody seemed uncomfortable. Matter of fact, the only person who looked remotely out of place was Fletcher, whose eyes bulged at the sight of all that girlhood. However, that was only his initial reaction. He eventually made himself comfortable on a stool up at the counter with my parents and Ms. Race and didn't miss a word we said. I caught him giving Shannon a complete inspection over the top of his milk glass.

Any other time I'd have said, "Dream on, kid." But at that point, I was way too brittle to be sarcastic.

"So how are you holding up, L'Orange?" Norie said, as Mom cleared away plates and brought out the brownies.

"Barely," I said. "One more attack from somebody—anybody—and I'm going to break. I know it."

"No way, girl," Brianna said. "And that is exactly why we're here."

There was a unanimous nod. I must have looked baffled.

"It was Marissa's idea," Norie said. "She came storming into the journalism room after school and said you were really getting shafted big-time, and we shouldn't let you go through this alone. So, here we are."

"Then let's pray," I said.

Everybody looked at Brianna.

"Well, now, we're going to pray . . ." She glanced at my father. "We're always going to do that, you know, but what I've been hearing from God—and I know this probably sounds weird or something, but I can tell when He's talking to me—what I'm hearing is that talking to the Lord is good, but if we don't do what He wants us to do, then we aren't listening. We're just talkin'."

"Which, of course, I picked right up on," Norie said. "Nothing does it for me like a plan of action."

"What plan of action?" I said.

"That's what we're here to figure out. And Ms. Race is here to tell us if any of it is illegal."

"Well, against school policy," she said. "I can't imagine this group coming up with anything illegal."

"I used to do illegal stuff," Cheyenne said. "But that was before. I'm clean now. It's been about six months since I—"

"Cheyenne," Brianna said, "have a brownie, girl."

Cheyenne chewed contentedly, and Norie stuck out her hands. "Let's pray first," she said.

We did, hand in hand, although all I could murmur was "thank you" about twenty thousand times.

When our heads came up, Norie grabbed a legal pad and a pencil and handed it to Shannon. "Take notes," she said.

Shannon started to write immediately, with Fletcher looking over her shoulder. Hands flew, lips flapped, and ideas poured out. When we were through, everybody had a job—even

Fletcher, although I was pretty sure that was more to impress Shannon than to help me. I could almost see a light, and I was thinking it was hope shining at me.

"Sounds like a wonderful plan, girls," Ms. Race said. "You know if you need anything I'm right there in the office."

"We have one more thing to do before we go," Marissa said. She shook her chopped-off shiny hair away from her face and looked shyly at my parents. "If it isn't getting too late?"

I could tell my parents had fallen in love with her—with all of them. Shannon was holding one of Mom's most recent teddy bear creations Mom had shown her during our bathroom break, and Dad nodded every time Norie opened her mouth. Go figure that one.

"Go for it," Mom said. "You have plenty of time."

"She's so cool," Cheyenne whispered to Brianna.

"You tell it, Marissa," Norie said. She had to nod to Marissa with her little sharp eyes piercing before Marissa could stop blushing and start talking.

"Okay, well, you know how we decided that one day right when we first started to meet we weren't allowed to fix each other, we could only tell our own story?"

It was my turn to get red. I'd been the Great Fixer that day, ready to show everybody how to defend their beliefs. Now I was the one needing the help because I was being kicked in the face for doing just that.

"So we had everybody put themselves in your place, Tobey," Shannon said, "and we each picked out the Scripture we would keep in our hearts if it was us in your shoes."

My father looked about as impressed as I'd ever seen him. Mom and Ms. Race looked at each other and both grabbed for the Kleenex at the same time. I didn't bother with facial tissue. I just let the tears run on down.

"You go first, Norie," Shannon said.

"Like I know so much about the Bible," Norie said. She took the one Brianna was holding and thumbed through it. "I always thought it was a rad piece of literature. I've only recently started looking at it as an operator's manual."

Dad chuckled.

"All right—Luke 21. This is what I'd want to be hearing in my head. 'They will lay hands on you and persecute you. But make up your mind not to worry beforehand how you will defend yourselves. For I will give you words and wisdom that none of your adversaries will be able to resist or contradict. You will be betrayed. All men will hate you because of me. But not a hair of your head will perish. By standing firm you will gain life.'" She shrugged. "It's a little dramatic, but you get the point."

I nodded tearfully.

"I'll do mine," Shannon said. I could tell this was one area where she felt sure of herself. She lifted her delicate little chin right up and read like a pro. "Psalm 64—just the first part. 'Hear me, O God, as I voice my complaint; protect my life from the threat of the enemy. Hide me from the conspiracy of the wicked, from that noisy crowd of evildoers." She cocked her head at me. The wispy strands of almost-white hair fell across her cheek like it would on an angel, I decided. "I'd think that. And then I'd know He was right there doing it. That's all."

"Okay," Brianna said, "now I'm into the Ol' Testament myself 'cause those people were always getting in some kind of trouble. I found what I would need—" She took her Bible back from Norie, who was currently absorbed in it. "Here it is—First Samuel 23, verse 18. 'The two of them made a covenant before the LORD.' And I'm thinkin', all right—there's six of us making a pact right here in front of God—and don't nobody try to tell me he isn't right here in this room tonight." She gave us all a searing glance. Nobody disagreed. "So I figure if it was me and I had all of you in here praying with me and making promises, I'd be good to go."

She snapped the Bible shut as if to say the matter was all but over. I wanted to hug her.

Norie elbowed Cheyenne.

"I didn't even know where to start, and I got all freaked out," Cheyenne said. "But Tassie made me sit down, and she helped me." She looked at Norie. "Is that okay?"

Everybody said yes.

"Okay, so she showed me a bunch of them, and I picked out this one." She opened the most used copy of the New Testament I'd seen since my grandmother's attic. Tassie, whoever she was, must be a Christian from way back. "Romans 12." Cheyenne cleared her throat, flipped back her hair, squinted at the page, and then wet her lips until I was sure Norie was going to climb up the wall. Finally, Cheyenne read, with painful slowness, "Honor one another above yourselves. Never be lacking in zeal, but keep your spiritual . . . fever—"

"Fervor," Dad whispered.

Cheyenne nodded at him, then blinked back at the page. After a brief search, she continued, "Share with God's people who are in need. Bless those who persecute you; bless and do not curse."

She grinned at us. "Tassie told me to put that in because I was swearing about those mean kids. I told her you'd never do that though, Tobey."

"Thanks," I said. It felt so good to laugh.

"You got one, Marissa?" Norie said.

Marissa nodded. "Mine's from *The Message*." She looked apologetically at my father. "It's not a translation, it's an interpretation."

"I use *The Message* all the time," Dad said. "Eugene Peterson does excellent work."

Marissa looked relieved. She turned to the page and took a deep breath before she started. Her face had this reverent glow, as if reading from the Bible to us was a big honor. She made me wish I had a piece picked out myself.

"Romans 11, verse 34," she said. "'In one way or another, God makes sure that we all experience what it means to be outside so that he can personally open the door and welcome us back in.'"

I really started to sob then. And Ms. Race passed the Kleenex box around. As I watched them all crying and laughing at each other blowing their noses into soggy tissue wads, I knew one very important thing for sure. The love in my Christian friends' eyes made up for the hate I'd been seeing in everybody else's.

CHAPTER SIXTEEN

THE PLAN WENT INTO EFFECT FIRST THING THE NEXT morning. Just as they had promised, Cheyenne and Brianna met Fletcher and me in the parking lot when we pulled in.

"Dude!" Fletcher said.

If he meant, "That is the biggest human being I've ever seen," I agreed with him.

A guy about six-foot-six was standing there with arms as big around as my thighs and a forehead that hooded his eyes and made him look like a brooding condor. A big, brooding condor.

When I got out of the car, Cheyenne hauled him toward me like he was a ninety-pound weakling she kept at her beck and call. "This is my brother I told you about," she said, gorgeous lips smiling proudly. "He's not really my brother, but I call him that because we both live at Tassie's, along with—"

"Cheyenne," Brianna said, "what's his name?"

"Oh." She grinned. "This is Diesel. He says he'll see nothing bad happens to you."

Unless he takes a dislike to me! I thought.

But Diesel took off his ball cap—to reveal a completely shaved head—and said to me, "You don't gotta worry 'bout nothin'."

I believed him. Especially when Brianna brought her boyfriend who stood next to her over to me. He wasn't as big as

Diesel—few people are—but with all those buffed-out muscles, he definitely looked as if he could take care of himself—like, in downtown Los Angeles or maybe Harlem.

He was African-American, too, and had caramel-colored eyes and the same hairstyle as Diesel. It gave him a clean, intelligent aura. So did the soft empathy on his face, and the polite way he said, "Nice to meet you," when Brianna said, "Ira, this is Tobey."

He got on one side of me with Diesel on the other.

"All right," Ira said, "where's your first class?"

Cheyenne and Brianna had told me the guys would spend the entire day walking me to every class and being there the minute the bell rang to take me to the next one. I hadn't believed it until they actually did it. I didn't ask how they managed. I didn't have to. Who would say no to either one of them if he said, "I'm leavin' now"?

The three of us definitely had an effect on people right off. We were on our way into the gym for first period, and the trio of baby vultures got the first taste. They descended on me in the hall, not seeming to notice Ira and Diesel at first. That's how perceptive those three were.

"I don't mean to be rude," Emily said. She shook her hopelessly frizzed hair out of her face—probably thinking that gesture made her look sultry. "But this whole Angelica Benitez thing—I think you've gone way too far."

"We knew you were a snitch before," Hayley piped up, freckles popping. "But now you've, like, gone off the scale or something."

Before Jennifer could add her two cents' worth, I put up a hand. It was time to try out what we had agreed on last night was the perfect answer. "I'm sorry you feel that way," I said. "But you know what—I'd still stand up for you if you were being abused."

That stopped them in mid-eyelash-bat for a second. Then Jennifer did that mouth-open-eyes-rolling thing and said, "Don't bother 'helping' me."

"I think you're the one who's going to need help," Emily said to me. "I've heard there are some kids—"

"Kids who were really close to Coach Mayno," Hayley put in, lip curled.

"Who are planning to—"

"To what?"

A dark shadow fell over us, created by the hulking form of Diesel-of-Tassie's-Place. The three vulturettes all gaped up at him with identical dumbfounded expressions. I almost laughed out loud.

"Planning what?" Diesel said again.

"Go on—don't hold nothin' back," Ira said. He actually smiled at them.

They hightailed it into the locker room as if they had been shot in the rear. Diesel and Ira looked at each other and gave a nonchalant high-five. I grinned at them.

"I think this is going to work out just fine," I said.

Although I did have one question, which I asked them after second-period English as we strolled to my locker.

"What if somebody doesn't back down when you move in?" I said. "Would you, like, hit them or something?"

"You want us to?" Diesel said. He was frowning so hard his eyes disappeared under the forehead hood.

"No," I said. "I just want you to keep them from hurting me."

Diesel gave that serious consideration. He looked at Ira, who rubbed his nose and looked back.

"Tell you what," Ira said. "I think my man Diesel here could pretty much hold anybody in this school up by the back of the shirt while I went and got a security guard."

"I think you're right," I said.

"Okay, then let's get on. What you got third period?"

We moved off in tandem toward trig class. I felt like a princess—and it wasn't all that bad a feeling.

The day was warm and sunny, and for once the wind wasn't strong enough to blow the potato chips out of your bag, so we ate lunch out on the front grass. I liked hearing the flag rope give an occasional clang against the pole. It was as comforting as Ira and Diesel sitting with their own friends within earshot.

And as reassuring as Shannon reporting that she was doing her part.

"The petition's all ready," she said. "I did it in computer typing this morning."

"Wow. Where did you find all those neat fonts and stuff?" Norie asked.

"Never mind that, girl," Brianna said. She held up the petition, which said the undersigned supported Tobey L'Orange remaining junior class president even in the event of the sponsor's resignation.

"Where's the sheet with the signatures?" Norie said.

Shannon bunched up her mouth. "I haven't gotten any yet." She looked at me, trying to smile. "Some people said it was because I'm only a sophomore—so what business is it of mine?"

"Give me that," Norie said. "I'll take it around."

"You don't have time," Brianna said. "You have to write that editorial, and it has got to be killer."

Norie smiled smugly. "Oh, it will be."

I had faith in her. I had faith in all of them. A tiny voice inside me started to chant, "It's going to be all right. You just wait. It's going to be all right."

"How are the dinner plans coming?" Norie said to Marissa.

Marissa turned her thumb up. "I already have my two cousins in on it with me. And I looked up Angelica's address in the office this morning." She looked at us sadly. "She lives in a motel, over on Second Street."

"Yikes," Shannon said.

"Can I go with you when you get it all set up?" I said.

I hadn't seen Angelica for days. Even though I sometimes thought that being on homebound she was having an easier time of it than I was, I knew that wasn't true. I wasn't the one who still had to recover from basically being raped. But I still felt responsible for helping her.

"Hey, Tobey," Shannon said, "isn't that your little brother?"

I grinned even before I saw him. He would die if he heard she had called him my little brother.

But seeing him made me absolutely guffaw. Fletcher was

crossing the lawn, hands shoved in his pockets, head back, silky hair swinging back and forth—with this gaggle of freshmen girls wrapped around his arms and clinging to the back of his shirt.

"Does he have enough women?" Norie said, snickering.

"Who are they?" Marissa said.

I could hardly answer for snorting. "That's Zena Thomas. She's a freshman on the track team and that other one, with the braid down to her fanny—that's Victoria somebody. She used to be on the track team. I don't know who the rest of them are."

"Doesn't matter," Norie said. "He's doing his job—get the freshman class in the know before these brainless upperclassmen corrupt them."

"He's hatin' it, isn't he?" Brianna said, cheeks dimpling.

"Hey, boy!" Ira called out to him. "How'd you get all them women on you?"

Fletcher flashed us an eat-your-heart-out smile and continued the victory walk across campus.

For a minute there I almost felt happy. Even for the rest of the afternoon I didn't cry, and I actually felt strong when I went in to Mrs. Quebbeman's office after school to tell her I wasn't going to step down from the judicial board—because I knew all five of the Flagpole Girls were standing outside in the hall, silently praying for me.

But the sickening sense of dread came back when Ira and Diesel dropped me off at the locker room for practice, promising to run with me if that's what it took to keep me safe. I opened my locker, and there was another note. This one dropped me right down on the bench.

You don't get the hint, do you? Let us use a reference you'll understand, then. JUDAS, get out—and go directly to the police to tell them you were wrong about Coach Mayno. If you don't, something BAD is going to happen.

The locker room emptied while I sat there staring at the paper. I must have read it fifty times, and still the words went in my brain and immediately out. They wouldn't stick anywhere. It's like that when you just won't believe something.

"Hey, L'Orange," a voice called to me from the direction of the coaches' office. "You still in here?"

It was Coach Gatney. "Yes ma'am," I answered. I threw the note in my locker and slammed the door. Then I leaned against it, closed my eyes, and tried to stop my heart from slamming against the inside of my chest.

"Are those two gorillas out there your personal bodyguards?" she said.

I lurched and opened my eyes. She was standing just a few feet from me, tossing her whistle from one hand to the other. She looked really awkward. I'd never seen her that way before.

"Yes ma'am," I said.

"Are you getting that much harassment from the other kids?" she said.

I nodded.

"Has anybody touched you?"

"No—just threats."

"Anybody touches you here on this team and you know to come to me, right?"

"Do I?" I said.

I shocked even myself. I hadn't really meant to say it out loud. I think she knew that.

"Where's this coming from?" she said.

I didn't want to answer her. I figured I'd said enough. But words curled around in my head like little wisps of smoke. *Make up your mind not to worry about how you will defend yourself—I will give you words and wisdom.*

"I haven't been getting much support from the faculty," I said. "You'd think Angelica and I were the criminals, not—well, you know—him."

She nodded, eyes squinted like she was struggling with her thoughts. "I'm making it a point not to talk about this one way or the other," she said. "Just let me say this though. I don't think you're a criminal, and you certainly don't deserve to be harassed. Anybody on this team gives you a hard time, threatens you—" She jabbed her thumb toward her chest.

"Okay," I said. "Then maybe you ought to read this."

I fumbled with my lock and finally opened the door so I could hand her the note.

"It's the third one," I said as she ran her eyes over it. "This is the worst."

She looked into me. "You're not quitting, are you?" she said.

"No."

She grunted. I think that meant, "Good," and then she folded up the note. "May I keep this?" she said.

"Sure," I said. "Do you think whoever wrote that means it?"

"Don't even think about it, L'Orange," she said. "You have enough to worry about."

The best I can say about the next couple of days is that I felt safe—but I didn't feel as if anything were being resolved. Shannon got about fifty signatures on the petition—out of 350 people in our class.

"That shows not everybody thinks you should quit," Marissa said.

"You're such an optimist, Marissa," Norie said. "Not only are people not signing this one, but they're signing the one they got up, saying you should resign."

"You have so much tact, Norie," Brianna said.

"I'm calling a spade a spade," Norie said briskly. "If we're going to fight this thing, we have to know how big it is."

"It's bigger than me," I said.

They got all over me, and I finally conceded that we hadn't even started yet, and I should be patient. At least I had my visit with Angelica to look forward to.

"Meet me at six at the Timberline Motel Apartments on Second Street," Marissa told me. "It's number fourteen."

"This was so nice of you to do," I told her.

"If there's one thing I can do it's cook," Marissa said. "And I figure she and her mama can use some comfort food about now."

That was for sure, I decided when I pulled into the potholed parking lot in about the most run-down section of Reno. With the multimillion-dollar casinos winking over us just a few blocks away, this part of town boasted about six bars, all with the doors hanging open to reveal smoke-filled caves I wouldn't have

gone into unless I'd had a death wish. Some of the houses probably were pretty neat in their time. Now they all had washing
machines on their front porches and toothless women going past
with shopping carts full of stuff they had pulled out of people's
trash cans.

"Welcome to the Biggest Little Disgrace in the World," I muttered to myself.

The Timberline Motel Apartments fit right into the look.
Their special touch was the dozens of skinny children racing
barefoot across the asphalt chasing even more emaciated cats
and trying out obscenities. Just as I pulled the Honda in, this
woman stuck her head out of a door on the first floor and
screamed, "Get in here before I bust your back end!"

No one heeded her call. I didn't blame them. I was afraid to
even get out of the car myself.

But Marissa appeared on the upper level and waved down to
me. Trying not to look as if I thought I was going to be mugged
at any moment, I slipped out and scampered up the steps.

I could smell the incredible aroma of real Mexican food before I even got in the door. We weren't talking burritos from Taco
Bell—yummy as those are when you're ravenous at your forty-
six-minute lunchtime. No, these were smells designed to bring
you to your knees—bubbling enchiladas, bean burritos smoth-
ered in cheese, sizzling spicy fajitas.

I was glad I enjoyed it while I was still outside, because all
joy went out of me the minute I stepped through the door. The
place wasn't dirty or anything. As a matter of fact, the smell of
Pine Sol and Lysol was as strong as the scent of salsa. Everything
looked neat and tidy, too. The blankets were folded tight and flat
as envelopes on the back of the couch, and candles were lined
up in a row on top of the television. I could see a Harrah's change
bucket on the bathroom counter neatly filled with hairbrushes
and Angelica's signature hair spray.

But I was kicked in the gut by something none of that could
cover up. These people were poor. And I learned right then that
abject poverty is dark and painful and, at best, clawing at hope.

Their whole "apartment" was smaller than my room. I hoped

the couch folded out because there was no bed and there wouldn't have been room for one if they had had one. Basically, I was looking at a sofa, a television, a rickety table with a matchbook under one leg, two unmatched chairs, and a dresser with the veneer peeling off. A square of linoleum was supposed to designate the kitchen I guessed. It consisted of a Barbie-sized refrigerator, a sink, and a hot plate. Marissa was performing a miracle, finding room for all the goodies she had brought in.

Even more shocking than any of that was Angelica herself. I've seen anorexics who weighed more than she did and looked healthier. The heaviest thing about her was her eyes, which were swollen and had navy blue rings under them like she hadn't slept in a week. I was pretty sure she hadn't.

"Hi," she said to me as she crossed the room—in two steps. Even her voice was weak, and the arms she put around my neck were as limp and thin as two pieces of cooked spaghetti. I was afraid if I hugged her she would dissolve.

"I want you to meet my mama," she said.

I don't know where Señora Benitez had been hiding. There weren't that many spots in the apartment. But she emerged from the shadows and held out her hand to me—a tiny brown one connected to a short body and an older, even more worried version of Angelica's face. Only she didn't smile. She looked like she had forgotten how.

"It's nice to meet you," I said.

She nodded and then hurried to the kitchen square. Marissa said something comforting-sounding to her in Spanish.

"Did I say something wrong?" I whispered to Angelica.

She shook her head as she continued to cling to me. "She's not really used to people," she whispered back. "She doesn't speak that much English."

Señora Benitez had looked a little more than shy to me, but for the time being, I was too busy concentrating on Angelica to give it much thought.

"Sit down," Angelica said, waving toward the Goodwill-material couch with one hand and still clutching my arm with the other.

I sank into the couch, half-expecting to feel springs poking me. "Are you okay?" I said. "Have you been sick or something?"

"I can't eat," she said.

At her elbow, Marissa's face fell. She was carrying a plate piled with enchiladas, burritos, fajitas, and rice.

"But I'm sure I can eat this!" Angelica said quickly. "This is just the nicest thing—"

"You just hush up and eat it," Marissa said to her in that soft voice.

Marissa ought to be a nurse or something, I thought. She confirmed that by handing me a plate that was just as loaded down as Angelica's. Then Marissa sat on the floor at Angelica's feet where she could watch both her and her mother, who was sitting at the table as if she were trying to become invisible.

"You haven't been eating because you're upset then," I said.

Angelica nodded as she put three grains of rice in her mouth.

"I thought it would be better since you aren't in school," I said. "At least you don't have people in your face about it all day."

She set down her fork. Marissa picked it up and filled it with enchilada for her.

"There are people here, too," Angelica said. "I had to talk to the woman from the district attorney's office for three hours yesterday and two hours today."

"Here," Marissa said. She made Angelica take three bites.

"Was she nice to you?" I said.

"Oh, yes, don't be afraid of her. She'll be coming to talk to you, too. At least you won't have to talk to a therapist to make sure you're not crazy and a doctor, and the State Child Protection Bureau and the County Family Services Agency—at least you don't have to do all that."

"I'm not worried about me. I just don't want people being mean to you. You don't deserve it."

She chewed slowly and looked down at her plate. Marissa filled up her fork again.

"So, if everybody's been nice to you, what's going on?" I said.

"I mean, I know you have a lot of recovering to do, but isn't anybody helping you?"

"Mama is," Angelica said.

At the sound of her name, Señora Benitez looked up, and for a second her eyes lit. But she went back to her plate, which as far as I could see she was just rearranging rather than eating from.

"And we're all praying for you," I said. "But is there anything else we can do?"

"I don't think so," Angelica said. She put her fork on the edge of the plate again and looked apologetically at Marissa. "There isn't anything you can do unless—"

"What?" I said.

Her black eyes grew wet. "Unless you can make people leave us alone!"

"What people?" I said. "What are they doing?"

"Angelica!"

It was the first time I'd heard Señora Benitez speak. Her voice was surprisingly commanding. It made me put down my fork, too.

"It's all right," Angelica said to me. "You've done so much. There isn't anything else you can do."

Her mother muttered something in Spanish under her breath—something that made Marissa jerk her head up and exchange glances with Angelica.

"What?" I hissed at her.

She was saved from having to answer by a pounding on the door. "Phone call!" a gravel voice yelled from outside.

"For who?" Angelica called back.

"The old lady."

"Yikes," I said. "Could he be a little more rude?"

"In English or Spanish?" Angelica said.

The man swore as if Angelica had asked him to rattle off the whole conversation word for word. It gave me the creeps. "English!" he said when he had finished calling her every name in the cuss-word book. "What do I know from Spanish?"

Angelica sighed and dragged herself up and beckoned to her mother. She said something to her in Spanish, and they both disappeared out the door.

"What's going on?" I said as soon as they were gone. "What did her mother say a minute ago?"

Marissa pretended to be chewing.

"Come on," I said. "I feel responsible for this whole thing. I need to know what's happening!"

Poor Marissa. She looked as if she would rather I just took her out and shaved her head than make her tell. "When Angelica said something about how you had already done so much, her mother said, 'Too much. That kind of help we don't need.'"

I shoved my plate away from me. "You're kidding me!"

Marissa shook her head.

"Her mother is mad at me?"

"It kind of sounds like it. When I was over there serving up the plates, she said something about she wished Angelica had just told her and they had left town. They don't need this kind of trouble."

"What kind of trouble? She's out of school so nobody there is hassling her. She said the lady from the DA's office was being really nice to her."

"That I couldn't tell you," Marissa said. "It's hard for immigrants though, especially if they don't speak English. When the law is involved, they just get scared even if they haven't done anything wrong. Where Señora Benitez comes from, the law can throw you in jail for no reason."

I felt lousy. "I should have talked to her first before I dragged Angelica down to the welfare office."

"It isn't your fault, Tobey," Marissa said. "You were all by yourself—and if you had talked to her mother first, she might have talked Angelica right out of it."

"Yeah," I said reluctantly, "and taken her out of town." I scraped my fingers through my hair, Roxy-style. "I'm not judging her or anything, but I can't imagine my parents running away instead of fighting for me."

"That's why we have to fight for her," Marissa said.

Her voice was still soft, but it was firm. It occurred to me that it had been getting stronger as the days had gone by. My first impression of her as this mousy little thing was gone.

"Okay," I said. "At least now I know how hard we have to fight."

But until the door to the apartment flew open, I didn't have a clue how hard that really was.

CHAPTER SEVENTEEN

SEÑORA BENITEZ FLEW IN THE DOOR FIRST, HANDS OVER her face, sobbing in big hoarse gasps. Angelica was right behind her, and she had nothing on her face but blank shock. Dishes clattered as Marissa and I dove at the two of them.

"What happened?" I said. "What's going on?"

Marissa questioned Angelica's mother in Spanish, but all the poor woman could do was shriek. Angelica dropped to the couch and stared straight ahead. I felt as if I were in some bad black-and-white movie. I fumbled for the wall switch and startled us all with the blaring light from a naked light bulb in the ceiling. That's when I saw the cut on Angelica's cheek.

I went to my knees in front of her. "Angelica," I said, "you have to tell me what happened!"

Her mother started to scream louder than ever. Only Marissa's grabbing the woman's arm kept her from coming across the room after me.

Angelica came to life then and said something to her mother. Señora Benitez sank into one of the chairs at the table and cried into her hands. Marissa stayed with her.

"Talk to me, Angelica," I whispered.

Her voice came out fragile as a piece of glass. "We went to answer the phone, only no one was there anymore. It's a pay phone, down at the end of the building on this floor. When I hung up, and we started back, a car squealed into the parking lot, and somebody in it threw something. It hit me on the cheek—that's all."

"That's all?" It took every ounce of self-control I had left to keep from charging to the phone myself and calling 911. "Okay, look," I said. "Did you see who it was? Recognize the car?"

"I wasn't really paying attention," she said. "When the tires squealed, I looked down, but that happens all the time around here so I wasn't that interested, you know? All I saw was a blur, and then something hit me."

"Let me see your face," I said.

She let me look at the V-shaped cut on her cheekbone. It didn't look deep, but it made me wince. I'm not sure whether it was the trickle of blood or the thought of some jerk aiming a projectile at her.

Marissa brought over a wet cloth and cleaned it, naturally.

"I'm going out to see what they threw," I said.

Before I could even get up off the floor, Señora Benitez was babbling loudly in Spanish, and Angelica was tugging on my arm. "Don't go out there!" she said. "They could be waiting for you."

"I'll keep down low," I said. "But we need to get the evidence before somebody picks it up. The police are going to need that—"

"No police, Tobey," Angelica said. "Mama says no police—no more trouble."

"But if we don't raise a stink, they'll just keep doing stuff to you!" The note dropped into my locker danced in front of my eyes. "They'll think they have power over you—and they don't!"

Angelica looked at me, imploring, pleading. She wanted to believe me.

Her mother had no intention of even trying. She rattled off a stream of Spanish I didn't have to have translated. The answer was no, and that was it.

"But you shouldn't stay here," I said. "It's pretty clear a bunch of people are working together. Somebody made the phone call to lure you guys out there, and then the others came in for the—"

I was going to say "kill." I was pretty worked up by then. I chewed on my lip instead.

"We don't have anyplace to go," Angelica said.

"Yes, you do," said Marissa. "We'll load the food and your clothes into my father's car when he gets here, and you can come to my house."

She turned to Señora Benitez and told her what I assumed was the same thing in Spanish, because the woman immediately started to shake her head. It took Marissa less than five minutes to talk her into it.

"You had better go now, Tobey," Angelica whispered to me. "I don't want you getting hurt, too."

I may never have felt lower in my life as I dragged myself out of that apartment and slunk to my car. I hated checking the shadows for possible assailants. Then I used the flashlight to make sure no vengeful high school idiots were in the backseat waiting to choke me. All the way home I wondered why our prayers didn't seem to be helping. And I found myself crying again, even though my stomach was already sore from so much sobbing.

"Where are you, God?" I said out loud as I drove. "What about all those Bible verses, huh?" I did the hiccup thing. "When are you going to open the door and welcome us back in?"

There was no answer that night. In fact, I didn't even start to get one until the next day—and that came in an unexpected way.

I started to hurry out of English class at the end of the period because I knew Ira and Diesel would be in the hall waiting for me, but Mr. Lowe stopped me—and Roxy and Gabe.

"I need to talk to you three for a minute," he said. "I'll write you a pass to your next class."

I quickly poked my head out the door. Ira and Diesel were standing there, arms crossed, watching Utley and Kevin go by. If those two had had tails, they would have been between their legs.

"You ready?" Ira said.

"I have to stay after class. You guys go on so you won't be late."

"We'll wait," Ira said.

Diesel grunted his assent.

There was nothing for me to do but go back inside. I didn't look at either Roxy or Gabe as I slid into a seat a few desks away from them. The room felt cold and uncomfortable. It didn't even seem like the same place where people like them joked with me and told me to write them notes when I walked past them.

"I wanted to give you the results of the Lions Club Speech Contest," Mr. Lowe said. He handed Roxy and Gabe their score sheets. He kept what I assumed was mine in his hand.

"Man, I lost again," Gabe said. He flopped his ponytail over his shoulder. "You'd think those old codgers would get a clue, you know?"

A pang went through me. A few weeks ago I would have thought that was pretty funny. Now, if I hadn't already had enough to be mad about, that comment would have ticked me off.

"Don't feel pregnant," Roxy said. "I didn't win either—as usual."

She raked her hand through her mop of red hair. That gave me a pang, too. I missed so many of the fun things about being around her.

Give me my results, Mr. Lowe, please, I thought. *I want to get out of here.*

Instead, he perched on the edge of his desk and lowered his head so the fluorescent lights shone on his baldness. When he looked up, his eyes were grave.

"Tobey took third place in the county," he said.

There were no "All rights!" and "Way to go, Tobeys," although I was pretty sure I heard Gabe give a barely audible snort.

"The judges wrote on here," Mr. Lowe went on, "that if you had had more passion for your subject matter, Tobey, you might have taken first. Everything else was in place."

"So what are we supposed to do to get passion?" Gabe said curtly. "Get up there and bulge our veins like Baptist preachers?"

Mr. Lowe shook his head. "You don't do anything to achieve passion," he said. "You just talk about something you really believe in, and you do it with courage and conviction, no holds barred, pull out all the stops."

"I can do that," Gabe said, bobbing his ponytail at Roxy. "I can do passion."

"I don't know that you can, Gabe," Mr. Lowe said. "Not at this point in your life. But if anybody can, it's Tobey."

He looked directly at me; I had no choice but to look straight back. His eyes were still serious, but they were kind. I'd never seen him look so soft before.

"Tobey, you've shown that you're willing to stand up for what you believe in, no matter what the consequences. A lesser girl would have backed off this Coach Mayno thing long ago."

Gabe gave a full-blown snort. "If you want to talk about the Mayno thing—"

"I don't," Mr. Lowe said.

"Yeah, but I've said what I believed about that—"

"Not with passion," Mr. Lowe said. "With cowardice perhaps."

Gabe opened his mouth. Mr. Lowe silenced him with a look. "But like I said, I don't want to talk about it. I'm proud of Tobey. I'm not proud of you—either of you."

Roxy's hair flew five ways. Her hazel eyes looked stung, and I felt sorry for her. I was sure she had no idea what Mr. Lowe was talking about.

Still, that session got me through the rest of the day. Through still another note in my locker—*We're still waiting, Judas. Don't think we're bluffing.* Even through seeing Damon sucking face with Pam at the water fountain after practice. I mean, right there in the hall. Tongues and all—

Anyway, I got through it because of Mr. Lowe. But it was the Flagpole Girls who got me through the worst part.

They were all waiting for me in my bedroom when I went

home from practice, except for Marissa who was home keeping Angelica and her mother company.

"We're kidnapping you," Norie said from her place at my desk in front of my computer. "You know, I could upgrade this thing for you."

Brianna poked her head out of the closet and tossed me a cream Lycra shirt and a double-layered skirt I once blew a whole weekend's baby-sitting money on. "You got any shoes besides Nikes in here, girl?" she said.

"Where are we going?" I said.

"Pneumatic Diner," Cheyenne said. She was sitting cross-legged in the middle of my bed, hugging the mangy stuffed rabbit I'd had since birth.

Shannon poked her head out of the closet. "I'm excited. I've never been there. Here's a pair of white sandals."

"No, girl," Brianna said. "I mean something that makes a statement."

"I have combat boots," I said.

"Keep looking," Brianna said to Shannon.

Norie came up behind me and pulled my backpack off me. "Get changed," she said.

I noticed then that they were all dressed up. Shannon was in something long and flowy and pastel, and Cheyenne had on new jeans and a cool-looking scarf tied around her head. Brianna looked like a model on the cover of *Seventeen*, and even Norie had on a to-die-for vest and mascara.

"I'll have to ask my parents," I said as Brianna went after my hair with a paddle brush.

"Done," Norie said.

"They even gave us money!" Cheyenne said.

Brianna stopped brushing. "Girl, you do not have to tell every piece of information you know."

"My parents are paying you to take me out?" I said.

"No," Norie said. "We told them we wanted to take you out, and then they chipped in."

"Which is why we can afford Pneumatic," Brianna said. "You have any hair gizzies?"

"Just a headband."

"Forget that. I'll make do."

She definitely did. I hardly recognized myself in the mirror, which at that point was not altogether a bad thing. I'd been looking red-eyed and haggard for days. She made me look like a normal person again—one with a friendship glow on her face.

"This is so cool, you guys," I said as we all piled into Norie's father's van.

"Nah, this is nothing. You ought to see his Porsche."

"I don't mean the car, I mean this—your taking me out. I just wish we had more to celebrate."

"We have a ton to celebrate," Norie said. "We were talking at lunch today, while you were with Marissa—"

"And we all feel," Brianna cut in, "like we have never been this good in our lives."

I laughed.

"No, I am so serious," Norie said. "I have this, like, exhilarating thing going on, like I am finally doing something that matters for somebody—"

"It's God," Shannon said.

It was her usual quiet voice, but nobody gave her the isn't-she-the-sweetest-thing look. She had basically summed it up for all of us.

The Pneumatic Diner, which I'd never been to, was this wonderful, funky place downtown on First Street. Located upstairs in a small hotel building, it was adjacent to a dance studio. In fact, as we were sitting there on high stools all crowded around a table the size of a large pizza, we could see the dancers doing their thing through a window. There was all this free-looking, blasts-of-color art on the wall, which Brianna was totally getting into. Even the menus were artsy. We all howled over food names like "schmear" and asked this bizarre-looking waiter with electric-socket hair to translate everything for us. As we sipped our apricot fizzes and blackberry dynoflows and waited for our ratatouille and potato bayard, I felt normal and calm and almost untouched by the Mayno thing. I told them what had happened with Mr. Lowe.

"You see, it's working," Shannon said.

"Well, I knew it would," Norie said. "But we can't slack off. We have to keep at it until people start cutting you some slack—"

"And start seeing things the way they really are," Brianna said. She narrowed her eyes into slits. "That is always my goal, y'all—to get people to see it like it is and tell it like it is. I am so sick of games, you know what I'm sayin'?"

She flung out her hand for emphasis, dumping her dynoflow across the table. It missed dripping on everybody but me. The cream-colored shirt took it heavy.

"Get cold water on that," Shannon said. She shrugged. "My mother is Queen of Laundry."

"I am so sorry, girl," Brianna said. "If it doesn't come out, I'll give you something of mine."

"Don't worry about it," I said. And I meant it. A friend like her was worth my entire wardrobe.

"Bathroom's down the hall," the waiter said behind me.

They were all hooting and shrieking about the cleanup as I went out the door. The hallway was pretty dim. We are not talking about a high-rent establishment, and I had to squint to see a rest-room sign. What I saw was movement from the stairs, somebody coming out of the shadows.

I don't think it would have made me stop in my tracks if the person hadn't moved as if he didn't want to be seen. I knew it was a he. He wasn't too tall, but he had broad shoulders and a head too sharp around the edges to belong to a woman. Yeah, it was a man. And when he stepped into the faded light, I saw what man. Coach Mayno.

The second it registered I started to back up.

"No, L'Orange, don't go," he said. "You have to listen to me—you owe me that."

I kept backing—until I bumped the wall.

"Relax, L'Orange," he said. "I'm not going to hurt you. What do you think I am?"

The voice went right up my backbone. I'd heard those words before from him, said to somebody else: *"I'm not going to hurt you—you know that."*

I couldn't say anything. All I could think was that I knew just how scared and immobilized Angelica must have been.

"Why don't you believe me?" he said. "Why do you believe that little bimbo instead of me?"

"She isn't a bimbo," I managed to get out.

He gave a dry laugh. "You don't even know what a bimbo is. You don't know anything about sex—I'd be willing to bet on that. Which is why you had no business ever starting this thing in the first place."

"What difference does it make whether I know anything about sex?" I said. "I'm not going to talk about this with you."

I started away from the wall. He stepped in my way. He didn't touch me. He was careful to keep his hands behind his back. But the way he stood there made me stop. It scared me.

"Then I'll do the talking," he said. There was no laugh, not even a smile. That close, I could see that his eyes were dull and baggy, and he had lines on his face I hadn't seen before. He didn't even smell the same. He had the vague odor of clothes that need to go to the dry cleaners.

I stood still.

"Now you listen," he said. "I know Angelica Benitez can be very convincing when she puts on that little girl act, but don't be fooled by it. I wasn't. She wanted to be with me."

I shook my head.

"No, now just listen," he said. "I'm not going to deny that I spent time with her. You're too sharp for that. Besides, I've always felt like you were one of the adults. We could always talk to each other."

My apricot fizz started to work its way up my esophagus.

"But what you have to understand is that Angelica was having the time of her life with me, until she found out you knew. And then she panicked. She knew she was going to be in big trouble. She knew that I have pull in the district, that I'm thick with Holden. So she did what every inexperienced tramp does: She turned it around to make it sound like she had been forced against her will. Suddenly I go from lover to rapist."

I put my hand over my mouth, and I could taste the bitterness of just-swallowed fruit juice on my tongue. This was the most sickening thing I'd heard yet. Not the explanation—that was nauseating enough—but that Coach Mayno believed everything he said. He really thought that was the way it had happened. And he really thought it was all right.

"It's hard to take," he was saying. "I'm sure you've become real attached to her. I did, too—I miss her. But you can't trust her, L'Orange. And this is never going to fly anyway, this whole thing. I'm too important to that school. You've already found out that people up there know I would never rape a girl. I don't want to see you getting hurt anymore. You know you're special to me—"

"Stop it!" I screamed at him. My voice cracked against the walls and sent him stepping backward toward the stairs.

"All right, if you can't stand to hear it, fine. Just stop screaming." He stopped at the top step and glinted his eyes at me through the darkness. "But don't say I didn't warn you. She'll flake out on you, and you're the one who's going to end up taking all the heat."

I bolted before he did, ramming my way back into the diner, bile spilling out onto my lips, shirt still dripping with juice. Brianna saw me first and knocked over a chair getting to me.

"Please, can we go home?" I said. "I don't think I can eat anything."

The minute I gave them the *Reader's Digest* version of what had happened, somebody took care of the check for food we never ate, and a couple of other somebodies got me to the van, which Norie pulled right up to the downstairs door, stopping traffic behind her. I knew it was Shannon who kept saying, "It's going to be all right, Tobey. We'll get you home," as she stroked my hair.

But we didn't make it home. We didn't even drive two blocks before the car phone rang. Norie answered it and pulled the van over to the side of First Street to listen. We sat there in frightened silence until she hung up.

"We're going to my house," she said.

"I want to go home," I said miserably. "Please, I'm sorry . . ."

"You can't go to your house," Norie said. She pressed her mouth in an adult-serious line. "You've had a bomb threat."

"Oh, uh-huh, girl," Brianna said. "You think some little ol' bent-out-of-shape jocks are going to bomb her house? They're just trying to scare her!"

"I don't think so," Norie said. She glanced over her shoulder and then pulled the van into traffic.

My sense of dread was rising, and it was becoming as reliable as an alarm clock. "Norie," I said, "what's wrong? What happened?"

Her eyes met mine in the rearview mirror. "Somebody just threw a bomb at the Timberline Apartments," she said.

CHAPTER EIGHTEEN

WE SAW IT FOR OURSELVES, AS MUCH AS WE COULD. I made Norie drive down Second Street until we reached the police detour. Even as we turned around in a used furniture store parking lot, we could see about a hundred red and blue flashing lights, and black smoke billowing out of the second story. Otherwise, it didn't look much worse than it had before.

I plastered my hand over my mouth again though, when I thought about all those skinny children in the parking lot.

"Was anybody hurt?" I said.

Norie shook her head. "My dad said it was a homemade job—barely enough to start a fire. It was aimed right at number fourteen."

"But nobody was there," Brianna said, "thanks to Marissa."

"There is a God," Norie said. "But then, was there ever any doubt?"

"Does Angelica know?" I said.

"I don't know," Norie said. "We can call her when we get to my house. Your parents and your brother are going to meet us there."

"I don't want to call her," I said. "I don't want her to know."

Brianna turned around in the front seat and stared at me, scandalized. "Girl, she has to know!"

"No," I said. "If she knows, her mother will just run with her—out of town someplace."

"After all she's already been through? No way!" Norie said.

"Oh, girl, you are right," Brianna said to me. "Like I told you before, it's always worse on minorities."

"I feel as if we're all a minority right now—all six of us," Shannon said.

"Not for long though, I don't think," Norie said. "Once word gets out about this—and Tobey tells what Mayno said to her—"

"Do you really think they'll believe me?" I said. I could hear the hopelessness in my own voice, but I couldn't stop it. God was definitely not opening any doors to let me back in. "It was just him and me in that hall," I said. "So it's still my word against his."

"And he was probably punctuating it by having his little helpers bomb Angelica's house. Just in case you didn't come around," Norie said.

"It happened too fast for that though, didn't it?" Shannon said.

"No," I said. I leaned my head wearily against the window. "You should have seen how fast it went down at Angelica's the other night. She answered the dead phone, the car squealed into the parking lot—boom, Angelica gets it in the face."

"He definitely has people helping him," Brianna said. "It's like they know everything you do—everywhere you go—"

"There's one thing they don't know," Cheyenne said.

I had to look at her, even as hagged out and hopeless as I was feeling. Her voice was the only vibrant, lively one in the car, and her eyes were shining as I looked at her in the light from on-coming traffic.

"What's that, girl?" Brianna said. "I can never wait to hear what you have to say."

"They don't know we've been praying," Cheyenne said. "They probably think we'll give up—and we won't—because God doesn't."

She said it as if we had just received a guilty verdict for Coach Mayno from the jury. Brianna smiled across at Norie.

But I sat up straight in my seat. "Do you really believe that, Cheyenne?" I said.

"Of course," she said. "I didn't used to, not till I started hanging out with you guys. If anybody should have ended up a loser, it was me." She smiled with her wonderful, full lips. "And now, I'm a total winner."

"You're a winner, all right—" Brianna started to say.

"Norie," I said, "step on it. We have stuff to do."

Even now I can't tell you exactly what it was that changed my attitude in, like, the snapping of a finger. I don't think God really lets us know every detail. But my best guess is that it just became obvious that—shoot—we'd helped save one little lost kid—why couldn't we help save another one—and keep trying—until we got her?

Norie pulled up the van to a cover-of-*House-Beautiful* home in exclusive Caughlin Ranch and herded us all in through the front door. I think Cheyenne and Brianna—maybe even Shannon and me, too—would have stood there in the foyer gaping at the crystal chandelier for an hour if Norie hadn't shoved us into "the den." I barely noticed the cherry paneling and whole-wall entertainment center that night. I headed straight for my dad.

"Everybody's all right," he said into my hair. "No one was hurt."

"What about your house?" Norie said.

"The police are there," I heard Mom say.

"You should have seen it," Fletcher said, more than likely to Shannon. "I think they had the whole SWAT team there."

He sounded like a ten-year-old who has watched too much TV. I didn't care. I squirmed so I could see Dad's face.

"Does Angelica know?" I said.

"Yes, when we called the police we told them where she was so they could be sure she's protected."

"That's good, right?" I said.

But his face didn't look like anything was good. I realized then that every adult in the room was trading a look with every other adult in the room. Norie didn't miss it either.

"What's going on?" she said.

Mrs. Vandenberger brought in a tray of something, and Dr. V. coaxed the girls onto the miles of white couches. Norie and I stood there staring at my father.

"This was the last straw for Angelica's mother, sugar," Dad said. I felt my mother's hands on my shoulders. "They're dropping the charges. She and Angelica are leaving for Fresno as soon as they can get packed up. They have family there."

"Dropping the charges?" I said—stupidly, I know. It was another case of not wanting to believe what I was hearing.

"Aw, man, she can't!" Norie said. "Can't they protect her?"

"Not if she doesn't want to pursue it anymore," Dr. Vandenberger said. He had a crisp, no-nonsense voice, the kind I didn't want to hear just then.

"Daddy," I said, "can't we do something? What if I talked to Angelica? What if we all did, and prayed with her—"

"Oh, honey," Mom said. She wrapped her arms around me from behind and buried her face in my cheek. She was pretty close to tears. "Angelica's mother told Marissa to be sure to tell you she doesn't want you to talk to Angelica."

I whirled around. "Ever?" I said.

Mom shook her head. Dad put his arm around me. Fletcher even looked sympathetic.

But I looked at the Flagpole Girls, all lined up on the couch watching me.

"From what I know about these things," Dr. Vandenberger said, "it sounds like it's over."

My eyes stopped on Norie, who was perched on the arm of the couch like a waiting hawk. Our gazes met like a pair of hands.

"I don't think it's over," I said. "I just don't think it is."

"Me either," Norie said. "Girls—" Her eyes swept over Cheyenne, Shannon, and Brianna. "Somebody tell Marissa—we keep praying—we keep working."

It was weird sleeping in our house while the police sat out front in a patrol car. Fletcher was still entranced by their presence when we left for school the next morning. I had other things on my mind, like getting through Friday, then tomorrow's track meet, then . . .

Ms. Race had ideas of her own. She grabbed me in the parking lot and took me to the office breakroom through a back door. I thought I knew everything about that school until I saw that maze of rooms they have in the back of the office. She plunked me down at a table, handed me a cup of tea, and sat down beside me. Her face was ashen.

"Okay," she said. "The word is out. I don't know how people find out this stuff, but they do. Every person I've talked to this morning knows that Angelica dropped the charges."

"I can handle it," I said. "I have friends, and you're one of them."

She smiled, kind of sadly. "I know—and that helps. But this means Coach Mayno will be back at King."

I heard myself swallow. "Okay. I can handle that, too. Is he going to be here today?"

"I doubt it. Nobody's been able to get in touch with him, and the school board has to confer on it. But, Tobey, that isn't the worst of it."

I frowned at her. "What do you mean?"

"Now that Angelica has dropped the whole thing, it casts doubt on your story. Three people this morning have asked me if you're going to be in trouble now, and doesn't this mean Angelica was lying all the time, so you were, too, blah, blah, blah."

"I don't care," I said. "I did what was right, and I'm sticking to it. Besides, the Girls would be disappointed in me if I caved in now. We've kind of made a commitment to each other to do it the way Jesus would, you know? Jesus wouldn't do it the easy way."

Ms. Race leaned back in her chair and folded her arms. Her eyes, if I wasn't mistaken, were misty. "You girls amaze me," she said. "Although I guess I shouldn't be surprised. God still works miracles."

"Then who knows?" I said. "Maybe one will happen."

"You're going to stay here for the day then?" she said.

"Of course."

"And run in the meet tomorrow?"

"Yes."

"All right then," she said.

She started to get up, but I touched her arm, which was clad in some kind of Eastern Indian sarong-looking top in pumpkin and bronze. Someday, when the world turned right side up again, I was going to have to ask her where she got such cool clothes.

"Will you be there?" I said. "At the meet?"

"You want me there?" she said.

"Yes ma'am."

"Then you can count on it," she said.

Ira and Diesel did everything but sit in classes with me that day. Nobody dared even speak to me—except the three vultures.

"Hey, Tobey," Emily said to me in the locker room. She flitted her eyes over to Hayley and then Jennifer, in her watch-me-do-this-chick-in way.

"Yeah," I said. I looked right at her, which I think knocked her off balance a little. But it didn't stop her.

"Do you think Coach Mayno will sue you now?" she said.

"For what?" I said.

"For—what's that thing called?"

"Declaration of character," Hayley said.

There were a few snickers in the locker room, even after Emily tried to glare them down. That was encouraging.

"I think you mean 'defamation,'" I said. "And no, I don't think he'll sue me. I'm a minor."

"And a liar," Emily pointed out. "And an opportunist and a manipulator."

"You pretty much know all the options, don't you?"

Every girl in the place whipped around. Coach Gatney was leaning against a bank of lockers, eyes riveted to Emily.

"Yeah, I know some big words," Emily said. Her tone was surly, but she was on the defensive. Big mistake with Coach Gatney.

"Do you know 'intimidation'?" Coach said. "'Intent to do bodily harm?' 'Accomplice?'"

"Yeah," Emily said. She tried to gather in Hayley and Jennifer with her eyes.

They didn't gather. They both looked as if they were about to wet their pants. I watched Coach Gatney carefully. Emily decided to go it alone.

"So, what's your point?" she said.

"I'm not ready to make it quite yet," Coach Gatney said. A slow, gap-toothed smile spread across her face. "But I might after we take our little written quiz today."

A chorus of protests went up in the locker room, and several of the girls looked at me. I had to shrug at them. I didn't know a thing about a written quiz.

"This is PE!" Jennifer said and then rolled her eyes and left her mouth hanging open.

"No kidding?" Coach Gatney said. "Imagine my surprise." She smiled again. "Bring pencils to the gym, ladies. I'll meet you there."

I waved off their questions and followed her. "What's up, Coach?" I said.

"I think you might find out," she said. "Just be patient."

The quiz turned out to be some lame little essay about sportsmanship. Emily, Jennifer, and Hayley were, of course, the first ones through. They knew absolutely nothing about sportsmanship. When all the papers were in, Coach Gatney handed them to me.

"Go in the coaches' office, L'Orange," she said, "and grade these for me, would you?"

I took them and started off across the gym. A screech from the class made me look back over my shoulder.

"How come she gets to grade them?" Emily was hollering. Her face was ashen. It was the most flipped-out I'd seen her do yet.

"Because she's my aide," Coach Gatney said mildly. She seemed to enjoy the whole scene tremendously.

Emily sank back to the floor with a face the color of cream of wheat. I cocked my head at Coach Gatney. She just waved me off toward the office.

I still didn't get it, but I was relieved to be away from the whole pack of them. *One period down, six more to go*, I told myself. *I can do this.*

I pulled the first paper off the stack and grinned to myself. Coach had made sure Emily's was the first one. I couldn't wait to get a load of her idea of what it meant to be a good sport.

I read about two words and broke into a cold sweat. I mean it—I got clammy from palms to soles.

"What's the verdict, L'Orange?" said Coach Gatney from the doorway. Closing the door behind her, she pulled two pieces of paper out of her pocket and spread them out on the desk. "Do these look like any of those?"

It was the two notes I'd given her, the ones I'd found in my locker. Sitting there, next to Emily Yates's essay, the two hand-writings were identical—so much the same, it was chilling.

"I don't get it," I said. "Maybe I'm dense, but Emily isn't on the cross-country team."

"Does she have friends on the team?"

"I doubt it, but I don't know that much about her." I closed my eyes. "I feel awful. I thought it was Pam."

"Does she know Pam? Pam's a senior. You know how these freshmen love to get in the upperclassmen's good graces."

"Pam hates freshmen," I said. I tried not to sound bitter. "It's one of the lovelier things about her."

"What about the guys?"

"Emily loves guys," I said. "She would do anything for any one of them that looked at her twice and had a nice body. It's a possibility, I guess, but I wouldn't even know where to start con-necting her with somebody on the team—"

"Leave it to me," Coach Gatney said. She patted my shoulder. "I haven't let you down so far, have I?"

"It's so weird," I said.

"What's that?" She sat on the desk, swinging her legs and glancing through the window out into the gym to check on the "little chickies."

"I got a note right after I stood up for Angelica that time they tripped her playing volleyball. It just said, you know, watch out,

Angelica is a tramp, don't stick up for her, blah, blah. It would have made sense that Emily or one of the others had written it, except it wasn't like any of these." I flipped through the quizzes. "It was more like a boy's handwriting."

Coach Gatney scratched her nose for a good fifteen seconds. "Do you still have it?" she said finally.

"It's in my backpack."

"Go get it," she said.

I did. She barely gave it a glance before she tossed it on the desk.

"You know whose handwriting that is?" she said.

I shook my head.

"Paul Mayno's," she said. "I know it like I know my own."

I sat back in the chair. Even after all this time, every new disgusting thing I found out was still numbing.

"He was trying to scare me off," I said, "and I didn't even suspect him then."

"He was covering his rear end," Coach Gatney said, "if you'll excuse my French. Not very carefully though, as we now know. He has such an ego, he probably thought he would never get caught."

"It's so sad," I said. "This note might have helped convict him, huh?"

"Yep," she said. "And it doesn't do anybody any good now." She slid off the desk. "I really thought somebody had him this time."

She caught herself in the same instant that I jerked up in my chair.

"You never heard me say that, L'Orange," she said quietly. "Because I can't prove a thing. I wasn't as slick as you; I could never catch him."

She gave my shoulder a squeeze and went for the door. "I'd better go teach the little chickies," she said. "And don't bother grading those papers. Just trash them—all except Emily's." She smiled. "I'll get back to you."

By lunchtime, anybody who didn't know about Angelica dropping the charges before was filled in. I was getting everything from black looks to gang signals to hisses in the halls. It would have been worse without Diesel and Ira. Ms. Race wanted us to hide out in the supply room to eat, but I wasn't doing that.

"Nobody can say or do anything worse to me than they've already done," I told the girls. "Let's just sit outside like we always do. It's gorgeous, and I like to be near the flagpole with you guys."

"You're so brave, Tobey," Cheyenne said. She glared at the rest of them. "And don't anybody tell me I can't say that."

"You're not going to get any argument from me," Norie said. "Tobey's my hero."

They had me bouncing back and forth between giggles and tears by the time we got outside. Ira and Diesel weren't taking any chances. They sat on either side of me, holding their faces like AK-47s every time somebody even looked at me crooked. When one guy yelled out, "Hey, Vandenberger, L'Orange made your editorial sound like a crock," Diesel stood up, and the kid took off like his jeans were on fire. After that, Ira and Diesel almost didn't let Fletcher near me, until Brianna reminded them he was my brother.

He had his entourage with him—at least, the abbreviated version—Zena and Victoria.

"They want to sit with you guys," Fletcher said, nodding his head at his female appendages. Their devotion to him was obviously losing its charm.

"Sure," I said. "Sit down, you guys."

I introduced them around. To my surprise, Zena answered everybody's "hi" with a muttered something. I didn't remember Victoria that well, but she, too, seemed cowed by us all. *So why did they want to sit here?* I thought.

Fletcher seemed glad they had somebody else to talk to for a change and devoted his attention to Shannon. She was so polite, I had to look the other way to keep from laughing.

"Tobey," Zena said to me, "is it true that girl Angelica said Coach Mayno didn't—you know—"

"She didn't say he didn't," I told her. "She just decided not to press charges—"

"Because she was getting threats from people," Norie put in.

"Not just threats," Cheyenne said. "They bombed her apartment!"

"Girl, you stick this apple right in your mouth!" Brianna said.

Victoria and Zena looked as if they were watching a Stephen King film.

"Nobody got hurt," I reassured them. "I think somebody was just trying to scare them. And unfortunately it worked. The police could have protected her. There was plenty of evidence to convict Coach Mayno, and they may even be able to find out who was doing all the threatening and who threw the bomb. Nobody would have gotten away with anything, but she was too scared to stay and fight it."

"I don't blame her," Victoria said.

I looked at her more closely. She had a fragile china oval face and a sweet little bow mouth. She was just a baby, like Angelica. Her innocence made me want to cry.

"That's why we wanted to talk to you guys," Zena said. She looked at Norie. "I read your article in the *King's Herald* this morning, and, see, I thought it was really good."

"You say that like some people didn't," Norie said. "Big surprise."

"Some kids are saying that what you wrote—about nobody seeing how much courage it took for Angelica and Tobey to accuse Coach Mayno and how much braver they are than the people who won't even look at the truth and try to change things for the better—anyway, they're saying that's all wrong now because Angelica quit." She turned her rich blue eyes on me. "Do you think she was wrong to drop it, Tobey?" she said. "Do you blame her?"

The Flagpole Girls were watching me. That was all I needed to know what to say. "I don't judge anybody," I said. "But I do know what's right. I wish she'd stuck with it because what she was doing was right."

"Do you guys always do what's right?" Zena said. She was looking around the circle of us.

Fletcher snorted, but the minute Shannon knitted her tiny eyebrows at him, he sat up and started to nod.

"Yes, Fletcher?" I said. I couldn't resist.

"They always do what's right," my precious baby brother said. "They do—I mean it—they're like these angels or something. It's—hey—it's uncanny."

Uncanny? I snickered to myself. I was going to have to ask him about that later. I didn't even think he knew what "uncanny" meant.

"I wouldn't say we were exactly angels," Norie said. "But we try, and we—uh—you know, we pray. I mean—" She shrugged, took a breath, swallowed until I thought the rest of us would crawl out of our skins—even Cheyenne. "Well, it's because we're Christians," Norie said at last. "Christians—if they're really sincere, you know, they'll always try to do what God wants them to do."

"Wow," Zena said. She looked at Victoria, who was playing with a cameo ring on her finger and not looking at anyone.

"Does that answer your question okay?" I said.

Zena gave me this serious look. "It does for me," she said. "Thanks, you guys."

"That was bizarre," Norie said when they had walked away with a reluctant Fletcher in tow.

"Everything is bizarre anymore," I said.

I stretched out on the grass and looked up at the mountains. I immediately came up on my elbows.

"Hey, you guys," I said. "Look how gold the trees are now. See, way up there in the Sierras."

"They're about done bein' gold, girl," Brianna said. "It's been fall for weeks. You been locked up someplace or what?"

"Yeah," I said. I grinned, a real grin. "But for some reason, I think I see the doors opening now."

CHAPTER NINETEEN

WE DID A LIGHT RUN AT PRACTICE THAT AFTERNOON—just up McCarran and back in twos along the sidewalk. Zena glued herself to me. She only skittered away when Damon edged in beside me.

"So I guess it's a done deal now, huh?" he said.

I kept my voice cool, and my eyes fixed uphill. "Not necessarily," I said. "And you know what, I really don't want to talk about it. I'm just trying to stay loose for the meet tomorrow."

"What if Coach Mayno's there for it? You have more guts than I do. I wouldn't even show up."

"Oh yeah, I forgot." I cut a glance at him. "You like girls with guts."

He clenched his jaw. It was really too bad. He was a good-looking guy—yet there were times he was downright ugly. Bummer. A real bummer.

He didn't say anything else, but he didn't show any inclination to move on either. As long as he was there, I had an idea.

"It's funny though," I said. "Pam's your latest, and she doesn't strike me as being incredibly brave. She kind of hides behind Utley and Kevin. Now Emily Yates, now there's a girl with guts—she's brazen, even."

"Who's Emily Yates?" he said.

I watched his eyes—the gold, blue, gray ones. They did look vacant.

"You know," I said, "freshman, big perm."

"Oh, her," Damon said. "Not my type. She's going out with Kevin anyway." He ran his hand over the dark, wavy hair. "Not that it's any of your business."

I just shook my head.

Wow. Kevin. And probably Utley and Pam, too.

But what about Damon? The angry part of me, the part that had been so hurt and disappointed I could just about wish the worst, wanted to think he was right in there with them, possibly making threatening phone calls and hurling bombs.

Most of me, though, knew it probably wasn't true. Damon didn't have enough passion in him to take a chance like that. Damon Douglas was too scared.

"I need to go talk to Coach Gatney," I said. "Have a good race tomorrow."

He looked at me for a minute, and then he looked away, almost as if he were embarrassed. "I hope this all dies down for you now," he said. "You really aren't a bad person. I mean, you were doing what you thought was—"

"I was right," I said. "And I hope it doesn't die down—not until it all works out the way it's supposed to."

He blinked at me with those curly eyelashes, and then he ran on. I watched his little running shorts and let myself feel sad one more time.

The next day was a "glorious" fall day, to use one of my dad's words. The sky was big and blue, the way only a Nevada sky can get, and there was this crispness in the air. Gold leaves I hadn't even noticed before were dancing around all over the ground.

It was a great day for running, and that was what I was trying to think about when I got to King. I'd told Coach Gatney what I'd found out about Kevin and Emily, and she said she almost had it put together. At least that part was going to be over soon. It wasn't the resolution I'd hoped for, but at least it was something. Now I could concentrate on the race—and maybe some of the other things that had gotten lost in my life since this all started. I wanted to get to know the Flagpole Girls better—find out who Cheyenne's Tassie was and why Shannon had such a thing about praying for kids on drugs. I laughed to myself. I really wanted to figure out what was up with the friendship that was blossoming between Norie and me.

The buses from the other schools in the county were all packed into the upper parking lot. Runners in different spirit-colored uniforms were warming up in clumps all over the football field for the race that would start here in the stadium and take us out into the desert and partway into the foothills. The sizzle that gets into the air before a race was there. I jogged over to the clump that was clad in royal blue.

Coach Gatney was there with her clipboard, checking off people's names. I let any anxiety that was left in me tingle right on out. Coach Mayno was still gone.

"I'm here, Coach," I said.

"Good. That makes everybody but Zena Thomas. Anybody seen her?"

I gave the sidelines a sincere search. It wasn't like Zena to be late. She was such a conscientious little thing it was almost disgusting. As I scanned the bleachers, my eyes snapped on a figure up at the top.

In sunglasses, a ball cap, and a big jacket he didn't need on a day like this, there was no mistaking him—Coach Mayno.

"Don't worry about it," said a quiet voice at my elbow. It was Coach Gatney. "I saw him, too. You just say your prayers and run. Everything else is being taken care of."

If that didn't reassure me, the group on the front row did. They were all there, cheering like they were about to see the Olympics—Mom, Dad, Ms. Race, Norie, Marissa, Shannon, Cheyenne and Diesel, Brianna and Ira, and Fletcher. I was surprised Victoria wasn't with him—disappointed, too. I could have asked her about Zena.

Coach Gatney tooted on her whistle. "All right, people, you know the way the pack lines up."

I listened and prayed at the same time. I also watched the main gate for Zena, which may have been the reason I was one of the first to see the two uniformed policemen march in the same way Norie does when she's on a mission. Mr. Holden marched behind them in a King High jacket and ball cap. Even from the middle of the football field I could tell he wasn't happy, just from the way he was clasping and unclasping his hands. I'd seen him do that before.

Utley and Kevin spotted them, too. They jockeyed their way in front of me and craned their necks like a pair of old women.

"Cops," Kevin said.

"No, duh," Utley said. "What was your first clue? The uniforms or the thirty-eights in their holsters?"

Kevin shifted from leg to leg. "What if—"

"Chill," Utley said. He hitched up his shorts. "It's cool—they're not even coming out here."

Damon sidled up to them and poked Kevin in the rib with his elbow. "What's the matter, Kev?" he said. "Did you think they were onto your cocaine ring or something?"

Kevin growled at him, but Utley threw his head back and gave this big fake laugh. I somehow wanted to laugh myself. Damon not only wasn't part of it—he didn't even know what they'd done. *Thank you, God*, I thought.

"Hey!" Pam crossed over to her little group with her ponytail swinging. "Did you guys see Coach Mayno up there?"

Kevin, Utley, and Damon all shielded their eyes, as did the rest of our team. Coach Gatney gave up trying to herd people into the lineup for the start of the first race. Nobody else was doing it. Every person in the stadium was watching the police make their way down the track and then start up the bleachers. Coach Mayno spied them, too; we could all see that. He took his elbows off his knees and pulled at his ball cap.

The closer the police got, the more he straightened and pulled—and then even glanced over his shoulder.

"There's nobody behind you, pal, if that's what you're thinking," Coach Gatney whispered near me. I don't know if she was talking to me or herself, but it was obvious what she meant. The police were headed right for him.

They reached him. He stood up. A hush fell over the crowd, as if everybody were trying to hear what was being said.

After about a minute, there was no need to hear. We watched, mesmerized, as one of the officers put his thumbs in his belt and talked like he was chanting, reading him his rights, no doubt. The other one pulled handcuffs off his belt. They glinted in the sun as he wrenched Coach Mayno's arms behind his back and snapped them on. It all had the quality of one of those slightly off paintings you see that is so real it hurts your eyes. Mine burned as I watched the two policemen lead him down the bleachers and off the track.

There wasn't an eye there that wasn't on him. He lowered his head and let them lead him out the gate.

I'd never seen a man look smaller.

"You've violated your sacred trust as a teacher, pal," I heard Coach Gatney mutter. "What do you expect?"

Meanwhile, Kevin was looking for a place to plant his fist. "What the heck, dude!" he shouted. "Not again!"

He whirled around and flailed his eyes until he found me. "What did you do, talk that little Hispanic broad into coming back?" he said.

Before I could even open my mouth, he lunged at me. I felt the heels of his hands hit the fronts of my shoulders, so hard it knocked the air right out of my chest. I stumbled backward into Coach Gatney. She gripped me by the arms and rolled me aside and then hurled herself right at Kevin. She had both of his arms behind his back and her face right in his from over his shoulder before the two sets of thundering footsteps arrived. Our team split like the Red Sea as Ira and Diesel roared toward me. Diesel scooped me up in his arms, and Ira made for Kevin as if Coach Gatney were holding him there for Ira to take his shot.

"Don't hit him, son," Coach Gatney said. "It isn't worth it."

"Is everything all right over here?" I heard my father say in an out-of-breath voice.

"Coach, you have this under control? What's happening?" That was Mr. Holden.

Coach Gatney thrust Kevin right toward him. "Here's a suspension for you, Mr. Holden," she said. "If you don't mind, I'd like him away from my team—now."

Mr. Holden nodded to the security guard who was just now trotting onto the field. He took Kevin by the arm and led him away. I'd have watched him go if Mr. Holden hadn't tapped Diesel, rather cautiously, on the shoulder. "Is she all right?" he said.

Diesel looked at me, forehead brooding. "You all right?" he said.

"Yeah," I said. "I'm fine."

"Then could you put her down?" Mr. Holden said. "I'd like to talk to her."

Diesel looked as if he would rather not, but I told him it was okay, and he reluctantly slid me to the ground. Mr. Holden stuck his hands into his pockets and said, "Would you mind stepping over here, Tobey?"

I looked around and spotted my father, still right there. "I want my dad to come, too," I said.

The three of us strolled off the field to the empty side of the track. Beyond us, a buzz started in the stadium. It was probably going to be half an hour before they settled everybody down enough to run.

"I wanted you to be the first one to know what just happened," Mr. Holden said. "I think we owe you that much at least."

"Okay," I said.

Mr. Holden blew out a sad puff of air. "Obviously, Coach Mayno was just arrested again. Another girl came forward and charged him with sexual abuse. You may know her—little girl named Victoria Ballard."

I had about decided I could never be surprised again. I was wrong. A pang went through me that cut off my air supply.

"Do you know her, Tobey?" Dad said.

"Yes sir," I said. "She's a friend of Fletcher's. She used to be on the team, and then she quit . . ."

My voice trailed off. Mr. Holden followed my thought and nodded. "She was too frightened to stay and too frightened to tell. Poor little thing has been struggling with it for weeks." He made a clicking sound with his mouth. "It turns out you were right about Coach Mayno after all, Tobey—and I am so sorry you've had to go through these past few weeks. I hope you'll understand that I had to have no doubt in my mind—from an administrative point of view as well as because the man is a dear friend of mine."

I started to prickle—big-time. "Could I ask a question?" I said.

"Certainly," he said.

I looked at my father, who nodded.

"How come Victoria is a 'poor little thing' and you take her word," I said. "But Angelica was suspected of being a liar from the minute she opened her mouth against Coach Mayno?"

"There's a very good explanation for that," Mr. Holden said. "Angelica didn't have an eyewitness. Victoria has left us with no doubt, which was the place I was trying to get to with Angelica's case."

"This girl had an eyewitness?" Dad said. His eyebrows were tangled the way my mind was. "Someone actually saw—and yet they took this long to say anything?"

"Zena Thomas isn't quite the brave young woman your daughter is, Rev. L'Orange," Mr. Holden said. "She probably doesn't have the strong family background—"

"Zena Thomas!" I said. "She was there when Coach Mayno was, like, touching, Victoria?"

"According to both Victoria and Zena, the two girls were in the locker room together after practice when Coach Mayno came in. Zena got scared and hid in her locker. She was there for the whole thing. We don't know the rest of the story at this point—"

"Nor do we need to," Dad said. He put his arm around me and pulled me close to him. I clung like a five-year-old.

"Of course," Mr. Holden said. "I just wanted to tell you myself, Tobey, because I know what you've been through."

I shook my head at him. He didn't have a clue what I'd been through.

He pursed his lips and nodded to us both. "I guess we'd better try to get on with this track meet, eh?" Mr. Holden put his hands in his pockets and walked slowly away from us across the football field. It was a sad walk, and it clutched at me a little. Maybe he didn't know what I'd been through right this minute, but I had a feeling he was about to. I didn't care what he had done to me—I wouldn't wish it on anybody.

The Flagpole Girls and I had a sleepover at my house that night. Although Mom gave everybody a handmade, miniature teddy bear and she baked double chocolate chip cookies, we didn't call it a celebration. It was hard to whoop it up about somebody going to jail and Zena and Victoria possibly facing what Angelica had been through with kids at school. We decided to call it a Plan of Action session.

"These little innocents—this Victoria and Zena," Norie said, "they're going to need our protection. It doesn't matter if six people witnessed the dude doing his thing, there are still going to be people who say Coach Mayno was right up there with the twelve apostles. We've been there."

"Let's let Fletcher be Zena and Victoria's bodyguard," I said.

Everybody howled, except for Shannon who said, "Now, you guys, be sweet."

We stayed up until three in the morning, planning, eating, and hugging, but we still managed to attend the eleven o'clock service at our church the next day. We all sat in a row and looked up at Dad when he was preaching. He didn't seem to look at anybody but us, and I loved every old-fashioned, unhip expression in the sermon. He was turning out to be a majorly cool father.

Then I slept almost all day Sunday. I don't think I had gotten a good night's sleep since that Friday when I found the underwear. But my personal part of it was over now, I thought. It was time to put it all to rest.

I wasn't quite right about that. Monday, some more mud hit the fan, and I was right behind it.

I got to first period PE, feeling a little naked without Ira and Diesel, and there was Coach Gatney with a pink pass.

"Go down to Mr. Holden's office," she said.

I groaned. She gave me the gap-toothed grin.

"Don't worry about it," she said. "I think if you have any evil in you at all, you might enjoy this."

The principal's office was pretty crowded. There was Kevin, Utley, Pam, and poor little Emily Yates. I never thought I would feel sorry for that girl, but she looked as if she were going to either puke her guts, pass out, or leap from the nearest twenty-story window. She was white-faced, curled up in the corner of the love seat, and begging Kevin with her eyes to look at her. He, naturally, didn't.

"Come in, Tobey," Mr. Holden said. "I have a room full of people here who are facing some pretty serious consequences, some of them not with us but with the law. Before I turn them out to their various punishments, I wanted you to have the opportunity to hear their explanations and apologies. Perhaps you'll accept them for Angelica Benitez as well as yourself."

I nodded, but I'm not sure I'd taken it all in yet. I sat in the chair he pulled out for me and waited while he stood behind me and said, "Emily, you go first. "

Poor Emily. I really expected her to toss her bacon on the floor.

"I let Kevin talk me into being his messenger," she said.

Kevin's face went scarlet. I had a feeling that wasn't entirely true, but Kevin wasn't talking.

"He would tell me what to write, and I'd write it and stick it in your locker at the end of PE after you were gone."

"And?" Mr. Holden said.

"I'm really sorry I was involved," she said to her knees.

You're really sorry you were caught, I thought. But I nodded at her. The pitiful little thing looked so miserable, maybe there was hope for her.

Mr. Holden nodded at Kevin. "Go," he said.

Kevin would rather have taken the electric chair, I know it. His lips barely moved as he spoke. I was actually surprised he would talk at all, without his uncle, the deputy DA, there.

"I told Utley we had to do something to get that girl to give up the whole thing." Kevin said. "She was such a liar—"

"Stick to the facts please," Mr. Holden said.

"So I said let's do something, and then I got Emily to help. That's all, and I'm sorry."

On the sincerity scale, I gave it about a minus two. The same for Utley, who admitted to being the mastermind. He actually told me more than I wanted to know.

"At first Coach Mayno didn't want to get involved with us," Utley said, but then he went on as if he were actually proud of the next part. "When we told him we knew where you were all the time and we could set it up so he could talk to you and try to get you to see where he was coming from, he was all over it. He said he knew he could change your mind." Utley shrugged. "We figured if anybody could, it was him."

But that didn't get to me as much as Pam did for some reason. She said she "just drove the getaway car," and I about choked.

"You mean at the Timberline?" I said. "At Angelica's place?"

"Yeah," she said. "I drove the car."

"While Utley threw a bomb into their apartment?"

"It wasn't going to hurt anybody," she said. "It was more like a firecracker."

"People have been blinded by firecrackers, okay?" I said. "Good grief, Pam, this just blows me away. Were you going to do that at my house if she didn't drop the charges?"

It was the first time I saw any of them look even an ounce remorseful. None of them would look at me, and I could see Pam's Adam's apple moving up and down.

"I can't even believe it," I said. "You guys were my friends. What you did to Angelica was worse—don't get me wrong—but turning on me, when you know me, you know what I'm like, I can't even imagine what you were thinking!"

Pam tried to shrug, but she couldn't pull it off. She tugged miserably at her ponytail. "I don't know," she said. "It just seemed like Coach Mayno—it couldn't be true. And you were being so self-righteous about it—"

"I wasn't and you know it," I said. "I was being right, and you couldn't face that."

"Yeah," Kevin said, "well you're sounding pretty self-righteous right now, if you ask me."

"No one did," Mr. Holden said dryly.

"That's okay," I said. "Think what you want. But I'm going to tell you something, all of you—"

They all kind of shrank, like they were ready for me to break out a whip and let them have it.

"I'm going to pray for all of you," I said. "And so are my friends."

They froze in mid-shrink.

"I just don't want you going on doing stuff like this," I said. "I know you're better than that."

I was suddenly drained, and I looked at Mr. Holden. "May I go now?" I said.

He nodded and gave me the nice smile. I think it was right then that I forgave him.

In the weeks that followed, I forgave everybody. That doesn't mean I felt the same about them, mind you. I knew, for instance, that Roxy and I were never going to be friends again like we were before.

When she came up to me one day in the library, her hazel eyes were overflowing with tears. "I feel so awful," she whispered to me.

"Roxy, it's done, okay? You did the best you could—what can I say?" And I meant that.

"But I should have told you," she insisted.

I stopped with my hand on the spine of a book in the 900-section and squinted at her. "Told me what?" I said.

"I knew Damon couldn't be trusted." She raked her hair with both hands.

"Damon?"

"Yeah. I heard him talking to some people in Port of Subs during lunch, right when you guys started going out. Somebody asked where you were, and he said you were at some Holy Roller meeting. Somebody else goes, 'How come you're going out with a Jesus Freak?' and he goes, 'How do you think I got her to go out with me? I told her I was a Jesus Freak!'" Roxy put her hand on my arm. "I should have told you, but you were so happy and all. I just don't like to make trouble, you know what I mean?"

I knew exactly what she meant. Poor Rox. I put her on my prayer list. *God, please help Roxy figure out what to really give a flip about in life.*

Coach Gatney apologized to me about eighty times. I finally told her I liked it better when we talked about my hair color, and she got the message. She was disappointed when I quit the track team, but I assured her it wasn't because of the kids. They were trying to put it behind us, most of them.

"I just want to spend my time doing something else," I told her. "I'm volunteering at the shelter for abused women, and Norie and I are helping the district put together a panel on sexual abuse for girls. That's more important to me."

"You know something, L'Orange? " she said. "You are amazing. Someday you better tell me how you do it."

"I don't do it," I said. "It's God."

She didn't have an answer for that. She just smiled the gap-toothed grin.

Mr. Ott mumbled some kind of apology to me, which I accepted without hesitation. He has enough problems without my giving him the evil eye.

Gabe never apologized, and I didn't expect him to. And for that matter, neither did Damon, really. What he did say proved to me that there are still surprises in this world.

He came up to me right after Kevin, Utley, and Pam were carted off to juvie, the same day I was in Mr. Holden's office. He looked as if he had been crying or something. His eyes were all red-ringed, and his hair was ruffled—I mean, as ruffled as it ever got. He said, "I heard you were in Mr. Holden's office with Pam and everybody this morning."

"Yeah," I said.

"Well," he darted the multicolored eyes all over the place. "Did they say anything about me?"

"You?" I said. "You weren't involved in that."

He looked a little startled. "You knew that?" he said.

"It's not your kind of thing," I said.

"I had a hard time convincing Holden of that," Damon said. "Coach Gatney just assumed since I'm friends with them I must be in on it, so I got called in. I asked if Utley or Kevin or anybody said I was involved, and he said no, but he kept asking me all these questions." Damon ran his hand down his neck. "I was like, hello, why doesn't anybody believe me?!"

I could feel a smile creeping onto my face. I hadn't been evil enough to enjoy the session in Mr. Holden's office, but I was going to enjoy saying this. "Don't you hate that?" I said. "When nobody will believe you?" I patted his arm. "It's a drag, but I tell you what, Damon, I'll pray for you."

I started to walk away, and he put a hand gingerly on my arm. I stared at it until he took it away.

"I just wanted to tell you," he said, "that I'm breaking up with Pam—I mean, today. I won't be involved with somebody who does the kind of stuff she was doing—I mean, they could get jail time!"

"That would be really bad for your reputation, wouldn't it?" I said.

His eyes cooled. "I just wanted you to know that I'm not some jerk, okay?"

"Thanks," I said.

Then I did walk away. It was the last conversation we ever had. Needless to say, I tossed out the butterfly ring and the pacifier, and I didn't spend much time at Virginia Lake for a while.

I did pray for him though, and Utley, Kevin, Pam, and Emily.

"I am so impressed that you can pray for those jackals," Norie said to me. "I'm not there yet."

"I've been wanting to ask you something," I said. "What is a 'jackal' exactly?"

"It's this species of wild dog that runs in packs and catches prey for like lions and then eats what's left over."

"Oh," I said. I shuddered.

She nodded. "Fits, huh?" she said.

Coach Mayno—I prayed for him also—and Angelica

wherever she was and Victoria and Zena, who got a mild case of the cold shoulder from some people who still wouldn't give up Mayno-worship. All of us prayed—all of us Flagpole Girls— every Friday when we met for lunch with the flag flapping and clanging hopefully nearby. They were the ones who helped me with the Mrs. Quebbeman decision. I'd already told her I was staying on the board, but she still wouldn't leave it alone.

"I know there are kids who want me off, just so they won't have to be reminded," I told the girls one day in mid-October. "But I like being in a group that's responsible for fairness and stuff."

"You should be there, girl," Brianna said. "Ain't nobody as fair as you around here."

"We have the homecoming election coming up and all, but it's hard to work with Mrs. Quebbeman. It's like ever since I wouldn't take her advice, she sees me as this uppity little snob who thinks she's better than the teachers. I'm not like that!"

"No, you are not like that," Marissa said. "I'd like to go in there and tell her what time it is, you know?"

We all grinned at each other.

"You used to be so shy, Marissa," Shannon said. "What happened?"

"You all happened," she said.

We didn't even hesitate. We said it in unison, "And God."

"Okay, so what's it gonna be?" Brianna said to me. "You gonna stay on and show them how the Christians do it, or you gonna let them chase you off?"

I looked at them all—my friends, my people-I-could-now-tell-anything-to. They were like sisters to me, and I'd made a commitment to them to do it the way Jesus would.

"Okay," I said. "I'm staying on—Mrs. Quebbeman or not."

They were cheering as Ms. Race floated across the lawn to the flagpole to join us. Today she was wearing a red silk dress with just a hint of some Oriental gold embroidery on the shoulder. I found out about her clothes, by the way. She went on a mission to a different country every summer, and she always included a shopping trip at the end to help support the country's economy. Wow, as Zena would say.

"Every time I'm late I miss something good," she said when she reached us.

"Tobey's staying on judges' board," Cheyenne said.

Nobody corrected her. But Norie did hold up her hand.

"What, Nor?" I said.

"I just want to say this one thing. You can stay on the board, you can run the election, and you can be sure the dust is going to settle on this whole thing before you graduate." She shook her head, eyes twinkling. "But, L'Orange—don't count on homecoming queen, okay?"

There was a unanimous squeal. I feigned puking.

"Why would I want to be homecoming queen?" I said.

"You were a prime candidate at the beginning of the year," Ms. Race said. "People told me that all the time."

I thought about that. It took me all of seven seconds to come up with a response. "But I'm not the same person I was then," I said. "I'm a whole other girl from the one who stood at the flagpole that day—I can tell you that."

"Wow," Cheyenne said. "I hope that happens for me."

"Only one way to insure that," Norie said. She stuck out her hands. "Girls, shall we pray?"

And, of course, we did.

If you or someone you know experiences sexual abuse and there's no one in your community to talk to, call the National Council on Child Abuse and Family Violence at 1-800-222-2000.

Join millions of other students in praying for your school! See You at the Pole, a global day of student prayer, is the third Wednesday of September each year.

For more information, contact:

See You at the Pole
P.O. Box 60134
Fort Worth, TX 76115
24-hour SYATP Hotline: 619/592-9200
Internet: www.syatp.com
e-mail: pray@syatp.com